ONCE BOUND

(A RILEY PAIGE MYSTERY—BOOK 12)

BLAKE PIERCE

BOOKS BY BLAKE PIERCE

THE MAKING OF RILEY PAIGE SERIES
WATCHING (Book #1)

RILEY PAIGE MYSTERY SERIES
ONCE GONE (Book #1)
ONCE TAKEN (Book #2)
ONCE CRAVED (Book #3)
ONCE LURED (Book #4)
ONCE HUNTED (Book #5)
ONCE PINED (Book #6)
ONCE FORSAKEN (Book #7)
ONCE COLD (Book #8)
ONCE STALKED (Book #9)
ONCE LOST (Book #10)
ONCE BURIED (Book #11)
ONCE BOUND (Book #12)
ONCE TRAPPED (Book #13)

MACKENZIE WHITE MYSTERY SERIES
BEFORE HE KILLS (Book #1)
BEFORE HE SEES (Book #2)
BEFORE HE COVETS (Book #3)
BEFORE HE TAKES (Book #4)
BEFORE HE NEEDS (Book #5)
BEFORE HE FEELS (Book #6)
BEFORE HE SINS (Book #7)
BEFORE HE HUNTS (Book #8)
BEFORE HE PREYS (Book #9)

AVERY BLACK MYSTERY SERIES
CAUSE TO KILL (Book #1)
CAUSE TO RUN (Book #2)
CAUSE TO HIDE (Book #3)
CAUSE TO FEAR (Book #4)
CAUSE TO SAVE (Book #5)
CAUSE TO DREAD (Book #6)

KERI LOCKE MYSTERY SERIES
A TRACE OF DEATH (Book #1)

PROLOGUE

As consciousness slowly returned, Reese Fisher realized that she was in pain all over. The back of her neck ached and her skull felt as though it would burst from throbbing.

She opened her eyes only to be blinded by glaring sunlight. She squeezed her eyelids tight again.

Where am I? she wondered. *How did I get here?*

Mingled with the pain was a tingling numbness, especially in her extremities.

She tried to shake her arms and legs to get rid of the tingling, but found that she couldn't. Her arms, hands, and legs were somehow immobilized.

She wondered …

Was I in some kind of accident?

Maybe she'd been hit by a car.

Or maybe she'd been thrown from her own car and was now lying on hard pavement.

Her mind couldn't get a hold on anything.

Why couldn't she remember?

And why couldn't she move? Was her neck broken or something?

No, she could *feel* the rest of her body, she just couldn't move anything.

She could also feel the hot sun on her face, and she didn't want to open her eyes again.

She tried hard to think—where had she been and what had she been doing just before this … whatever this was?

She remembered—or thought she remembered—getting on the train in Chicago, finding a good seat, and then she'd been on her way home to Millikan.

But had she gotten to Millikan?

Had she gotten off the train?

Yes, she thought she had. It had been a bright, sunny morning at the train station, and she was looking forward to the mile-long walk to her house.

But then …

What?

The rest was all fragmented, even dreamlike.

It was like one of those nightmares of being in terrible danger but unable to run, unable to move at all. She'd wanted to struggle, to free herself from some threat, but she couldn't.

She also remembered a malignant presence—a man whose face she now couldn't bring to mind at all.

What did he do to me? she wondered.

And where am *I?*

She realized she could at least turn her head. She turned away from the glaring sunlight and finally managed to open her eyes and keep them open. At first, she was aware of curving lines stretching away from her. But at the moment they seemed abstract and incomprehensible.

Then she could see why the back of her neck was in such pain.

It was lying against a long curving stretch of reddish steel, hot under the bright sunlight.

She wriggled slightly and felt a sharp roughness against her back. It felt like crushed rock.

Little by little, the abstract lines came into focus and she could see what they were.

In spite of the hot sun, her body felt cold as she understood.

She was on a railroad track.

But how had she gotten here?

And why couldn't she move?

As she struggled, she realized that she *could* move, at least somewhat.

She could writhe, twisting her torso, and also her legs, although she couldn't separate them for some reason.

The tingling numbness she hadn't been able to shake off was now turning into surges of fear.

She was tied here somehow—tied to railroad tracks, with her neck fastened to the rail.

No, she told herself. *This is impossible.*

It had to be one of those dreams—a dream of being immobilized and helpless and in terrible danger.

She closed her eyes again, hoping the nightmare would go away.

But then she felt a sharp vibration against her neck, and a rumbling reached her ears.

The rumbling was getting louder. The vibration became

piercingly strong, and her eyes snapped back open.

She couldn't see very far along the curve of the tracks, but she knew what the source of that vibration was, that crescendo of noise.

It was an oncoming train.

Her pulse pounded, and terror erupted through her whole body. Her writhing became frantic, but completely futile.

She couldn't tear her arms and legs free, and she couldn't pull her neck away from the rail.

The rumbling was now a deafening roar, and suddenly it came into view …

… the reddish-orange front of a massive diesel engine.

She let out a scream—a scream that sounded supernaturally loud to her own ears.

But then she realized—it wasn't her own scream she'd heard.

It was the piercing noise of the train whistle.

Now she felt a weird rush of anger.

The engineer had sounded his whistle …

Why the hell doesn't he just stop?

But of course, he couldn't—not nearly fast enough, not hurtling along at his current speed.

She could hear a screeching sound as he tried to bring the mountain of metal to a stop.

The engine filled her whole field of vision now—and peering out through the windshield was a pair of eyes …

… eyes that looked as terrified as she felt.

It was like looking in a mirror—and she didn't want to see what she was seeing.

Reese Fisher closed her eyes, knowing it was for the last time ever.

CHAPTER ONE

When Riley heard the car pull up in front of her townhouse, she asked herself …

Am I really going to be able to go through with this?

She studied her face in her bathroom mirror, hoping it didn't look too obvious that she'd been crying. Then she went downstairs, where her family was already gathered in the living room—her housekeeper, Gabriela; her fifteen-year-old daughter, April; and Jilly, the thirteen-year-old girl Riley was in the process of adopting.

And standing among them, flanked by a couple of large packed suitcases, was fifteen-year-old Liam, smiling rather sadly at Riley.

It's really happening, she thought. *Right now.*

She reminded herself that this was all for the best.

Even so, she couldn't help but feel sad.

Then came the sound of the doorbell, and Jilly rushed to open the front door.

A man and woman in their late fifties came inside, all smiles. The woman hurried over to Liam, but the man approached Riley.

"You must be Ms. Paige," he said.

"Riley, please," Riley said, her voice choking just a little.

"I'm Scott Schweppe, Liam's uncle," he said. He turned toward his wife, who was giving Liam a big hug. "And this is my wife, Melinda."

With a slightly awkward chuckle he added, "But I guess you already know that. Anyway, I'm so glad to meet you."

Riley shook his offered hand. She noticed that his handshake was warm and strong.

Unlike Riley, Melinda didn't bother to hold back her tears. Looking up at her nephew, she told him, "Oh, Liam! It's been such a long time! You were so little when we last saw you. Such a handsome young man you've become!"

Riley took several long, slow breaths.

This really is for the best, she told herself again.

But until a couple of days ago, it was about the last thing she'd expected to happen.

It seemed like only yesterday when Liam had come to live with

Riley and her family. In fact, he'd been here less than two months, but Liam had fit in perfectly and everyone in the household was already very attached to him.

But now it had turned out that the boy had relatives who wanted him to come live with them.

Riley said to the couple, "Please, sit down. Make yourselves comfortable."

Melinda dabbed her eyes with a tissue, and she and Scott sat down on the couch. Everybody else found places to sit except Gabriela, who hurried away to the kitchen for refreshments.

Riley was a bit relieved when April and Jilly started making small talk with Scott and Melinda—all about their two-day drive from Omaha, where they had stopped for the night, and how the weather had been along the way. Jilly seemed in good spirits, but Riley detected sadness behind April's cheerful demeanor. After all, she had been closer to Liam than any of them.

As Riley listened, she observed the couple closely.

Scott and his nephew looked a lot alike—the same lanky build, bright red hair, and freckled complexion. Melinda was on the stout side and looked like a perfectly conventional, good-natured housewife.

Gabriela quickly returned carrying a tray with coffee, sugar and cream, and some delicious home-baked Guatemalan cookies called champurradas. She served everybody as they talked.

Riley noticed that Liam's aunt was looking at her.

With a warm smile, Melinda said, "Riley, Scott and I can't thank you enough."

"Oh—it was my pleasure," Riley said. "He's a delight to have around."

Scott shook his head and said, "I'd had no idea how bad things had gotten with my brother, Clarence. We'd been estranged for such a long time. The last I'd heard from him was years ago, when Liam's mother left him. We should have stayed in better touch, if only for Liam's sake."

Riley wasn't sure what to say. How much had Liam told his aunt and uncle about what had happened?

She remembered it all too vividly.

April had just started dating Liam, and Riley had taken a liking to him right away. But after a frantic call from April, Riley had rushed to Liam's house and found him being beaten savagely by his drunken father. Riley had subdued the man, but leaving Liam in his care had been unthinkable. Riley had brought Liam home and set up a place for him to sleep in her family room.

This living situation had been precarious, of course.

Liam's father kept calling and texting his son, promising to change and not to drink anymore—emotional blackmail, pure and simple. And it had been awfully hard for Liam.

Scott continued, "You could have knocked me over with a feather when Clarence called out of the blue last week. He sounded like he was out of his mind. He wanted my help getting Liam back. He said ... well, he said some stuff, let me tell you."

Riley could imagine some of the "stuff" Liam's father had said—probably including what a vile, horrible person Riley was for taking Liam away from him.

"Clarence said he'd stopped drinking," Scott said. "But I was sure he was drunk even when he called. Sending Liam back to him was a crazy idea. So there seemed to be only one thing to do."

Riley felt an emotional jolt those words ...

"... only one thing to do."

Of course, that one thing wasn't to let Liam stay and live with Riley's family.

It was simple common sense.

He should go and live with his nearest relatives.

Melinda squeezed Scott's hand and said to Riley, "Scott and I are empty nesters, you know. We raised three kids, two sons and a daughter. Our girl is finishing her last year of college, and the boys are married and successful and ready to start families of their own. So we're alone in our big house and we miss hearing young voices. For us, this is the perfect time."

Again, Riley felt a sharp twinge.

"... the perfect time ..."

Of course it was the perfect time. What was more, these were obviously perfect people—or as nearly perfect as parents could be.

Probably a lot better at it than me, Riley thought.

She was a long, long way from balancing everything in her own complicated life—the duties of being a parent and the often conflicting, sometimes dangerous duties of being an FBI field agent.

In fact, she sometimes found it to be almost impossible, and having Liam here hadn't made her life any easier.

She'd often felt as though she wasn't giving nearly enough attention to her kids—including Liam. She had stretched herself much too thin when she took him in.

Besides, how could he keep living in that family room until he went to college?

Just how was Riley going to send him to college, anyway?

No, this really was for the best.

Jilly and April kept the conversation going, asking all about the couple's children.

Meanwhile, Riley's head was filling with worries.

She felt as though she'd gotten to know Liam well in just a short time. After years of estrangement from him and his father, what did these people know about him? She knew that Scott was the owner of a thriving bicycle store. He also seemed to be in remarkably good shape for his age.

Would he understand that Liam was by nature clumsy and nonathletic?

Anything but a jock, Liam loved to read and study, and he was the captain of his school chess team.

Would Scott and Linda know how to relate to him? Would they enjoy talking with him as much as Riley did? Would they share any of his interests?

Or would he wind up feeling lonely and out of place?

But Riley reminded herself that she had no business worrying about these things.

This really is for the best, she told herself again.

Soon—much too soon, as far as Riley was concerned—Scott and Melinda finished their cookies and coffee and thanked Gabriela for the delicious refreshments. The time had come for them to go. After all, it was going to be a long drive back to Omaha.

Scott picked up Liam's suitcases and headed out to the car.

Melinda took Riley's hand warmly.

She said, "Again, we simply can't thank you enough for being there when Liam needed it."

Riley simply nodded, and Melinda followed her husband outside.

Then Riley found herself face to face with Liam.

His eyes were wide, and he looked to Riley as if he'd just now realized that he was going away.

"Riley," he said, his voice squeaking in that charming adolescent way of his, "we never got a chance to play a game of chess."

Riley felt a stab of regret. Liam had been teaching April the game, but somehow Riley had never gotten around to playing with him.

Now she felt that she'd never gotten around to too many things.

"Don't worry," she said. "We can play online. I mean, you *are* going to stay in touch, aren't you? We all expect to hear from you. A lot. If we don't, I'll come out to Omaha. I don't think you'll want the FBI knocking on your door."

Liam laughed.

"Don't worry," he said. "I'll stay in touch. And we'll play chess for sure."

Then he added with an impish smile, "I'm really gonna kick your ass, you know."

Riley laughed and hugged him.

"In your dreams," she said.

But of course, she knew he was right. She was a pretty good chess player, but not nearly good enough to win against a brilliant kid like Liam.

Looking like he was on the verge of tears, Liam dashed out the door. He got into the car with Scott and Melinda, and they pulled out of the driveway and drove away.

As Riley stood watching, she heard Jilly and Gabriela cleaning up in the kitchen.

Then she felt someone squeeze her hand. She turned and saw that it was April, looking at her with concern.

"Are you OK, Mom?"

Riley could hardly believe that April was the one to show sympathy right now. After all, Liam had been her boyfriend when he'd moved it. But their romance had been put on hold since then. They'd had to be *"hermanos solamente,"* as Gabriela had put it—brother and sister only.

April had handled the change with grace and maturity.

"I'm OK," Riley said. "How about you?"

April blinked a little, but she seemed remarkably in control of her emotions.

"I'm fine," she said.

Riley remembered something April had planned to do with Liam when school was out.

She said, "Are you still planning to go to chess camp this summer?"

April shook her head.

"Without Liam, it just wouldn't be the same."

"I understand," Riley said.

April squeezed Riley's hand a little harder and said, "We did a really good thing, didn't we? Helping Liam, I mean."

"We sure did," Riley said, squeezing April's hand back.

Then she stood gazing at her daughter for a moment. She seemed so incredibly grown up right now, and Riley felt deeply proud of her.

Of course, like all mothers, she worried about April's future.

She'd become especially concerned recently, when April announced to her that she wanted to be an FBI agent.

Was that the kind of life Riley wanted for her daughter?

She reminded herself yet again …

What I want doesn't matter.

Her job as a parent was to do all she could to make her daughter's dreams possible.

April was starting to look just a little restless under Riley's intense, loving gaze.

"Um, is something wrong, Mom?" April asked.

Riley simply smiled. She'd been waiting for the right moment to bring up something special with April. And if this wasn't the right moment, she couldn't imagine when it would be.

"Come on upstairs," Riley said to April. "I've got a surprise for you."

CHAPTER TWO

As Riley led April up the stairs, she found herself wondering if she had really made the right decision. But she could feel that April was excited about what the "surprise" would be.

She thought that April also seemed a little nervous.

No more nervous than I am, Riley realized. But she didn't figure she could change her mind now.

They both went into Riley's bedroom.

A glance at the expression on her daughter's face convinced Riley not to make any advance explanations. She went to her closet, where a new little black safe was on the shelf. She punched numbers into the keypad, then took something out and laid it on the bed.

April's eyes opened wide at what she saw.

"A gun!" she said. "Is it …?"

"Yours?" Riley replied. "Well, legally it's still mine. Virginia law says you can't own a handgun until you're eighteen. But you can learn with this one until then. We're going to work our way into this slowly, but if you've learned to handle it well, it'll be yours."

April's mouth was hanging open.

"Do you want it?" Riley asked.

April didn't seem to know what to say.

Was this a mistake? Riley wondered. Maybe April actually didn't feel ready for this.

Riley said, "You said you wanted to become an FBI agent."

April nodded eagerly.

Riley said, "So—I thought it might be a good idea to start you on some weapons training. Don't you?"

"Yes—oh, yes," April said. "This is wonderful. Really, really amazing. Thanks, Mom. I'm just kind of overwhelmed. I really hadn't expected this."

"I hadn't either," Riley said. "I mean, I hadn't expected to do anything like this at this point. Owning a gun is a huge responsibility and one that a lot of adults can't handle."

Riley took the gun out of the case and showed it to April.

She said, "This is a Ruger SR22—a .22 caliber semiautomatic

handgun."

"A .22?" April asked.

"Believe me, this is not a toy. I don't want you training with a larger caliber yet. A .22 can be just as dangerous as any other gun—maybe more so. More people are killed by this caliber than any other. Treat it with care and respect. You'll only be handling it for training purposes. I'll keep it in my closet the rest of the time. It will be in a gun safe that can only be opened with a combination. For now, I'll be the only one with that."

"Of course," April said. "I wouldn't want to have it just lying around."

Riley added, "And I'd rather you didn't mention this to Jilly."

"What about Gabriela?"

Riley knew it was a good question. As far as Jilly was concerned, it was simply a matter of maturity. She might get jealous and want a gun of her own, which was out of the question. As for Gabriela, Riley suspected that she might be alarmed at the idea of April learning to use a weapon.

"I might tell her," Riley said. "Not just yet."

Riley clicked out the empty cartridge and said, "Always know whether your weapon is loaded or not."

She handed the unloaded gun to April, whose hands were shaking a little.

Riley almost joked …

"I'm sorry I couldn't get one in pink."

But she thought better of it. This was not a thing to joke about.

April said, "But what do I do with it? Where? When?"

"Right now," Riley said. "Come on, let's go."

Riley put the gun back in its case and carried it with her as they went back down the stairs. Fortunately, Gabriela was working in the kitchen and Jilly was in the family room, so they didn't have to discuss what was in the case.

April went to the kitchen and told Gabriela that she and Riley were going out for a while, then went to the family room and told Jilly the same. The younger girl seemed to be fascinated by something playing on the TV, and she just nodded.

Riley and April both went out the front door and got into the car. Riley drove them to a gun store called Smith Firearms, where she'd bought the gun a couple of days ago. When she and April went inside, they were surrounded by firearms of every type and size, hanging on the walls or in glass cases.

They were greeted by Brick Smith, the store owner. He was a large, bearded man wearing a plaid shirt and a wide, hearty smile.

"Hello there, Ms. Paige," he said. "It's good to see you again. What brings you around today?"

Riley said, "This is my daughter, April. We came by to try out the Ruger I bought here the other day."

Brick Smith seemed slightly amused. Riley remembered when she'd brought her own boyfriend, Blaine, here to buy him a gun for self-defense. Back then, Brick had seemed a little nonplussed to see a woman buying a gun for a man. His surprise had waned when he'd found out that Riley was an FBI agent.

He didn't look the least bit surprised now.

He's getting used to me, Riley thought. *Good. Not everybody does.*

"Well, well, well," he said, looking at April. "You didn't tell me you were buying the gun for your little girl."

Those words jarred Riley a little …

"… your little girl."

She wondered—had April taken offense?

Riley glanced at April and saw that she was still looking a bit overwhelmed.

I guess she kind of feels like a little girl at the moment, Riley thought.

Brick Smith led Riley and April through a door into the surprisingly large shooting range behind the store, then left them alone.

"First things first," Riley said, pointing to a long list on the wall. "Read these rules. Ask me if you've got any questions."

Riley stood watching as April read over the rules, which of course covered all the safety essentials, including *never* pointing a gun in any direction except downrange. As April read with an earnest expression, Riley felt an odd sense of déjà vu. She remembered when she had brought Blaine here to buy and try out his new weapon.

It was a somewhat bitter memory.

Over breakfast at his house after their first night of lovemaking, Blaine had hesitantly told her …

"I think I need to buy a gun. For home protection."

Of course, Riley had understood why. His own life had been in danger since he'd come to know her. And as things turned out, he'd needed that gun only days later to defend not only himself but also

Riley's whole family from a dangerous escaped convict, Shane Hatcher. Blaine had almost killed the man.

Riley now felt again the pang of guilt over that terrible incident.

Is no one safe with me in their lives? she wondered. *Will everyone I know need guns because of me?*

April finished reading the rules, and she and Riley went to one of the empty booths, where April put on ear and eye protection gear. Riley took the gun out of the box and put it in front of April.

April looked at it with a daunted expression.

Good, Riley thought. *She ought to feel intimidated.*

April said, "This is different from the gun you bought for Blaine."

"That's right," Riley said. "I got him a Smith and Wesson 686, a .38 caliber revolver—a much more powerful weapon. But his needs were different. He only wanted to be able to defend himself. He wasn't thinking about going into law enforcement like you."

Riley picked up the gun and showed it to April.

"There are some big differences between a revolver and a semiautomatic. A semiautomatic has a lot of advantages, but a few disadvantages as well—occasional misfires, double feed, failure to eject, stovepipe jams. I didn't want Blaine to have to deal with any of that, not in a case of emergency. But as for you—well, you might as well start learning about them right away, in a safe setting where your life isn't in danger."

Riley began to show April what she needed to know next—how to put rounds into the cartridge, how to put the cartridge into the weapon, and how to unload it again.

Demonstrating, Riley said, "Now this weapon can be used in either single-action or double-action mode. Single-action is when you pull back the hammer before pulling the trigger. Then the gun takes over and automatically cocks the gun again and again. You can fire off rapid shots until your cartridge is empty. That's the great advantage of a semiautomatic."

Fingering the trigger, Riley continued, "Double-action is when you do all the work with the trigger. As you begin to pull, the hammer cocks, and when you finish, the gun fires. If you want to fire another shot, you have to start all over again. That takes more work—your finger is pulling against eight to eleven pounds of pressure—and the firing is slower. And it's what I want you to do to get started."

She pushed a button to bring the paper target to seven yards away from the booth, then showed April the proper stance and hand positions for firing, and also how to aim.

Riley said, "OK, your gun isn't loaded. Let's try some dry firing."

As she had done with Blaine, Riley explained to April how to breathe—to inhale slowly while aiming, then exhale slowly as she pulled the trigger so that her body would be most still when the weapon fired.

April aimed carefully at the vaguely human shape on the target, then pulled the trigger several times. Then, at Riley's instruction, she put the loaded cartridge into the gun, resumed her position, and fired a single shot.

April let out a startled squeal.

"Did I hit anything?" she asked.

Riley pointed to the target.

"Well, you hit the target, anyway. And for your first try, that's not bad. How did it feel?"

April let out a nervous giggle.

"Kind of surprising. I expected more of a ..."

"Recoil?"

"Yeah. And it wasn't as loud as I'd expected."

Riley nodded and said, "That's one of the nice things about a .22. You won't develop a flinch or other bad habits. As you work your way up to larger weapons, you'll be ready to deal with their power. Go ahead, empty the cartridge."

As April slowly fired the nine remaining rounds, Riley noticed a change in her face. It was a determined, fierce expression that Riley realized she had seen in April sometime before. Riley tried to remember ...

When was that? Only once, she thought.

Then the memory hit her like a thunderbolt ...

Riley had pursued the monster named Peterson down to a riverbank. He was holding April hostage, bound hand and foot with a gun to her head. When Peterson's gun misfired, Riley lunged at him and stabbed him, and they struggled in the river until he pushed her head underwater and was about to drown her.

Her face surfaced for a moment, and she saw a sight she would never forget ...

Her wrists and feet still bound, April was on her feet holding

the shotgun that Peterson had dropped.
April slammed its butt against Peterson's head ...

The fight had ended a few moments later, when Riley smashed Peterson's face in with a rock.

But she'd never forgiven herself for allowing April to be in such danger.

And now, here April was, firing away at the target with the same fierce expression on her face.

She's so much like me, Riley thought.

And if April really put her heart and soul into it, Riley was sure that she'd become as good an FBI agent as she'd ever been— perhaps better.

But was that a good thing or a bad thing?

Riley didn't know whether to feel guilty or proud.

But during the half-hour training session, April fired with ever increasing confidence and accuracy at the target. By the time they left the gun store and drove home, Riley was definitely feeling proud.

April was exhilarated and chatty, asking all kinds of questions about the training she had to look forward to. Riley gave the best answers she could, trying not to show her ambivalence about the future April seemed to want so much.

As they neared home, April said, "Look who's here."

Riley's heart sank when she saw the expensive BMW pulled up in front of the townhouse. She knew it belonged to the last person in the world she wanted to see right now.

CHAPTER THREE

As Riley parked her own modest vehicle behind the BMW, she realized that things were likely to get very unpleasant in her house. When she turned off the engine, April picked up the box with the gun in it and started to get out of the car.

"Better leave that here for now," Riley said.

She certainly didn't want to explain the weapon to the unwelcome visitor.

"I guess you're right," April replied, shoving the box under the front seat.

"And don't forget—don't tell Jilly about this," Riley said.

"I won't," April said. "But she's probably figured out already that you got something for me, and she'll wonder all about it. Oh, well, on Sunday you'll be giving her a present of her own and she'll forget all about this."

Present of her own? Riley wondered.

Then she remembered—Sunday was Jilly's birthday.

Riley felt her face flush with alarm.

She'd almost forgotten that Gabriela had planned a family party for Sunday evening.

And she still hadn't bought Jilly a present.

Don't forget! she told herself sternly.

Riley and April locked up the car and walked on into the house. Sure enough, the owner of the luxury car—Riley's ex-husband— was sitting there in the living room.

Jilly was in a chair across from him, her stony expression showing that she wasn't the least bit happy to have him there.

"Ryan, what are you doing here?" Riley asked.

Ryan turned toward her with that charming smile that had too many times weakened her resolve to shut him out completely.

He's still handsome, damn it, she thought.

She knew that he went to a lot of trouble to look that way and spent many hours at the gym.

Ryan said, "Hey, is that any way to greet family? I *am* still family, aren't I?"

Nobody spoke for a moment.

The tension was palpable and Ryan's expression turned to one of disappointment.

Riley wondered—what kind of greeting had he expected?

He hadn't even been to see them in about three months. Before that, they had made an attempt at reconciling. He'd spent a couple of months more or less living here, but he'd never completely moved in. He'd kept the comfortable house he had once shared with Riley and April before the separation and divorce.

The girls had been happy to have him around—until he lost interest and wandered off again.

The girls had been crushed by that.

And now, here he was again, out of the blue and without warning.

The silence continued to hang in the air. Then Jilly crossed her arms and scowled.

Turning to Riley and April, she asked, "Where did the two of you take off to, anyway?"

Riley gulped.

She hated to lie to Jilly, but this would surely be a bad time to tell her about April's gun.

Fortunately, April said, "We just had an errand to run."

Ryan looked up at April.

"Hey, sweetie," he said. "Don't I get a hug or something?"

April didn't make eye contact with him. She just stood there shuffling her feet for a moment.

Finally she said in a sullen voice, "Hi, Daddy."

Looking like she was about to burst into tears, April turned around and trotted up the stairs to her room.

Ryan's mouth dropped open.

"What was *that* all about?" he said.

Riley sat down alone on the couch, trying to figure out how best to handle the situation.

She asked again, "What are you doing here, Ryan?"

Ryan shrugged.

"Jilly and I are talking about her schoolwork—or at least I'm trying to get her to talk about her schoolwork. Have her grades been slipping? Is that what she doesn't want to tell me?"

"My grades are fine," Jilly said.

"So tell me all about school, why don't you?" Ryan asked.

"School's fine—Mr. Paige," Jilly said.

Riley cringed, and Ryan looked wounded.

Jilly had started calling Ryan "Dad" just before he had left.

Before that, she had called him "Ryan." Riley was sure that Jilly had never called him Mr. Paige before. The girl was expressing her attitude very clearly.

Jilly got up from her chair and said, "If it's OK with everybody, I've got some homework to do."

"Do you want any help?" Ryan asked.

Jilly ignored the question and trotted up the stairs.

Ryan looked at Riley with a stricken expression.

"What's going on here?" he said. "Why are the girls so mad at me?"

Riley sighed bitterly. Sometimes her ex was just as immature as they'd both been when they married so young.

"Ryan, what on earth did you expect?" she asked, as patiently as she could manage. "When you moved in, the girls were just thrilled to have you around. Especially Jilly. Ryan, that poor girl's father was an abusive drunk. She almost became a prostitute to get away from him—and she's just thirteen years old! It meant so much to her to have a father figure like you in her life. Don't you understand how crushed she was when you took off?"

Ryan just stared at her with a puzzled expression, as if he had no idea what she was talking about.

But Riley remembered all too well what Ryan had told her on the phone.

"I need some space. This whole family thing—I thought I was ready for it, but I wasn't."

And he hadn't shown a lot of concern about Jilly at the time.

"Riley, Jilly was your decision. I admire you for it. But I never signed up for it. Somebody else's troubled teenager is too much for me. It's not fair."

And now here he was, acting hurt because Jilly didn't want to call him "Dad" anymore.

It really was infuriating.

Riley found it small wonder that the two girls had stormed off just now. She more than half wanted to do the same thing. Unfortunately, somebody had to be an adult in this situation. And since Ryan seemed to be incapable of that, Riley was stuck with the job.

Before she could think of what to say next, Ryan got up from his chair and sat down beside her. He reached toward her.

Riley pushed him away.

"Ryan, what are you doing?"

"What do you think I'm doing?"

Ryan's voice sounded amorous now.

Riley's fury was mounting by the second.

"Don't even think about it," she said. "How many girlfriends have you been through since you've been gone?"

"Girlfriends?" Ryan asked, obviously trying to sound baffled by the very question.

"You heard me. Or did you forget? One of them mistakenly called here while you were still around. She sounded drunk. You said her name was Lina. But I don't guess Lina was the last. How many more have there been? Do you even know? Do you even remember all their names?"

Ryan didn't reply. He looked guilty now.

Everything was starting to make sense to Riley. This whole thing had happened before, and she felt stupid for not having expected it.

Ryan was between girlfriends, and he figured Riley would do under the circumstances.

He didn't really care about the girls at all—not even his own daughter. They were just a pretext for getting together with Riley.

Riley clenched her teeth and said, "I think you'd better leave."

"Why? What's the matter? You're not seeing anyone, are you?"

"As a matter of fact, I am."

Now Ryan looked genuinely perplexed, as if he couldn't imagine why Riley would take an interest in any other man.

Then he said, "Oh my God. It's not that cook again, is it?"

Riley let out a growl of anger.

She said, "You know very well that Blaine is a master chef. You also know that he owns a nice restaurant, and April and his daughter are best friends. He's terrific with the girls—everything you're not. And yes, I am seeing him, and it's getting pretty serious. So I really, really want you to get out of here."

Ryan stared at her for a moment.

Finally he said in a bitter voice, "We were good together."

She didn't reply.

Ryan got up from the couch and headed for the door.

"Let me know if you change your mind," he said as he left the house.

Riley was tempted to say ...

19

"Don't hold your breath."

… but she managed to not say it. She just sat still until she heard the sound of Ryan's car pulling away. Then she breathed a little easier.

Riley sat there in silence for a little while, thinking about what had happened.

Jilly called him "Mr. Paige."

That had been cruel, but she couldn't deny that Ryan had deserved it.

Even so, she worried—what should she say to Jilly about that kind of cruelty?

This motherhood thing is tough, she thought.

She was about to call Jilly down from her room to talk about it when her phone buzzed. The call was from Jenn Roston, a young agent she'd worked with on recent cases.

When Riley took the call, she could hear the stress in Jenn's voice.

"Hey, Riley. I just thought I'd call and …"

A silence fell. Riley wondered what was on Jenn's mind.

Then Jenn said, "Listen, I just want to thank you and Bill for … you know … when I …"

Riley was on the verge of telling her …

"Don't say it. Not over the phone."

Fortunately, Jenn's voice faded without finishing her thought.

Even so, Riley knew what Jenn was thanking her for.

During the case they'd just finished, Jenn had gone AWOL for most of a day. Riley had persuaded Bill that they should cover for her. After all, Jenn had covered for Riley in a somewhat similar situation.

But Jenn's delinquency from her job had been due to the demands of a woman who had once been her foster mother, but who was also a master criminal. Jenn had stepped outside of legal boundaries to take care of a problem for "Aunt Cora."

Riley didn't know exactly what it had been. She hadn't asked.

She heard Jenn make a slight choking sound.

"Riley, I've been thinking. Maybe I should just turn in my badge. What happened before might happen again. And it might be worse next time. Anyway, I don't think it's over."

Riley sensed that Jenn wasn't telling her the real truth.

Aunt Cora is pressuring her again, Riley thought.

It was hardly surprising. If Aunt Cora's hold was strong

enough, Jenn could serve as a real resource from inside the FBI.

Riley briefly wondered …

Should Jenn resign?

But she quickly told herself …

No.

After all, Riley had had a similar relationship with a master criminal—the brilliant escaped convict Shane Hatcher. It had ended after Blaine had shot Hatcher, almost fatally, and Riley had captured him. Hatcher was back in Sing Sing now, and he hadn't spoken a word to anybody ever since.

Jenn knew more about Riley's relationship with Hatcher than anybody except Hatcher himself. Jenn could have destroyed Riley's career with the knowledge she had. But she had kept quiet out of loyalty to Riley. Now it was time for Riley to show the same loyalty to Jenn.

Riley said, "Jenn, remember what I said to you when you first talked to me about this?"

Jenn was silent.

Riley said, "I told you we'd deal with this. You and me, together. You can't quit. You've got too much talent. Do you hear me?"

Jenn still said nothing.

Instead, Riley heard the beep of her call-waiting service telling her that she had another caller.

Ignore it, she told herself.

But the beep came again. Riley's gut told her that the other call was something important. She sighed.

She said to Jenn, "Look, I've got to take another call. Stay on the line, OK? I'll try to make it quick."

"OK," Jenn said.

Riley switched to the incoming call and heard the gruff voice of her team chief at the BAU, Brent Meredith.

"Agent Paige, we've got a case. It's a serial killer in the Midwest. I need to see you in my office."

"When?" Riley asked.

"Already," Meredith grumbled. "Sooner if possible."

Riley could tell by his tone that this really was an urgent matter.

"I'll leave right now," Riley said. "Who else are you putting on the team?"

"That's up to you," Meredith said. "You and Agents Jeffreys

21

and Roston did good work together on the Sandman case. Take both of them if it suits you. And all of you get your asses right over here."

Without another word, Meredith ended the call.

Riley got back on the line with Jenn.

She said, "Jenn, turning in your badge isn't an option. Not right now. I need you on a case. Meet me at Brent Meredith's office. And hurry."

Without waiting for an answer, Riley ended the call. As she dialed the number of her partner, Bill Jeffreys, she thought …

Maybe another case is just what Jenn needs right now.

Riley hoped so.

Meanwhile, she felt a familiar heightening of her own alertness as she hurried to find out what the new case might be.

CHAPTER FOUR

About a half hour later, Riley pulled into the parking lot at Quantico. When she'd asked Meredith how soon he wanted her there, she'd heard real urgency in his voice …

"Already. Sooner if possible."

Of course, when Meredith called her at home, time was almost always running out—sometimes literally, as in her last case. The so-called Sandman had used sand timers to mark the hours that would elapse before his next brutal murder.

But today, something in Meredith's tone told her that this situation was pressing in some unique way.

As she parked, she saw that Bill and Jenn were also just arriving in their own vehicles. She got out of her car and stood waiting for them.

Without exchanging many words, the three walked toward the building. Riley saw that, like her, Bill and Jenn had brought their go-bags along. None of them had needed to be told that they'd likely be flying out of Quantico in short order.

They checked into the building and headed toward Chief Meredith's office. As soon as they got to his door, the burly, imposing African-American man burst out into the hallway. He'd obviously been notified of their arrival.

"No time for a conference," he growled at the three agents. "We'll talk and walk."

As they hurried along with Meredith, Riley realized that they were headed straight to Quantico's airstrip.

We really are in a hurry, Riley thought. It was unusual not to have at least a brief meeting to bring them up to speed on a new case.

Striding along beside Meredith, Bill asked, "What's this all about, Chief?"

Meredith said, "Right now there's a decapitated dead body on a train track near Barnwell, Illinois. It's a line out of Chicago. A woman was bound to the tracks and run over by a freight train, just a few hours ago. It's the second such killing in four days and there are apparently striking similarities. It looks like we're dealing with a serial."

Meredith began to walk a little faster, and the three agents scurried to keep up.

Riley asked, "Who called for the FBI?"

Meredith said, "I got the call from Jude Cullen, the Chicago area Deputy Chief of Railroad Police. He says he wants profilers there right away. I told him to leave the body where it was until my agents got a look at it."

Meredith grunted a little.

"That's a pretty tall order. Three more freight trains are scheduled along that track today, and a passenger train as well. Right now, they're all on hold, and it's already getting to be a mess. You need to get out there ASAP and get a look at the crime scene so the body can be moved and the trains can start running again. And then ..."

Meredith grunted again.

"Well, you've got a killer to stop. And I'm pretty sure we all agree on one thing—he *will* kill again. Aside from that, you now know as much about the case as I do. Cullen will have to fill you in on anything else."

The group stepped out onto the tarmac of the airstrip where the small jet was waiting, its engines already rumbling.

Over the sound, Meredith called out, "You'll be met at O'Hare by some railroad cops. They'll drive you straight to the crime scene."

Meredith turned around and headed back into the building, and Riley and her colleagues mounted the steps and boarded the plane. The hastiness of their departure almost made Riley dizzy. She couldn't remember Meredith ever rushing them out like that.

But it was hardly any surprise, considering that railroad traffic was stalled. Riley couldn't imagine that enormous difficulties that might be causing right now.

Once the plane was airborne, the three agents opened their computers and got online to look for what little information they might find at this point.

Riley quickly saw that news of the most recent killing was already spreading, although the current victim's name wasn't yet available. But she saw that the previous victim's name was Fern Bruder, a twenty-five-year-old woman whose decapitated body had been found on a train track near Allardt, Indiana.

Riley couldn't find much else online about the murders. If the railroad police had any suspects or knew of any motive, that information hadn't leaked to the public yet—which was a good thing as far as Riley was concerned.

Still, it was frustrating not to be able to learn more right now.

With so little to think about regarding the case, Riley found herself mulling over what had happened so far today. She still felt a pang about losing Liam—although she also realized …

"Losing" isn't exactly the right word.

No, she and her family had done their very best for the boy. And now things had turned out for the best, and Liam was in the care of people who would love him and take good care of him.

Even so, Riley wondered …

Why does it feel like a loss?

Riley also had mixed feelings about buying April a gun and taking her to the shooting range. April's show of maturity had certainly made Riley proud, and so had her budding marksmanship. Riley was also deeply touched that her daughter wanted to follow in her footsteps.

And yet … Riley couldn't help but remind herself …

I'm on my way to view a decapitated body.

Her whole career was one long string of horrors. Was this really a life she wanted for April?

It's not up to me, Riley reminded herself. *It's up to her.*

Riley also felt strange about that awkward phone conversation she'd had with Jenn a little while ago. So much had been left unspoken, and Riley had no idea what might be going on right now between Jenn and Aunt Cora. And of course, now was no time to talk it out—not with Bill sitting right here with them.

Riley couldn't help but wonder …

Was Jenn right? Should she turn in her badge?

Was Riley doing the young agent any favors by encouraging her to stay with the FBI?

And was Jenn in the right frame of mind to take on a new case right now?

Riley looked over at Jenn, who was sitting in her seat staring raptly at her computer.

Jenn certainly seemed fully focused at the moment—more so than Riley was, anyway.

Riley's thoughts were interrupted by the sound of Bill's voice.

"Tied to railroad tracks. It almost sounds like …"

Riley saw that Bill was also looking at his computer screen.

He paused, but Jenn finished his thought.

"Like one of those old-time silent movies, huh? Yeah, I was thinking the same thing."

Bill shook his head.

"I sure don't mean to make light of it … but I keep thinking of some mustachioed villain in a top hat tying a young damsel to the train tracks until some dashing hero comes along to rescue her. Isn't that what always happened in silent movies?"

Jenn pointed at her computer screen.

She said, "Actually, not really. I've been doing some research on that. It's a trope, all right, a cliché. And everybody seems to think they've seen it at one time or another, like some sort of urban legend. But it never seemed to show up in actual silent movies, at least not seriously."

Jenn turned her computer screen around so that Bill and Riley could see it.

She said, "The first fictional example of a villain tying someone to railroad tracks seems to have appeared long before movies even existed, in an 1867 play called *Under the Gaslight.* Only—get this!—the villain tied a *man* to the tracks, and the leading lady had to rescue him. The same sort of thing happened in a short story and a few other plays around that time."

Riley could see that Jenn was quite caught up in what she'd found.

Jenn continued, "As far as old-time movies are concerned, there were maybe two silent comedies in which this exact thing happened—a screaming, helpless damsel got tied to the tracks by a dastardly villain and got rescued by a handsome hero. But they were played for laughs, just like in Saturday morning cartoons."

Bill's eyes widened with interest.

"Parodies of something that was never real to begin with," he said.

"Exactly," Jenn said.

Bill shook his head.

He said, "But steam locomotives were a part of everyday life back in those days—the first few decades of the twentieth century, I mean. Weren't there any silent movies portraying someone in danger of getting run over by a train?"

"Sure," Jenn said. "Sometimes a character would get pushed or fall onto tracks and maybe get knocked unconscious when a train was coming. But that's not the same scenario, is it? Besides, just like in that old play, the movie character in danger was usually a man who had to get rescued by the heroine!"

Riley's interest was thoroughly piqued now. She knew that Jenn wasn't wasting her time looking into this sort of thing. They needed to know about anything that could be driving a killer. Part of that could be understanding all the cultural precedents of whatever scenarios they happened to be dealing with—even those that might be fictional.

Or in this case, nonexistent, Riley thought.

Anything that might have influenced the killer was of interest.

She thought for a moment, then asked Jenn, "Does this mean that there have never been any real-life cases of people being murdered by getting tied to train tracks?"

"Actually, it has happened in real life," Jenn said, pointing to some more information on her computer screen. "Between 1874 and 1910, at least six people were killed that way. I can't find many examples since, except for one very recently. In France, a man bound his estranged wife to train tracks on her birthday. Then he got in front of the oncoming high-speed train, so he died along with her—a murder-suicide. Otherwise, it seems to be a rare way to murder anyone. And none of those were serial killings."

Jenn turned her computer screen back toward her and fell quiet again.

Riley mulled over what Jenn had just said …

"… a rare way to murder anyone."

Riley thought …

Rare, but not unheard of.

She found herself wondering—had that string of murders between 1874 and 1910 been inspired by those old stage plays in which characters had been tied to train tracks? Riley knew of more recent instances of life imitating art in some horrible way—in which murderers were inspired by novels or movies or video games.

Maybe things hadn't changed all that much.

Maybe *people* hadn't changed all that much.

And what about the killer they were about to look for?

It seemed ridiculous to imagine that they were hunting some psychopath who was emulating a dastardly, melodramatic, mustache-twirling villain who had never really existed, not even in the movies.

But what *could be* driving this killer?

The situation was all too clear and all too familiar. Riley and her colleagues were going to have to answer that question, or more people would be killed.

Riley sat watching as Jenn continued to work on her computer. It was an encouraging sight. For the time being, Jenn seemed to have shaken off her anxieties about the mysterious "Aunt Cora."

But how long will it last? Riley wondered.

Anyway, the sight of Jenn so focused on research reminded Riley that she ought to be doing the same. She'd never worked a case involving trains before, and she had a lot to learn. She turned her attention back to her computer.

*

Just as Meredith had said, Riley and her colleagues were greeted on the tarmac at O'Hare by a pair of uniformed railroad cops. They all introduced themselves, and Riley and her colleagues got into their vehicle.

"We'd better hurry," the cop in the passenger seat said. "The railroad bigwigs are really breathing down the chief's neck to get that body off the tracks."

Bill asked, "How long will it take us to get there?"

The cop who was driving said, "Usually an hour, but it won't take us that long."

He turned on the lights and siren, and the car started wending its way through the heavy late afternoon traffic. It was a tense, chaotic, high-speed drive that eventually took them through the small town of Barnwell, Illinois. After that, they passed through a railroad crossing.

The passenger cop pointed.

"It looks like the killer turned off the road right next to the tracks in some kind of off-road vehicle. He drove alongside the tracks until he reached the place where he did the killing."

Soon they pulled over and parked next to a wooded area. Another police vehicle was parked there, and also a coroner's van.

The trees weren't very dense. The cops led Riley and her colleagues straight through them to the railroad tracks, which were only some fifty feet away.

Just then, the crime scene came into full view.

Riley gulped hard at what she saw.

Suddenly gone were any corny images of mustachioed villains

and damsels in distress.

This was all too real—and all too horrible.

CHAPTER FIVE

For a long moment, Riley stood staring at the body on the tracks. She'd seen corpses mangled in all kinds of horrifying ways. Even so, this victim presented a uniquely shocking spectacle. The woman had been beheaded cleanly by the wheels of the train, almost as if by a guillotine's blade.

Riley was surprised that the woman's headless body seemed unscathed by the train that had passed over it. The victim was bound tightly with duct tape, her hands and arms taped to her sides, and her ankles taped together. Clothed in what had been an attractive outfit, the body was twisted in a desperate, writhing position. Where her neck was severed, blood was spattered on the crushed stones, the wooden ties, and the rail. The head had been thrown some six or seven feet down the embankment along the tracks. The woman's eyes and mouth gaped up at the sky in an expression of frozen horror.

Riley saw several people standing around the body, some of them wearing uniforms, some not. Riley figured they were a mix of local police and railroad cops. A man in a uniform came toward Riley and her colleagues.

He said, "You're the FBI folks, I take it. I'm Jude Cullen, Deputy Chief of Railroad Police for the Chicago region—'Bull' Cullen, folks call me."

He sounded proud of the nickname. Riley knew from her research that "Bull" was general slang for a police officer on the railroad. Actually, in the railroad police organization they held the titles of Agent and Special Agent, much like the FBI. This one apparently preferred the sound of the more generic term.

"It was my idea to get you guys here," Cullen continued. "I hope the trip proves to be worth it. The sooner we can get the body away from here, the better."

As Riley and her colleagues introduced themselves, she looked Cullen over. He seemed remarkably young and had an exceptionally muscular physique, his arms bulging below the uniform's short sleeves and the shirt stretched tight across his chest.

The nickname "Bull" suited him pretty well, she thought. But

Riley always found herself put off rather than attracted by men who obviously spent many hours in a gym to look this way.

She wondered how a muscle-bound guy like Bull Cullen actually found time for much of anything else. Then she noticed that he wasn't wearing a wedding ring. She figured that his life must be about his job and working out, and not much else.

He appeared to be good-natured and not especially shocked by the unusually grisly nature of the crime scene. Of course, he'd been here for a few hours now—long enough to get somewhat numbed to it. Even so, the man immediately struck Riley as rather vain and shallow.

She asked him, "Have you identified the victim?"

Bull Cullen nodded.

"Yeah, her name was Reese Fisher, thirty-five years old. She lived right near here in Barnwell, where she worked as the local librarian. She was married to a chiropractor."

Riley looked up and down the tracks. This stretch was curved so that she couldn't see very far in either direction.

"Where is the train that ran over her?" she asked Cullen.

Cullen pointed and said, "About a half mile down there, exactly where it stopped."

Riley noticed an obese, black-uniformed man who was crouching next to the body.

"Is that the medical examiner?" she asked Cullen.

"Yeah, let me introduce you to him. This is the Barnwell coroner, Corey Hammond."

Riley crouched down beside the man. She sensed that, in contrast to Cullen, Hammond was still struggling to contain his shock. His breathing was coming in gasps—partly due to his weight, but also, she suspected, from revulsion and horror. He'd surely never seen anything like this in his jurisdiction.

"What can you tell us so far?" Riley asked the coroner.

"No sign of sexual assault that I can see," Hammond said. "That's consistent with the other coroner's autopsy of the victim four days ago, over near Allardt."

Hammond pointed to mangled pieces of wide silvery tape around the woman's neck and shoulders.

"The killer bound her hand and foot, then taped her neck onto the rail and immobilized her shoulders. She must have struggled like mad trying to get loose. But she didn't stand a chance."

Riley turned toward Cullen and asked, "Her mouth wasn't

31

gagged. Would anybody have heard her screaming?"

"We don't think so," Cullen said, pointing toward some trees. "There are some houses through those woods, but they're out of earshot. A couple of my guys went from door to door asking if anybody had heard anything or had any idea what had been happening at the time of the murder. No one did. They found out all about it on TV or on the Internet. They've been instructed to stay away from here. So far, we haven't had any trouble with gawkers."

Bill asked, "Did it look like anything was stolen from her?"

Cullen shrugged.

"We don't think so. We found her purse right here beside her, and she still had identification and money and credit cards. Oh, and a cell phone."

Riley studied the body, trying to imagine how the killer had managed to get the victim into this position. Sometimes she could get a powerful, even uncanny, feeling of the killer just by tuning in to her surroundings at a crime scene. Sometimes it almost seemed that she could get into his thoughts, know what was on his mind as he committed the murder.

But not right now.

Things were too jangled here, with all these people milling about.

She said, "He must have subdued her somehow before he bound her up like this. What about the other corpse, the victim that was killed earlier? Did the local coroner find any drugs in her system?"

"There was flunitrazepam in her bloodstream," Coroner Hammond said.

Riley glanced at her colleagues. She knew what flunitrazepam was, and she knew that Jenn and Bill did as well. Its trade name was Rohypnol, and it was commonly known as the date rape drug or as "roofies." It was illegal, but all too easy to buy on the streets.

And it certainly would have subdued the victim, rendering her helpless although possibly not fully unconscious. Riley knew that flunitrazepam had an amnesiac effect once it wore off. She shuddered to realize …

It might well have worn off right here—just before she died.

If so, the poor woman would have had no idea how or why such a terrible thing had happened to her.

Bill scratched his chin as he looked down at the body.

He said, "So maybe this started off date-rape style, with the killer slipping the drug into her drink at a bar or a party or something."

The coroner shook his head.

"Apparently not," he said. "There wasn't a trace of the drug in the other victim's stomach. It must have been given to her as an injection."

Jenn said, "That's odd."

Deputy Chief Bull Cullen looked at Jenn with interest.

"Why so?" he asked.

Jenn shrugged slightly.

She said, "It's a little hard to imagine, that's all. Flunitrazepam doesn't take effect right away, no matter how it's delivered. In a date-rape situation, that typically doesn't matter. The unsuspecting victim maybe has drinks with her soon-to-be assailant for a little while, starts feeling woozy without knowing quite why, and pretty soon she becomes helpless. But if our killer stabbed her with a needle, she'd immediately know she was in trouble, and she'd have had a few minutes to resist before the drug took effect. It just doesn't sound … very efficient."

Cullen smiled at Jenn—a little flirtatiously, Riley thought.

"It makes sense to me," he said. "Let me show you."

He walked behind Jenn, who was markedly shorter than he was. He started reaching around her neck from behind her. Jenn stepped away.

"Hey, what are you doing?" Jenn said.

"Just demonstrating. Don't worry, I'm not really going to hurt you."

Jenn scoffed and kept her distance from him.

"Damn right, you're not," she said. "And I'm pretty sure I know what you've got in mind. You're thinking the killer used some kind of choke hold."

"That's right," Cullen said, still smiling. "Specifically, a so-called blood choke."

He twisted his arm to illustrate his point.

"The killer approached her unexpectedly from behind, then crooked his arm like this around the front of her neck. The victim could still breathe, but her carotid arteries were shut off completely, cutting off the blood flow to the brain. The victim lost consciousness within seconds. Then it was easy for the killer to administer an injection that rendered her helpless for a longer period."

Riley easily sensed the friction between Cullen and Jenn. Cullen was obviously a classic "mansplainer" whose attitude toward Jenn was condescending as well as flirtatious.

Jenn clearly didn't like him one bit, and Riley felt the same. The man was shallow, all right, with a poor sense of appropriate behavior when it came to dealing with a female colleague—and an even worse sense of how to behave at a murder scene.

Still, Riley had to admit that Cullen's theory was sound.

He might be obnoxious, but he wasn't stupid.

In fact, he might be genuinely helpful to work with.

That is, if we can stand to be around him, Riley thought.

Cullen stepped off the tracks and down the slope and pointed at a space where the ground had been taped off.

He said, "We've got some tire tracks, from where he drove down here after turning off the main road back at the railroad crossing. They're big tracks—obviously some kind of off-road vehicle. Here are some footprints too."

Riley said, "Have your people take pictures of these. We'll send them to Quantico and have our technicians run them through our database."

Cullen stood with his arms akimbo for a moment, taking in the scene with what seemed to Riley almost like a sense of satisfaction.

He said, "I've got to say, this is a new experience for me and my guys. We're used to investigating cargo theft, vandalism, collisions, and the like. Murders are few and far between. And something like this—well, we've never seen anything like it before. Of course, I guess it's nothing really special for you FBI folks. You're used to it."

Cullen got no reply and he fell silent for a moment. Then he looked at Riley and her colleagues and said, "Well, I don't want to take too much of your precious time. Just give us a profile, and my team will take it from here. You can fly back home today, unless you really want to spend the night."

Riley, Bill, and Jenn looked at each other with surprise.

Did he seriously think they could wrap up their work here that quickly?

"I'm not sure what you mean," Riley said.

Cullen shrugged and said, "I'm sure you've figured out something in the way of a profile by now. That's what you're here for, after all. What can you tell me?"

Riley hesitated for a moment.

Then she said, "We can give you a few generalizations. Statistically, most murderers who leave the body at the scene have a prior criminal record. Over half of them are between the ages of fifteen and thirty-seven—and over half are African-American, employed at least part time, and have at least a high school education. Some such killers have had prior psychiatric problems, and some have been in the military. But ..."

Riley hesitated.

"But what?" Cullen asked.

"Try to understand—none of this is really useful information, at least not at this point. There are always outliers. And our killer is starting to look like one already. For example, the kind of killer we're talking about usually has some kind of sexual motivation. But that doesn't seem to be the case here. My guess is that he's not typical in a lot of ways. Maybe he's not typical at all. We've still got a lot of work cut out for us."

For the first time since she'd arrived, Cullen's expression darkened a little.

Riley added, "And I want her cell phone rushed to Quantico. And the other victim's cell phone as well. Our technicians need to see if they can get any information out of them."

Before Cullen could reply, his own cell phone buzzed and he scowled.

He said, "I already know who that is. It's the railroad administrator, wanting to know if he can get the trains moving again. The line has got three freight trains piled up and a passenger train running late. There's a fresh crew ready to drive away the train that's still sitting on the tracks. Can we move the body yet?"

Riley nodded and said to the coroner, "Go ahead, get her into your van."

Cullen turned away and took the call, while the coroner called his people together and got to work with the body.

When Cullen got off the phone, he seemed to be in a genuinely sour mood.

He said to Riley and her colleagues, "So I guess you folks are going to make yourselves at home for a while."

Riley thought she was starting to understand what was bothering him. Cullen was positively looking forward to solving a sensational case, and he hadn't expected the FBI to rob him of his thunder.

Riley said, "Look, we're here at your request. But I think you'll be needing us—for a while longer anyway."

Cullen shook his head and shuffled his feet.

Then he said, "Well, we'd all better head on into the Barnwell police station. We've got something pretty unpleasant to deal with there."

Without another word, he turned and headed away.

Riley glanced at the body, which was now being loaded onto a gurney.

She wondered …

More unpleasant than this?

Her mind boggled as she and her colleagues followed Cullen back the way they'd come.

CHAPTER SIX

Jenn Roston was seething as she turned to follow her colleagues away from the crime scene. She trudged through the trees behind Riley and Agent Jeffreys as Deputy Chief Jude Cullen led the way toward the parked vehicles.

"Bull" Cullen, he calls himself, she remembered with contempt.

She was glad to have two people between her and that man.

She kept thinking …

He tried to demonstrate a blood choke on me!

She doubted that he'd been looking for an excuse to grope her—not exactly, anyway. But he sure was looking for a chance to show physical control over her. It was bad enough that he felt the need to mansplain the blood choke hold and its effects to her—as if she didn't know all about it already.

She thought they were both lucky that Cullen hadn't actually gotten his arm around her neck. She might not have been able to control herself. Although the man was ridiculously muscular, she would most likely have made short work of him. Of course, that would have been pretty unseemly at a murder scene and would have done nothing to promote good relations among investigators. So Jenn knew it was just as well things hadn't gotten out of hand.

On top of everything else, now Cullen seemed to be pissed off that Jenn and her colleagues weren't going away just yet, and that he wasn't going to hog all the glory of solving the case.

Tough luck, asshole, Jenn thought.

The group emerged from the trees and got into the police van with Cullen. The man said nothing as he drove to the police station and her FBI companions were quiet too. She figured that they, like her, were thinking about the grisly crime scene and Cullen's comment about having "something pretty unpleasant to deal with" at the station.

Jenn hated riddles, maybe because Aunt Cora was so often cryptic and threatening in her attempts at manipulation. And she also hated living with the sense that something in her past could destroy her present dream-come-true of being an FBI agent.

37

When Cullen parked the van in front of the police station, Jenn and her colleagues got out and followed him inside. There, Cullen introduced them to Barnwell's Chief of Police, Lucas Powell, a middle-aged man with a sagging chin.

"Come with me," Powell said. "I've got the guys right in here. My people and I just don't know how to deal with this kind of thing."

Guys? Jenn wondered.

And what kind of "thing" did he mean?

Chief Lucas Powell led Jenn, her colleagues, and Cullen straight to the station's interview room. Inside, they found two men seated at the table, both wearing neon yellow vests. One was lean and tall, an older but vigorous-looking man. The other was about Jenn's own shorter height, and probably not much older than she was.

They were drinking cups of coffee and just staring at the table.

Powell introduced the older man first, the younger man second.

"This is Arlo Stine, the freight conductor. And this is Everett Boynton, his assistant conductor. When the train stopped, they're the ones who had to walk back and find the body."

The two men barely looked up at the group.

Jenn gulped. Surely they must be terribly traumatized.

There definitely was "something pretty unpleasant" to deal with here.

Interviewing these men wasn't going to be easy. To make matters worse, they weren't likely to know anything that would help lead to the killer.

Jenn stood back as Riley sat down at the table with the men and spoke in a soft voice.

"I'm awfully sorry you've had to deal with this. How are you guys holding up?"

The older man, the conductor, shrugged slightly.

"I'll be all right," he said. "Believe it or not, I've seen this kind of thing before. People killed on the tracks, I mean. I've seen bodies mangled up a lot worse. Not that anyone ever gets used to it, but …"

Stine nodded toward his assistant and added, "But Everett here has never been through this before."

The younger man looked up from the table at the people in the room.

"I'll be OK," he said with a shaky nod, obviously trying to

sound like he meant it.

Riley said, "I'm sorry to ask this—but did you see the victim just before …?"

Boynton winced sharply and said nothing.

Stine said, "Just a glimpse, that's all. We were both in the cab. But I was on the radio making a routine call to the next station, and Everett was making calculations for the curve we were taking just then. When the engineer started braking and sounded the whistle, we looked up and saw … something, we weren't sure what it was really."

Stine paused, then added, "But we sure knew what happened when we walked back to the spot for a look."

Jenn was mentally reviewing some of the research she'd done on the plane flight. She knew that freight train crews were small. Even so, there seemed to be one person missing.

"Where's the engineer?" she asked.

"The hogger?" Bull Cullen said. "He's in the custody suite."

Jenn's mouth dropped slightly.

She knew that "hogger" was railroad slang for an engineer.

But what the hell was going on here?

"You put him in a jail cell?" she asked.

Powell said, "We didn't have much choice."

The older conductor added, "The poor guy—he won't talk to anybody. The only words he's said since it happened are, 'Lock me up.' He just kept saying that again and again."

The local police chief said, "So that's what we wound up doing. It seemed the best thing for now."

Jenn felt a flash of anger.

She asked, "Haven't you brought in a therapist to talk to him?"

The railroad deputy chief said, "We've asked for a company psychologist to come in from Chicago. It's union rules. We don't know when he's going to show up."

Riley looked truly startled now.

"Surely the engineer doesn't blame himself for what happened," she said.

The older conductor looked surprised at the question.

"Of course he does," he said. "It wasn't his fault, but he can't help it. He was the man at the controls. He's the one who felt the most helpless. It's eating him up inside. I hate it that he's shut himself off like this. I really tried to talk to him, but he won't even look me in the eye. We shouldn't be waiting around for some damned railroad shrink to show up. Rules or not, somebody ought to do something right now. A good hogger like him deserves better."

Jenn's anger sharpened.

She said to Cullen, "Well, you can't just leave him in that cell by himself. I don't care if he insists on being alone. It can't be good for him. Somebody needs to reach out to him."

Everyone in the room looked at her.

Jenn hesitated, then said, "Take me to the custody suite. I want to see him."

Riley looked up at her and said, "Jenn, I'm not sure that's such a good idea."

But Jenn ignored her.

"What's his name?" Jenn asked the conductors.

Boynton said, "Brock Putnam."

"Take me to him," Jenn insisted. "Right now."

Chief Powell led Jenn out of the interview room and down the hall. As they walked along, Jenn wondered whether Riley might be right.

Maybe this isn't such a good idea.

After all, she knew that empathy was hardly her strong suit as an agent. She tended to be blunt and outspoken, even when a softer touch was needed. She certainly didn't have Riley's ability to turn on the compassion at appropriate moments. And if Riley herself didn't feel up to this task, why did Jenn feel like she ought to take it on?

But she couldn't help thinking …

Somebody's got to talk to him.

Powell led her into the row of cells, all with solid doors and tiny windows.

He asked, "Do you want me to come in with you?"

"No," Jenn said. "I'd better do this one-on-one."

Powell opened a door to one of the cells, and Jenn stepped inside. Powell left the door open but stepped away.

A man in his early thirties sat on the end of the cot, staring directly at the wall. He was wearing an ordinary T-shirt and backward baseball cap.

Standing just inside the doorway, Jenn said in a soft voice …

"Mr. Putnam? Brock? My name is Jenn Roston, and with the FBI. I'm so terribly sorry about what happened. I just wondered if you wanted to … talk."

Putnam showed no indication of even hearing her.

He seemed especially determined not to make eye contact with her—or with anybody else, Jenn felt sure.

And from her research flying out here, Jenn knew exactly why he felt that way.

She swallowed hard as a knot of anxiety filled her throat.

This was going to be a lot harder than she'd even imagined.

CHAPTER SEVEN

Riley uneasily kept her eye on the door after Jenn left the room. As Bill kept asking the conductor and his assistant questions, she worried about how Jenn was going to deal with the engineer.

She was sure that the engineer was probably having a terrible time of it. She didn't like the idea of waiting a lot longer for a railroad psychologist—possibly some official flunky who might be more concerned about the company's well-being than the engineer's. But what else were they supposed to do?

And might the young agent only make things worse for the man? Riley had never seen any sign that Jenn was especially skillful at dealing with people.

If Jenn did just upset the man further, how might that affect her own morale? She had already been contemplating leaving the FBI because of pressures from a criminal former foster mother.

Despite her concerns, Riley managed to listen to what was being said in the room.

Bill said to Stine, "You said you've seen this kind of thing before. Do you mean murders on railroad tracks?"

"Oh, no," Stine said. "Actual murders like that are really rare. But people getting killed on the tracks—that's a lot more common than you might think. There are several hundred victims a year, some of them just stupid thrill-seekers, but a lot of them suicides. In the business, we call them 'trespassers.'"

The younger man twisted in his chair uncomfortably and said, "I sure don't want to see anything like that again. But from what Arlo tells me … well, I guess it's part of the job."

Bill said to the conductor, "Are you sure there wasn't anything the engineer could have done?"

Arlo Stine shook his head.

"Damned sure. He'd already slowed the train down to thirty-five miles per hour for the curve we were on. Even so, there was no way to stop a diesel locomotive with ten freight cars behind it anywhere near fast enough to save that woman. You can't break the laws of physics and stop several thousand tons of moving steel on a dime. Let me explain it to you …"

The conductor started talking about the mechanics of braking. It was highly technical talk, and of no real interest or use to Riley or Bill. But Riley knew that it was best to let Stine just keep talking—for his own sake, if for no one else's.

Meanwhile, Riley still found herself looking toward the door, wondering how Jenn was doing with the engineer.

*

Jenn stood next to the bed looking anxiously at Brock Putnam's back as he stared silently at the wall.

Now that she was actually with the man, she found that she had no idea what to do or say next.

But from her research on the plane, she understood why he was incapable of looking at her or anyone else right now. He was traumatized by a single detail that often haunted "hoggers" who'd been through what he had just been through.

A few moments ago, the conductor had said that he and his assistant had only gotten a glimpse of the victim before she died.

But this man had gotten much more than a glimpse.

He'd seen something uniquely horrifying from his window in that cab—something that no innocent human being deserved to see.

Would it help for him to say it aloud?

I'm not a shrink, she reminded herself.

Even so, she felt more and more anxious to reach out to him.

Slowly and cautiously, Jenn said …

"I think I know what you saw," she said. "You can talk to me about it if you like."

After a pause, she added …

"But not if you don't want to."

A silence fell.

I guess he doesn't want to, Jenn thought.

She almost got up to leave, but then the man said in a nearly inaudible whisper …

"I died back there."

The words chilled Jenn to the bone.

Again, she wondered whether she had any business trying to do this.

She said nothing. She figured it was best to wait and see if he wanted to say more. She waited for many seconds, more than half-hoping the man would stay silent and she could leave quietly.

Then he said …

"I saw it happen. I was looking … in a mirror."

He paused for a moment, then added …

"I saw myself die. So why … why am I here?"

Jenn gulped hard.

Yes, what had happened to him was exactly the sort of thing she'd read about on the plane. Hundreds of people died on railroad tracks every year. And all too often, the engineers endured an unimaginably horrifying moment.

They made eye contact with the person who was about to die.

The exact same thing had happened to Brock Putman. The reason he couldn't make eye contact with anyone else was that it made him relive that moment all over again. And his identification with the poor woman was eating him up inside. He was trying to cope by denying that anyone else had been killed. Guiltily, he was trying to convince himself that he—and only he—was dead.

Jenn spoke even more cautiously than before.

"You didn't die. You weren't looking in a mirror. Someone else died. And it wasn't your fault. There was no way on earth you could stop it from happening. You know that—even if you have trouble accepting it. It wasn't your fault."

The man still faced away from her. But a sob escaped from his throat.

Jenn was momentarily alarmed. Had she just pushed him over some kind of edge?

No, she thought.

She had a gut feeling that this was good, that it was necessary.

The man's shoulders shook slightly as his quiet sobbing continued.

Jenn touched him on the shoulder.

She said, "Brock, could you do something for me? I just want you to look at me."

His shoulders stopped shaking, and his sobbing ebbed away.

Then, very slowly, he turned around on his bed and looked at Jenn.

His bright blue eyes were wide and pleading and brimming with tears—and they were gazing straight into Jenn's own eyes.

Jenn had to fight back her own tears.

As blunt, brusque, and sometimes even tactless as she normally was, it dawned on her that she'd never had this kind of interaction with anybody before, at least not professionally.

She swallowed hard, then said, "You're not looking into a mirror right now. You're looking at me. You're looking into my eyes. And you're alive. You've got every right to be alive."

Brock Putnam opened his mouth to speak, but no words came.

Instead, he nodded.

Jenn almost gasped with relief.

I did it, she thought. *I drew him out.*

Then she said, "But you deserve something more. You deserve to find out who did this terrible thing—not just to that poor woman, but to you. And you deserve justice. You deserve to know that he'll never do anything like this again. I promise—you'll get justice. I'll make sure of it."

He nodded again, with just a trace of a smile.

She smiled and said, "Now let's get out of here. You've got two pals out there who are worried about you. Let's go see them."

She got up from the cot, and so did Brock. They walked outside the cell, where Chief Powell was still waiting. Powell looked astonished at the change in Putnam's demeanor and behavior. They all walked back to the interview room and headed on inside. Riley, Bill, and Cullen were still there, and so were the two conductors.

Stine and Boynton sat gaping for a moment, then got up and exchanged emotional hugs with Brock Putnam. They all sat down at the table together and started talking quietly.

Jenn looked at the railroad deputy chief sternly and said, "Light a fire under somebody's ass and get that railroad psychologist down here ASAP."

Then, turning to the local police chief, she said, "Go get this man a cup of coffee."

Powell nodded mutely and left the room.

Riley took Jenn aside and asked quietly, "Do you think he'll ever be able to get back to work?"

Jenn thought for a moment and said, "I doubt it."

Riley nodded and said, "He'll probably be struggling for the rest of his life. It's a horrible thing to have to live with."

Riley smiled and added, "But you did some good work just now."

Jenn felt flooded with warmth at Riley's praise.

She remembered back to how her day had started—how her communication with Aunt Cora had left her feeling inadequate and unworthy.

Maybe I'm of some use after all, she thought.

After all, she'd always known that empathy was a quality she lacked and needed to cultivate. And now at last, she seemed to have taken at least a few steps toward being a more empathetic agent.

She also felt energized by the promise she'd just made to Brock Putnam:

"I promise—you'll get justice. I'll make sure of it."

She was glad she'd said it. Now she was committed to it.

I won't let him down, she thought.

Meanwhile, the two conductors and the engineer continued to talk quietly, commiserating about the awful experience they had all endured, but which had been especially awful for Putnam.

Suddenly, the door to the room opened and Chief Powell looked inside.

He said to Cullen and the FBI agents, "You'd better come with me. A witness just showed up."

Jenn felt a jolt of excitement as she and the others followed Cullen down the hall.

Were they about to get the break they needed?

CHAPTER EIGHT

As Riley followed Powell down the hall along with the other FBI agents and Bull Cullen, she wondered …

A witness? Are we really going to get a break this fast?

Years of experience told her that it wasn't likely.

Even so, she couldn't help hoping that this time might be different. It would be wonderful to wrap this case up before anyone else was killed.

When the group arrived at a small meeting room, a stout woman in her fifties was pacing inside. She wore heavy makeup and her hair was an unnatural shade of blond.

She hurried toward them. "Oh, this is awful," she said. "I saw her picture on the news a little while ago, and I recognized her right away. Such a horrible death. But I had a feeling about her—a bad feeling. A premonition, you might even call it."

Riley's hopes sank a little.

It usually wasn't a good sign when witnesses started talking about "premonitions."

Bill guided the woman to a chair.

"Sit down, ma'am," he said. "Take it easy and let's start from the beginning. What's your name?"

The woman sat down, but she just fidgeted in her chair.

Bill sat in a nearby chair, turning it a little to talk with her. Riley, Jenn, and the others also took chairs around the meeting room table.

"Your name?" Bill asked again.

"Sarah Dillon," she said, giving him a wide smile. "I live right here in Barnwell."

Bill asked, "And how did you know the victim?"

The woman looked at him as if surprised at the question.

"Well, I didn't actually *know* her. We exchanged words on occasion."

Bill asked, "Did you see her this morning—before she was killed?"

Sarah Dillon seemed more surprised than before.

"No. It's been a couple of weeks or more since I last saw her.

47

Why does that matter?"

Riley exchanged glances with Bill and Jenn. She knew they were all thinking the same thing.

A couple of weeks or more?

Of course it mattered a great deal.

When Powell had said a witness had shown up, Riley had imagined someone who either knew the victim personally or had seen something truly material to the case—the actual abduction, perhaps. Still, she knew that they needed to follow up on every possible lead. So far, they had nothing else to go on.

Riley said, "Tell us about your interactions with the victim."

Sarah Dillon scratched her chin.

"Well, I've seen her around town. Occasionally, I mean. In stores, on the streets. Also at the train stations, both here and in Chicago. I take the train to Chicago every week or so, to see my sister and her family there. I've seen her getting on or off the train, either here or in Chicago. Sometimes we've been in the same car together."

Sarah Dillon's eyes darted about for a moment.

Then she asked in a near-whisper, "Do you think I'm in any danger right now?"

The woman was striking Riley as less coherent by the moment. She didn't know how to answer her question. Why did the woman imagine she might be in danger? Did she have any good reason to worry at all?

Offhand, Riley doubted it. For one thing, she'd gotten a good look at the corpse at the crime scene, and she'd seen a photo online of the other victim. Both women were slight of build and dark-haired. Their faces were somewhat similar. If the killer was obsessed with a particular type of victim, this much more robust woman certainly didn't fit it.

Riley asked, "What information do you have?"

Sarah Dillon squinted.

"Information? Well, maybe not information exactly. But a strong feeling—really, really strong. Something was very wrong about that woman. I've known it for a while now."

"How so?" Jenn asked.

"Once, on the train up to Chicago, I tried to strike up a conversation with her. Just small talk, the weather, the kind of day I'd had, my sister in Chicago and her family. She seemed friendly enough at first. But she started getting standoffish when I asked her about herself. I asked her, 'What do you do in Chicago?' She said she went there to visit her mother, who was in a nursing home."

Sarah Dillon fingered her purse nervously.

"Then I started asking questions about her mother—what her health was like, how long she'd been in a home, that kind of thing. She started getting defensive, and in a few minutes she didn't want to talk to me at all. She got out a book and pretended to read it, like I wasn't even there. Whenever I've seen her on the train since then, she does the same thing—acts like she's never met me. I just thought she was rude, standoffish. But now … well, I'm sure it was something else."

"Like what?" Jenn asked.

The woman let out a grunt of disapproval.

"Well, you're the people in law enforcement. You tell me. But she was hiding something. I'll bet she was mixed up in something illegal. Something that got her killed. And now …"

She shivered all over.

"Do you think I'm in any danger?" she asked again, peering nervously around the room.

"Why would you think that?" Bill asked.

Sarah Dillon looked like she could hardly believe the question.

"Well, it's obvious, isn't it? There were other people on that train. Lots of people. None of them are exactly friendly these days. And ever since I talked to her, I've noticed some of them looking at me strangely. Any one of them might have been the killer. She didn't tell me what she was mixed up in, I don't know anything about it. But the killer doesn't know that. He might think she actually told me something—something he doesn't want me to know."

Riley suppressed a sigh of impatience.

She said, "I really doubt that you're in any danger, Ms. Dillon."

The fact was, Riley was quite sure of it. The woman was paranoid, pure and simple.

"But you don't *know* that," the woman said, her voice growing more shrill. "You can't know for sure. And I've got such a terrible feeling. You've got to do something. You've got to protect me."

Chief Powell got up and patted her gently on the shoulder.

"You wait here for just a moment, ma'am," he said. "I'll be right back."

The woman nodded, then sat silently. She looked as if she were on the verge of tears.

49

The police chief quickly returned with a uniformed policeman.

He said to the woman, "This is Officer Ring. He'll watch after you for a while. Right now, you should just go home. Officer Ring will make sure you get there safely."

The woman let out a gasp of relief. She got up from her chair and left the room with the policeman, gazing happily up at him as he held the door for her.

Bill shook his head and said to Chief Powell, "What are you going to do? Give her round-the-clock protection? Because that's just going to be a waste of time and resources."

Powell chuckled slightly.

"Don't worry," he said. "Landry Ring has got a calming effect on people. He's almost uncanny that way. That's why I picked him to take her home. By the time they get there, I'll bet Landry will have her convinced that she's in no danger at all."

Jenn was frowning.

"That sure was a waste of time," she said.

Maybe, Riley thought.

But she had a nagging gut feeling about what the "witness" had just said ...

"Something was very wrong about that woman."

... and ...

"She was hiding something."

Riley sensed that Sarah Dillon might not be altogether wrong.

She asked Powell and Cullen, "Did Reese Fisher have any family members living here in Barnwell?"

Powell said, "Just her husband, Chase. A local chiropractor."

"And has he been interviewed?"

"Of course," Bull Cullen said. "Chief Powell here and I both talked to him. He's got a clean alibi—he was in his office this morning when it happened."

"I want to talk to him again," Riley said.

Cullen and Powell glanced at each other with surprise.

Powell said, "I'm not sure what good that will do. He's pretty shaken up about all this."

Riley wasn't sure what she expected to find out. But if Reese Fisher was harboring some sort of secret, her husband might be able to tell them what it was.

"I want to see him," Riley insisted. "Right now."

CHAPTER NINE

The railroad's deputy police chief looked thoroughly annoyed by Riley's request to re-interview Reese Fisher's husband. But Riley was in no mood to back down.

Bull Cullen said, "When I asked you FBI guys to come out here, I didn't expect you to waste my time."

Feeling her temper escalate, Riley pressed her lips together to prevent snapping back at the man. She heard Bill let out a low grumble beside her.

Before Riley could think of a civil response, Jenn spoke up. The young agent sounded just as condescending and patronizing as Cullen had been toward her back at the crime scene.

"Oh, we won't interfere with your excellent work, *sir*. Just give us a car and we'll go see Mr. Fisher on our own. We'll get out of your way for a while. You and your team can keep right on doing the really important stuff. You might start by booking a comfortable place for those three men back in the interview room to stay the night."

Cullen grimaced at Jenn's obvious contempt for him.

"I'll do that," he said, puffing up his considerable physique in an attempt to exert male authority. "And I'll book a place for the three of you as well. Meanwhile, Chief Powell here will show you to a vehicle."

Powell's heavy, bloodhound-like jowls hung in an expression of bewilderment as he watched Cullen stalk away. Riley knew what Powell must be thinking. Surely he was worried that an FBI team and the railroad police were starting to look like a bad mix, and he was going to get caught in the middle of an ugly situation.

Finally Powell shook his head and led Riley and her team outside to a parked vehicle. He gave them the keys and directions to the Fisher home.

As Riley drove, she said, "Jenn, I don't blame you for not liking Deputy Chief Cullen, but—"

Jenn interrupted, "Huh-uh, that's not it. I don't like having hangovers or bronchitis. I don't like it when my car won't start. I don't like TV commercials. I don't like anchovies on my pizza. But that guy …"

She let out a slight growl, then added, "He's a whole special kind of unlikable, if you ask me. He practically stinks of testosterone."

Bill let out a hearty laugh, but he made no comment.

Riley couldn't help but be impressed by how vividly Jenn expressed her dislike.

But still …

Riley said, "Well, you're going to have to work with him. We all will. So get used to him—for as long as it takes to solve this case, anyway."

In her rearview mirror, Riley saw Jenn cross her arms in a gesture of silent annoyance.

Riley hoped Jenn was listening to what she'd just said and would take it seriously. On the other hand, she guessed that there might be an upside to Jenn's hostility toward Cullen. Maybe it would give her something to think about besides whatever might be going on between her and the mysterious Aunt Cora.

Anyway, Riley couldn't complain about Jenn's work so far today. In the past, she'd always felt that Jenn could be like the proverbial bull in the china shop. But she'd handled the situation with the engineer—the "hogger"—surprisingly well.

And it was no small accomplishment as far as Riley concerned. The ability to show empathy toward victims really was an important item in a BAU agent's toolbox. That didn't seem to come naturally to Jenn, but she was learning it well.

It was only a short drive across town to the address they were looking for. As Riley parked in front of the place, she noticed that it was of a familiar design—a cluster of clean new apartment buildings with pitched roofs, arched windows, and balconies. Based on similar places she'd seen before, she felt pretty sure the buildings surrounded an open area that included a large swimming pool.

Riley, Bill, and Jenn took the elevator to the third floor, then knocked on the apartment door.

Riley was startled when the door first opened. Due to some trick of the light, she almost mistook the man inside for Ryan. They were of similar height and build and complexion. His blond hair was barely touched with gray.

But the resemblance quickly faded, at least somewhat, and Riley felt herself relax a little.

"May I help you?" the man asked.

"Are you Chase Fisher?" Riley asked.

"I am."

Riley and her colleagues showed their badges and introduced themselves.

The man looked somewhat distressed.

"The police were here this morning," he said. "I answered a lot of questions. This is a really hard time for me."

"I know, and I'm very sorry," Riley said. "But we've just joined the case, and we're looking for a fresh perspective. We're extremely anxious to catch your wife's killer. We're hoping you might be able to help us."

She recognized that this man was of a different temperament from Ryan. Her ex-husband would be annoyed, but Chase Fisher just sounded tired.

He nodded and led them inside. It was a fair-sized apartment with lush rugs and a balcony. Riley guessed that it had three bedrooms, and that at least one of them was used as an office. She remembered hearing that Chase Fisher was a chiropractor, and his wife had been a librarian. Riley guessed that his practice must be elsewhere. And it must have been a reasonably prosperous practice for him and his wife to live in a place like this.

There were no family portraits, and Riley sensed right away that the couple had had no children. There were a few tasteful paintings on the wall, and a glass case was filled with golf and bowling trophies.

Overall, the place seemed studiously respectable and pleasant. Even so, Riley caught a scent of melancholy in the air. Her instincts told her that this hadn't been an entirely happy household even before Reese Fisher's murder.

The group sat down on the comfortable furniture.

Riley said, "Mr. Fisher, I know you've been asked this before. But where were you at the time of your wife's murder?"

"I was in my office in town," Fisher said.

"And can anyone account for your whereabouts?"

"Certainly. My receptionist, and at least a couple of my morning patients. I guess you already know that I'm a chiropractor."

Riley was still paying close attention to his demeanor. She was sure that that his alibi checked out. Bull Cullen might be obnoxious, but he wasn't stupid. He wouldn't have overlooked a detail like that. But at this point, Riley was more interested in *how* Fisher answered her questions than in what he actually said.

"Did you see your wife at all this morning?" Riley asked.

"No," he said. "She'd spent the night in Chicago, visiting her mother who is in a nursing home there. She came in on the morning train. As far as I know, she never got home."

Riley felt an odd tingle, a feeling that Fisher was leaving something important unsaid.

Probe gently, she told herself.

She asked, "Has her mother been told what happened?"

Fisher shifted slightly in his chair.

"Yes, I talked to Nadine as soon as I could. The poor woman— she's not very coherent anymore, and she had a hard time grasping it. She was very upset, and the call didn't go well. I hope the people who take care of her can help her understand and cope with it. She's in no condition to come down for the funeral. I'll have to pay her a visit soon."

A silence fell. Riley let it settle for a moment.

Then she nodded toward the trophies and said, "I see you're a golfer. And a bowler too."

He looked surprised at the comment. Of course, Riley knew that it seemed like a strange thing for a detective to mention at such a moment. But Riley had her reasons.

"Yeah," he said uncertainly. "Just an amateur at both. I do OK, I guess. A pretty good golfer. I'm not the best bowler in our local team, but we do pretty well."

Riley noticed an odd shift in his tone. He was being modest, of course, judging by the trophies. But she also sensed something else.

Shame? she wondered.

Why would anybody be ashamed of playing recreational sports? Especially somebody who was pretty good at them? Ryan bragged about his golfing scores at every opportunity.

She said slowly, "Did your wife like golf and bowling, Mr. Fisher?"

Fisher looked at her with a curious expression.

"Well, she didn't play, but ..."

Riley added, "I mean, was she at all interested in the games? As a spectator or a fan or anything? Or in how well you were doing?"

Fisher shook his head.

"No," he said. "She wasn't interested in sports at all. Why do you ask?"

Riley didn't reply. But she knew that this little fact was more important than it seemed. After all, sports trophies were the most prominent objects in this living room. And yet Reese Fisher had had no interest in sports.

Riley asked gently, "Mr. Fisher, were you and your wife happy together?"

Fisher looked into Riley's eyes and blinked a few times.

"Of course we were," he said.

Again, Riley let a silence settle in the room.

She was sure that either Bull Cullen or Chief Powell had asked that same question, and Fisher had given them the same answer. But Cullen and Powell had brushed it aside too easily.

Riley held Fisher's gaze.

She didn't say so aloud, but with her eyes she said to him …

You're lying.

He nodded ever so slightly in reply to her unspoken observation.

She sat waiting for him to tell her the truth.

CHAPTER TEN

Chase Fisher lowered his gaze and slumped in his chair. Riley remained quiet, and so did Bill and Jenn. She sensed her colleagues' anticipation at whatever was about to be said.

Finally, Fisher said in a nearly inaudible voice …

"Reese was having an affair."

Riley let his words hang in the air for a moment.

Then she said, "Did you mention this to the detectives who talked to you this morning?"

"No," Fisher said.

Jenn broke her silence sharply. "Why the hell not? Didn't it occur to you it might be important?"

Riley stifled a sigh. Jenn was regressing to her old bull-in-the-china-shop style. Riley darted her a look that told her to keep quiet.

Then Riley asked Fisher, "Who was she having an affair with?"

Fisher shook his head sadly.

"Somebody in Chicago," he said.

"You don't know who?" Riley said.

"No."

"She wouldn't tell you?"

Fisher heaved a long sigh.

"We never talked about it. I'm not sure she even knew that I knew. But I *did* know. First it was just a feeling. But then I did some … well, snooping. I'd call the hotel in Chicago where she was supposed to be staying, and she wasn't registered there. I'd call her mother's rest home too, and the staff would say she hadn't been there—at least not when she'd said she'd been."

As the room fell quiet again, Riley's mind clicked away, trying to process what she was hearing.

Finally Fisher said, "I—I should have told the detectives this morning. I don't know why I didn't. It's just that …"

His words faded away. Riley sensed that he was grappling with a tangle of thoughts and feelings.

Then he said, "This sounds weird, but I feel like it was all my fault. Her affair, I mean. It wasn't that I … well, I loved her, and I treated her well, and I don't think I was a bad lover. We were married for twelve years, and I did everything ... everything *right*, I thought. Everything a good husband is supposed to do. I built up a good practice, earned good money, tried to give her everything she wanted."

"What about children?" Riley asked.

Fisher shook his head again.

"We just kept putting it off. It never seemed like the right time somehow. Neither of us could say exactly why. Maybe we had doubts about ourselves, whether we'd be good parents. And as the years passed by, it just seemed to get less likely that it ever would be the right time."

Fisher let out a sad, bitter chuckle.

He said, "Did you know that that Barnwell, Illinois, has been ranked the third most boring town to live in, in the whole Unites States? Except for golf. It's not a bad town for golf. Even the bowling is considered lousy. Reese and I both grew up here. I don't guess it occurred to either of us to go anyplace else until we were way too settled—until it was too late."

He shrugged slightly.

"Small wonder she was bored—not just with the town, but with me. She loved literature and the arts. I wish I did too, but I don't, and I've never been able to fake it. And Barnwell is dead to the world as far as that kind of thing is concerned. She did everything she could to liven up this town, like start a choral group, put on plays, organize reading clubs. But nothing took hold. She tried not to act like it, but she was miserable."

He squinted pensively.

"I guess I hoped that whoever she was seeing ... could really help fill what was missing from her life. Sometimes I try to imagine what he must be like. Rich, maybe—or at least comfortably well off, with all the taste and culture that I just don't have. Somebody who could take her to art galleries, plays, symphonies, the opera. I hoped he could do everything that I couldn't do."

Riley asked slowly, "Were you ever unfaithful?"

Fisher shook his head.

"No," he said. "I don't feel especially virtuous about it. I never took enough interest in anyone else, I guess. I'm just too ..."

He didn't finish his sentence, but Riley knew what he was leaving unsaid.

"I'm just too boring to do something like that."

Riley was feeling strangely uncomfortable now. She wasn't

sure just why. But for some reason, this man was reminding her of Ryan again.

Why? she wondered.

Aside from a certain physical resemblance, how were they in any way alike? Ryan was vain, self-centered, amoral, and impervious to self-criticism. This man seemed introspective and empathetic, perhaps to a fault—that is, if Riley could believe anything he was saying.

Be careful, she told herself. She knew that credulity could be dangerous at a moment like this.

She said, "Mr. Fisher, what you're telling us could be very important. Do you have any idea how we might find out who your wife's lover was?"

"No. I've snooped through her office and her computer, looking through letters and emails. I've never found anything suspicious."

Riley was on the verge of asking …

"So are you really sure she was having an affair?"

It was quite possible that the man's insecurity had made him paranoid.

She reminded herself that Reese Fisher's cell phone was supposedly on its way to Quantico to be examined by technicians there. Maybe Sam Flores and his team could find significant text messages or calls.

Riley leaned toward Fisher slightly.

"Mr. Fisher, do you think your wife's involvement with another man might have had anything to do with her murder?"

Fisher's eyes widened, as if the possibility hadn't occurred to him.

"I—I don't know," he stammered. "I can't imagine …"

He seemed to be searching for the right words.

He said, "Surely Reese would never have been involved with anybody who meant her any harm. I just can't believe that."

He sounded perfectly sincere.

But was he?

Why couldn't she tell?

Riley turned toward Bill and gave him a nod, a familiar signal for him to ask his own questions. Bill complied, asking about routine details. Did Reese have any relationship with Fern Bruder, the earlier victim? Did Fisher personally know of anyone with grudges or grievances against Reese? Had she been acting strangely lately?

As Fisher kept saying no in answer to all of Bill's questions, Riley studied him carefully, trying to be alert for any trace of dishonesty or evasion. She got no clear gut feelings about him at all.

That worried her—and worried her badly.

She knew that his alibi was almost worthless. He was certainly well off enough to hire out his wife's murder if he wanted to.

And now it appeared that he had ample reason to want to.

His self-effacement and self-blame might be nothing more than an act.

I ought to be able to tell, Riley thought.

In fact, she prided herself on being able to see through facades, to detect evil when it was in the same room with her.

But for some reason, her instincts didn't seem to be engaged right now.

Why? Was his resemblance to Ryan clouding her thinking? The possibility disturbed her deeply.

Finally, there seemed nothing more to ask.

Riley said, "Mr. Fisher, we're terribly sorry for your loss, and we're deeply grateful for your time. Do you have any plans to leave Barnwell in the next few days?"

"No," Fisher said.

Riley handed him her card and said, "We'd rather you don't. In fact, we want you to keep in close touch with us. We may need to talk to you again in the near future."

Fisher took the card and nodded.

When Riley and her colleagues left the building, she was surprised at how dark it had gotten. She looked at her watch and saw that it was after nine o'clock.

As they walked toward the car that the local police chief had lent them, Jenn asked, "So what do we think? Is he our killer?"

Riley hesitated.

Then she said, "I don't know. But somebody had better keep a close eye on him."

CHAPTER ELEVEN

As they walked toward the car, Riley was worried, but not about the man they had just interviewed. She had no idea whether or not he could be the killer, and that's what disturbed her.

Why were her instincts floundering right now?

What was she going to do about it?

She was grateful for the distraction when Bill's cell phone buzzed.

Bill took out the phone and looked at it, then said, "It's a text from Bull Cullen. He says he's put the three railroad men up in a local motel, and he's made a reservation for us as well. He wants us to meet him there."

Riley was about to protest, but she realized she had no alternate course of action in mind. The day had slipped away quickly and there didn't seem to be anything more they could look into tonight. Uncertainty was all they had to show for their efforts.

Her spirits sank further as she got into the driver's seat and drove the short distance to the motel. It didn't help to see Bull Cullen waiting for them when she pulled the car up to the motel office. With a wide smile, he directed them to the parking spot outside a numbered door.

Riley thought that Cullen looked positively gleeful as they got out of the car and followed him into the room he had rented for them. Then she understood why he was so pleased with himself.

The room was small, with two single beds and a sofa that had been opened up to make a third bed. There was small desk with a chair, a shabby cabinet with an old TV, and very little space left to walk around in. It had to be the cheapest room available.

Not that Riley cared especially, and she knew that Bill didn't either. Over the years they'd shared much sparser lodgings and had even slept overnight in cars and vans when it had been necessary. Of course she was sure that these meager lodgings weren't a matter of necessity.

This was nothing short of a deliberate slight.

She could see that Bill was trying to control his amusement, but Jenn looked thoroughly disgusted.

Trying to sound nonchalant, Cullen asked, "How did your interview go with Chase Fisher? I don't assume you learned anything new."

Riley gave him a sharp look.

"Actually, we did," she said. "He thinks his wife was having an affair with a man in Chicago. We don't know who her lover is yet, or if he had anything to do with her death. Or for that matter whether Chase Fisher is a viable suspect. But …"

She paused, then asked, "Or did you find all that out yourself? I just don't remember seeing it in any of the reports."

Looking stunned, Cullen just shook his head.

Riley commented mildly, "I guess your interview skills need some work."

Cullen looked stung.

Riley added, "You'd better put a few plainclothes cops to work watching Fisher's every move. Starting tonight. Starting right now."

"I'll do that," Cullen said curtly. His face twisted with anger, but he got it under control and asked, "What's on your agenda for tomorrow?"

"It depends," Riley said. "Did the other victim, Fern Bruder, have any relatives in Allardt, Indiana?"

"Yeah," Cullen said. "She lived at home with her family."

"Did you interview them?"

"I did. The day after Fern Bruder died."

Riley didn't like being petty, but she couldn't help twisting the knife.

"Well, then," she said. "I guess Agents Jeffreys and Roston and I will need to go there and interview them again. Send me the notes you took, and also the contact information for the police chief there. I'll want to let him know we're coming. We'll drive to Allardt first thing tomorrow morning."

Cullen's face turned red, but he still managed to hold his temper.

"Great," he said through clenched teeth. "Then I'll see you later tomorrow."

As he turned to walk out of the room, Jenn said, "Wait a minute. Are those railroad guys we talked with today staying in this same motel?"

"They are," Cullen replied.

"What kind of room did they get?"

Cullen seemed to be surprised by the question.

"One that's pretty much the same as this," he said.

Jenn crossed her arms.

"Huh-uh," she said. "No way you're going to stick those poor guys in a coop like this. Go right to the front desk and get them the nicest rooms you can get."

"They're traumatized," Cullen said. "Maybe they don't want to be isolated. Maybe they want to be together."

"Yeah, maybe," Jenn said. "Did you ask them?"

Cullen didn't reply, but his face was reddening again.

"Ask them and find out," Jenn demanded. "Even if they do want to be together, get them some kind of suite with adjoining rooms or something. Something that's a hell of a lot better than this, anyway. If this motel doesn't have a place nice enough, take them someplace else. Get on it right now. Or else I will."

Cullen opened his mouth to speak, then seemed to think better of it. He left the room without another word.

Riley could see that Jenn was seething again.

"That man!" Jenn said, pacing back and forth. "He's really got some nerve. I don't care if he wants to stick us in a little hole like this. But disrespecting those poor guys after what they've been through? What a bastard!"

Riley shook her head and said, "Jenn …"

"What?" Jenn said. "Was I wrong? Tell me."

Riley sighed.

"No, but I keep telling you—we've got to work with him. Try not to let him push your buttons. I've got a feeling this is going to be a tough enough case as it is."

She tested one of the beds and sat down on it.

She said, "We haven't had anything to eat since this morning. Let's order some food and talk about where things stand."

Bill made a call for some pizza and beer. Then the three of them settled into their crowded quarters and went over the case. The topic of discussion, of course, was the victim's husband they had just interviewed and what little they had learned from him.

"One thing bothers me," Jenn said. "He didn't cry. Was it because he was still in shock, or crying just isn't in his nature? Or was it because he's as guilty as hell?"

Riley gave Jenn a cautioning look.

"Be careful not to jump to conclusions on account of that," she said. "People process grief in very different ways. I can't say for sure that he wasn't acting, but he seemed deeply shaken to me."

"Yeah, but marital jealousy is a classic motive," Jenn said. "Alibi or no alibi, he could have hired somebody to do it."

Jenn thought for a moment, then added, "Of course, there's still the first victim in Indiana to account for. I'm not sure how she fits into that theory."

Riley suppressed a discouraged sigh.

"Oh, she fits your theory, all right," she said. "Reese Fisher's death might just be a copycat murder. Her husband seems like a smart enough guy. He might have read about the earlier killing and seen it as an opportunity to make his wife's murder look like the second in a series of serial murders. It wouldn't be the first time something like this has happened."

Bill let out a grunt of dismay.

"Or," he said, "Chase Fisher might be innocent, and Reese's lover might be the killer, using the same copycat scenario you just mentioned."

"But we don't know who her lover is," Jenn added.

"Or if he exists at all," Riley added, shaking her head. "I don't like any of these possibilities. If either Chase Fisher or his wife's lover committed the second murder, we probably have two killers to deal with—one of whom might be planning another murder right now. If neither Fisher nor the lover is the murderer, we're wasting valuable time even thinking about them. There's a serial killer at large, and we're nowhere near stopping him."

There seemed to be nothing more to say. The group finished their pizza and beer in silence.

Finally Riley said, "Well, maybe we'll learn more tomorrow when we talk to Fern Bruder's family. If we can just find a connection between the two victims, that would be progress. Meanwhile, we'd all better get a good night's rest."

Riley called the front desk to schedule a wakeup call. The three agents took turns taking showers, then agreed on sleeping arrangements. Bill and Jenn got the two beds, while Riley took the sofa bed. It wasn't very comfortable, but Riley had slept in far worse.

In a matter of minutes, Riley could hear Bill's noisy snoring, followed by Jenn snoring more quietly.

Riley couldn't help but envy them. She was having trouble keeping her eyes closed, to say nothing of falling asleep. She kept thinking about Chase Fisher and the impressions she'd gotten of him during their visit.

Why had he kept reminding her of Ryan?

She found herself thinking about something Fisher had said about his wife's affair.

"I feel like it was all my fault."

Why did those words keep resonating in Riley's mind?

As she lay there staring into the darkness, it started to occur to her ...

Maybe Fisher didn't remind Riley so much of Ryan as he reminded her ...

Of myself.

She shuddered at the thought.

Fisher felt guilty—or at least claimed to feel guilty—about Reese Fisher's life of gnawing, bitter boredom that had driven her to wander away from her marriage.

Did Riley feel the same way toward Ryan?

Did she harbor some feeling that she'd been in some way responsible for his failings and infidelities?

No, she thought. *It doesn't make sense.*

At the same time, she knew perfectly well that making sense was beside the point. Irrational, unfounded, unconscious guilt could eat away at her as deeply as guilt that was based on any real wrongs she had committed.

All the logical thinking in the world wasn't going to help.

She felt a lump of despair form in her throat.

I can't let myself feel this way, she said.

But despairing thoughts started crowding in from all directions, and she found herself obsessing again about the last couple of days—over Liam's departure, April's hopes to follow in her footsteps, and whether she had any business trying to be a mother and an FBI agent at the same time.

It was a feeling of awful and senseless futility. Riley had to swallow down a sob of despair.

Don't cry, she told herself.

The last thing she wanted to do right now was wake up Bill and Jenn.

Little by little, she felt sleep creeping up on her, but she took no comfort from it.

Soon, she realized, the nightmares would start.

CHAPTER TWELVE

The man shuddered as his computer screen filled up with photos of the grisly murder scene.

The body, bound by tape to the railroad tracks, looked like some sort of decapitated mannequin—at least until he brought up the hideous close-up photos of the victim's neck. Then he was looking at images of an almost clinically clean cross-section of her trachea, esophagus, and spine, like something out of an anatomy textbook.

And here was the head, lying where it had rolled down the stony embankment. The woman's expression of horror looked much too wild, too exaggerated, to be real, as if it had been painted onto a mannequin's head.

But the man knew that it was all too real.

This was all his doing.

He had bound this woman in place, where she couldn't escape her fate. And he had done the same with another whose pictures were also here on this site.

But until now, he hadn't seen the results that were on display here. He'd had to rush away from both murder scenes before the victims even began to regain consciousness. He'd had to get as far away as he could in order not to get caught.

In fact, he'd never intended to even see these abominable images—and he certainly hadn't intended for them to be on display before the whole world.

But he should have known better.

What he'd done was evil, even he harbored no delusions about that, and yet …

What kind of a world is this? he wondered.

What kind of people would studiously photograph these images and display them where even a small child could unwarily stumble across them?

He was a sick man and he knew it.

But he was living in a truly sick world, in which people's worst cravings were provoked and slaked. The people who'd taken these photographs and put them on display had done so of their own free will.

He'd had no choice.

He'd been obeying the power that held him in its thrall—the visions and the voice that wouldn't leave him alone.

Now he felt a terrible nausea welling up inside him. But was it at the sight of these photographs?

No, some evil spirit was tormenting him again, just like yesterday, and four days before that. After the killing near Allardt, where these pictures were taken, he'd sworn to himself never to do this again.

He'd fought against the spirit until he'd become violently, physically ill.

And now?

Fight it, he told himself.

Surely looking these images of what he'd done ought to be enough to deter him from ever doing such a thing again.

But even now, he felt the fight ebbing out of him, and physical pain surged through his entire body, and emotional pain seared his brain—pain that could only be eased in one terrible way.

He could hear an audible voice whisper in his ear …

"Soon. Very soon."

CHAPTER THIRTEEN

It was night.

Riley was walking along a length of railroad tracks, enjoying the fresh warm air and the bright, moonlit sky.

Then she heard a whimpering voice directly behind her.

She turned around and saw a woman bound with duct tape to the tracks, her neck against one of the rails.

Riley felt as though her heart jumped up in her throat.

How was this possible?

She'd just passed that spot a second or two ago. No one had been there then.

She rushed to the woman and knelt down beside her. The woman seemed to be just regaining consciousness.

"Where am I?" the woman murmured. "What's happening?"

Riley said, "Don't worry, I'll get you loose."

But as she began to struggle with the seemingly endless coils of duct tape, the task quickly seemed impossible. The tape ripped off in sticky loops, but the woman was still bound.

Then she heard another whimpering voice.

She looked up saw another woman bound the same way just a short distance off.

Riley gasped aloud and ran toward her, trying again to pull loose the tape that bound her. Again the tape looped and snarled, but this woman, too, was still tied to the track. Then she heard another whimpering voice and looked up and saw another bound woman, and beyond her another, and beyond her another ...

Riley couldn't count the number of women who lay bound to the tracks before her.

Then she heard a heavy rumbling and saw a light blazing up ahead.

It was an oncoming train.

Riley stood waving frantically.

"Stop!" she yelled at the top of her lungs. "Please stop!"

She heard a grim, gravelly chuckle behind her.

She turned around. Standing on the tracks a short distance away stood a tall, gangly man wearing the full-dress uniform of a

Marine colonel. His face was heavily lined with bitterness and drink.

"What are you thinking, girl?" the man said with a laugh. "Do you think you can stop a goddamn locomotive?"

Riley recognized him instantly.

It was her own father.

But how could it be him? He'd died last October.

"Daddy, you've got to help me," she said. "We've got to get these women loose."

"I'm afraid you're on your own, girl. Now maybe if you'd bothered to come to my funeral ..."

He shook his head and let out a scoffing chuckle.

"Naw, I didn't care a damn about that. I'd have skipped it myself, except I didn't have much choice, being the corpse and all."

Riley could hear the crescendo of rumbling behind her. The light from the approaching locomotive threw her own shadow over the tracks and illuminated her father brightly.

"Daddy, what can I do?" Riley asked.

She heard a pleading tone in her own voice.

"Your job," her father said. "Do your goddamn job. Just don't get any ideas that you'll do any good. Remember the laws of physics. An object in motion stays in motion—unless it's stopped by something bigger."

He laughed a mean, ugly laugh.

"And there's no bigger object in all the world than evil. It's like some locomotive hurtling through outer space until it hits a planet or gets swallowed up by a star or something even bigger."

"How can I stop it?" Riley asked.

"Don't be stupid. You can't. Still, it's your job to stop it. That really stinks, doesn't it? It was like that for me in 'Nam, fighting a war that couldn't be won. Well, now it's your turn to fight and lose. It's all for shit, everything you do. And it's in your blood. It's your inheritance. Good luck with it. I'm through with it."

Riley's father turned and walked off the tracks and disappeared into the surrounding darkness.

Riley whirled back around to face the long row of bound women and the ever-brightening headlight and the roaring crescendo of the engine. She could feel an intense vibration beneath her feet.

Now she knew the locomotive, the oncoming train, was nothing less than the juggernaut of evil itself, an endless succession *of sadistic monsters and helpless victims, and they'd keep coming one right after another no matter how hard she tried to stop them.*

But her father's advice was all she had in life:

"Do your goddamn job."

She dashed forward, stepping over the victims one by one, yelling over the deafening noise and blinded by the engine's blazing light, waving her arms frantically.

"Stop! Stop! Stop!"

Suddenly the air was split by the deafening shout of the train whistle.

Then Riley realized that it wasn't a train whistle at all.

It was the motel room phone ringing beside her sofa bed.

It was her wakeup call.

Riley groggily picked up the phone and thanked the receptionist making the call.

She turned toward her colleagues, who were turning in their beds and grumbling to themselves.

"Wake up, guys," she said. "We've got a job to do."

*

Riley and her colleagues were soon on the road making the two-hour trip from Barnwell, Illinois, to Allardt, Indiana. Bill was driving, and Jenn was sitting beside him in the front passenger seat.

Riley sat behind them trying to keep herself occupied, doing her best to push last night's ugly dream out of her mind.

She exchanged text messages with the chief of police in Allardt, alerting him to their upcoming visit. Then she studied Bull Cullen's report of his interview with Fern Bruder's family in Allardt. He'd sent it to her last night at her request. According to Cullen, the family didn't have any idea why their daughter had been murdered, or by whom.

Cullen's report struck Riley as perfectly thorough and competent, and it was entirely possible that she and her colleagues weren't going to learn anything else from the victim's family. But Riley knew better than to leave any stone unturned.

Words still rang in her mind …

"Do your goddamn job."

She also studied official reports of the first killing, searching for any variations between the two murders. It was an important consideration. Contradictory details might support their "copycat" theory, that either Chase Fisher or his wife's lover had deliberately imitated the earlier murder.

But Riley soon realized that she simply couldn't tell one way or the other. Grisly photos of the first murder were circulating all over the Internet. Reporters and gawkers had apparently gotten past the barriers that the local police had set up to close off that crime scene. A would-be copycat could find all the information he needed online. It wouldn't be at all difficult to duplicate the first murder quite precisely.

While Riley was poring over this information, she listened to Bill and Jenn chatter away as Bill drove. He was telling Jenn stories about Riley herself. Riley had to admit that some of them were hilarious. Bill regaled Jenn about Riley's more outrageous detective methods, and the many times she'd been taken off a case, or suspended, or fired. Jenn laughed and laughed, thoroughly amused by it all.

Riley felt embarrassed, of course, and she half-wished that Bill would keep his mouth shut about her. Still, she couldn't help but be pleased that Bill and Jenn were finally starting to hit it off. During the last case the three of them had worked on together, Bill hadn't been entirely confident about Jenn.

Maybe we'll wind up making a good team, she thought.

At the same time, she couldn't help but worry about when or if something in Jenn's dark past was going to catch up with her.

If it did, was Riley going to wind up in trouble along with her?

After all, Riley was already covering for her.

And what about Bill, who knew nothing about Jenn's involvement with the sinister Aunt Cora? Would he wind up in trouble as well?

Riley wished she could get Jenn alone and ask what had been bothering her yesterday. But so far there had been no opportunity, not with Bill around.

And that was what made Riley most uncomfortable—not being completely open with Bill. In all their years together, they'd always been able to confide in each other completely. Was that no longer true?

And was it Riley's own fault?

Riley's thoughts were interrupted by the sound of Bill's voice.

"We're just entering Allardt."

Riley looked up to inspect the areas they passed through.

Allardt had upscale neighborhoods that must be populated by commuters, which she understood to be true of all stops on the train lines from Chicago. But they soon drove past those, into an older district that must have been in place long before the affluent sections came into being.

This part looked like a perfectly ordinary Midwestern town, with bungalows and ranch-style houses and old buildings. None of it looked especially prosperous, and they passed through a poor area on their way downtown. Poverty seemed to be creeping in, and some businesses were boarded up.

Riley also saw graffiti here and there. Gangs had obviously found their way into Allardt, as they had into too many American small towns in recent years.

And Riley knew that gangs meant drugs, and drugs meant despair.

Riley remembered what Chase Fisher had said about Barnwell—that it had been ranked the third most boring town to live in.

She wondered what list Allardt might top.

When they reached the police station, Bill parked their car in front of it and they all went inside. They identified themselves and were promptly taken to Chief Bryce Dolby's office.

Of course, the chief had been expecting them, and he greeted them pleasantly and offered them seats.

"Such an awful thing about what happened to Fern Bruder," he said. "I hated to hear that it happened again over in Barnwell. A serial killer! We don't get that kind of thing here in Allardt."

Chief Dolby immediately struck Riley as a kindly man. But his face looked tired, and she guessed that he was younger than he actually looked. She was used to that sort of weary expression on the faces of big-city cops, who routinely saw too much of violence and the worst in human nature. But in her experience, small-town cops usually looked much more cheerful and light-hearted.

He continued, "I wish I could be of more help to you about all this. My people and I are out of our depth with this kind of case. The truth is, I haven't got a single shred of information that might help you."

"That's understandable," Riley said. "The fact that a murder happened here doesn't make it a local case. The killer might be absolutely anywhere. That's why we've been called in."

Chief Dolby drummed his fingers on his desk.

He said, "I understand that you want to re-interview Fern Bruder's family. I called them to let them know you'd be paying them a visit this morning. They'll be expecting you."

He paused for a moment, then added, "If it's all right with you, I'd just as soon not come with you."

Riley was surprised.

"Why not?" she asked.

"I went there with Deputy Chief Cullen just the other day. One visit to Weston Bruder—Fern's dad—will hold me for a while. I hadn't seen him lately, and I'd rather not see him again until I absolutely have to."

He smiled slightly and added, "I guess that sounds rather petty of me. The truth is, we just don't like each other very much."

Riley looked at him carefully and asked, "Anything we should know about?"

"It's personal, nothing for you to worry about."

Riley couldn't help but feel uneasy about what Dolby might be leaving unsaid.

She asked, "How do people feel about him generally here in Allardt?"

Chief Dolby knitted his brow. Riley sensed that he was trying to choose his words carefully.

"Well, it depends on who you talk to," he said. "Some folks will tell you that Weston Bruder is one of the town's finest citizens, a good Christian and a pillar of the community. But other folks …"

He shrugged.

"I don't want to speak ill of him," he said. "And anyway, it doesn't matter—not for your purposes."

Riley wasn't sure why, but she wished Dolby would tell them more. But what was the point of asking? She and her colleagues weren't here to indulge in small-town gossip. They were here to solve a murder case.

As they left the station and got back into the car, Riley felt apprehensive.

It already seemed obvious to her that Allardt fell far short of being a quaint and charming Midwestern town. And she sensed that she and her colleagues were about to get a lesson in what was wrong with it deep down.

CHAPTER FOURTEEN

Sitting in the back seat again as Bill drove across the town of Allardt, Riley kept wondering …

Just who is this Weston Bruder?

Chief Dolby had expressed a definite aversion to the father of the first victim.

She told herself that must be the reason for her own bad gut feeling about him.

She pulled up the notes that Cullen had taken when he'd interviewed the Bruder family. They were informative enough as far as they went. The Bruders were a tight-knit, old-fashioned family.

The father, Weston Bruder III, owned a local hardware store that had been founded by his great-grandfather. His wife, Bridget, was a stay-at-home mother. The twenty-five-year-old victim, Fern Bruder, had been living with her parents and two younger siblings before she'd been killed. Riley found that a little odd for a woman Fern's age, but hardly anything to get really suspicious about. These days, lots of kids were slow to leave the nest.

In fact, Riley didn't see any red flags in Cullen's notes. He apparently hadn't noticed anything odd about the father or the family.

All the same, her bad feeling grew as they arrived at the Bruders' house and pulled into the driveway.

There was nothing outwardly sinister about the place. It was an older ranch-style house that had been added to over the years, and the medium-sized yard was immaculately kept. Even so, Riley was struck by …

What?

She wasn't quite sure.

Perhaps it was how bland and characterless the place looked, even from outside. Absolutely nothing was out of place, which she thought made it look like some kind of facade or movie set, not a real house. Riley somehow found it hard to believe that anyone actually lived here, much less a family of five.

When they knocked on the door, they were greeted by a rather plain, slender woman in her forties. She was wearing a simple, conservative, full-sleeved dress that modestly covered her legs well below the knees, almost down to her ankles.

She looked at her visitors a bit nervously.

"Are you the FBI folks?" she asked.

Riley and her colleagues produced their badges and introduced themselves.

Riley asked, "Are you Bridget Bruder?"

The woman nodded and said, "Come on in. Weston is expecting you."

Riley and her colleagues walked on into the small living room. She was startled to see three people standing stiffly together, almost as if posing for a family portrait.

Joining the group, Bridget said, "This is my husband, Weston. And our daughter Mia. And our son, Bobby."

Everyone was well dressed, with Mia looking like a miniature of her mother. From reading the files, Riley remembered that the girl was in her late teens. Weston was wearing a suit and tie, and so was his nine-year-old son. They had thin, pinched, expressionless faces. Only the young boy's features showed any sign of sadness.

As for the living room, it filled Riley with the same feeling as the outside of the house. The furniture was plain and ordinary, the carpet practical and perfectly clean, and everything seemed to be in its precise place. Decorations were few, but there were some religious paintings on the walls.

The room chilled Riley a little. It reminded her of a living room inside a dollhouse. It felt impossible to imagine that anything was ever spilled or broken or messy here. Was it really possible for a family to live like that?

Still standing stiffly, flanked by his family, Weston Bruder said, "I hope this is important. We missed our morning church service. If we don't leave soon, we'll be late for the next service."

The chill Riley was feeling suddenly deepened.

The family seemed too cold to even be distraught about Fern's death.

Riley said, "We do have some questions. But first I want to say that we are terribly sorry for your loss."

The wife said in a solemn tone, "'The Lord is near to those who are broken-hearted and saves those who are crushed in spirit.'"

It took Riley a moment to register that the woman was quoting from the Bible. Before she could think of anything to say in reply,

Jenn nodded and said …

"'Blessed are those who mourn, for they will be comforted.'"

In near unison, all four family members said, "Amen."

Riley looked at Jenn with surprise.

Was Jenn religious? She had never given Riley any reason to think so.

Nevertheless, Riley realized that Jenn had managed to say exactly what needed to be said under these circumstances. The family suddenly seemed much more at ease, and Weston actually invited the three agents to sit down with them.

Then he said, "We're sad about Fern's loss, of course. But she'd been straying away from us lately."

"How so?" Jenn asked.

Riley decided to let Jenn take the lead asking questions. She seemed to know exactly what she was doing right now. And she certainly was showing an appropriate degree of empathy.

Bridget said, "We'd hoped she would settle down and marry and raise a family right here in Allardt. This is a good town with good people. But she was restless. She longed for big-city life. She wanted to move to Chicago. She'd been going there a lot lately by train—looking for jobs, she said."

"What types of jobs?" Jenn asked.

"Some sort of secretarial work, I suppose," Bridget said. "She'd learned some office and computer skills at the local community college. But she never talked to us about it, because we didn't approve."

With a frown, Bridget added, "Not that our feelings mattered. She was a grown woman. Her choices were up to her."

As Riley listened, she thought she was starting to understand certain things that were being left unsaid. Both Bridget and Weston had deep family roots right here in Allardt, perhaps all the way back to frontier days. To them, the city of Chicago must seem to be a sinful and dangerous place. Even though Fern's murder had happened nearby, they somehow blamed her attraction to the city. It seemed almost as if it hadn't come as a surprise to them that their daughter had died a violent death.

Riley felt unsettled by another realization—that the family's grief was blunted by their resentment that Fern wanted to leave them.

Do they think she deserved this? Riley wondered.

It was a shocking possibility.

75

Jenn asked, "Are you aware of a similar murder that took place near Barnwell, Illinois, just yesterday?"

A look of vague surprise crossed the family's faces.

"No, we hadn't heard of that," Weston said.

Jenn said, "I won't go into details, except to say that the victim was killed in almost exactly the same way as your daughter. Her name was Reese Fisher, and she lived in Barnwell. Is the name familiar to you?"

Bridget and Weston and their daughter shook their heads no. The boy, Bobby, sat looking sadly at the floor.

Jenn asked, "Are you sure she never mentioned anybody by that name?"

Bridget Fisher shrugged and said, "None of us knew anybody in Barnwell. I don't know how she could have known her. Unless she met her on one of her trips to Chicago."

Weston gave his wife a stern look. Riley sensed that she was saying more than he wanted her to.

Are they hiding something? Riley wondered.

In a slow, cautious voice, Jenn said, "Mr. and Mrs. Bruder, I have to ask you a routine question, and I'm sure you've been asked it already. But can you both account for your whereabouts at the time of your daughter's murder?"

Weston Bruder straightened up in his chair.

He said, "I suppose that question is directed at me in particular."

"Not necessarily," Jenn said.

But of course, Riley knew that Bruder was exactly right. The woman and the daughter looked too physically slight to have carried out the murders, and the boy was out of the question.

Bridget Bruder said, "Mia and Bobby and I were at home."

"Wasn't it a school day?" Jenn asked.

"Yes," Bridget said. "We home teach."

Jenn directed her gaze directly at Weston Bruder.

In a tight voice, he said, "I was at home."

Riley felt a sharp tingling. She knew that her colleagues felt the same.

Jenn said to the mother, "Can you confirm that your husband was at home?"

The woman seemed to hesitate for a moment.

"Yes," she said.

A short silence fell.

Still speaking in a soft, sympathetic-sounding voice, Jenn said, "I believe we all know that that's a lie."

CHAPTER FIFTEEN

Riley held her breath for a moment. How would the Bruders respond to Jenn's pronouncement?

She was sure that Jenn was right, that Bruder and his wife were both lying. She felt it keenly, and had no doubt that Bill did as well.

Weston Bruder twisted his lips and said, "It's not a lie."

"Explain, please," Jenn said.

Bruder said, "My home is wherever I find the Lord's work to do."

Riley had to stop herself from asking what he meant by that. She reminded herself …

Let Jenn handle this.

The young agent seemed calm and unflappable.

She said, "Mr. Bruder, what church do you and your family belong to?"

"The Congregation of Ephesian Elders."

Jenn squinted slightly and said, "I'm not familiar with that denomination."

Bruder said, "That's because we only have one church, right here in Allardt. And now, if you'll allow me to explain …"

He paused for a moment.

"Aside from our minister, every male member of our church is a lay preacher. We are required to travel, spreading the gospel in other communities door to door."

Jenn nodded and said, "I believe Paul says something in the Book of Acts …"

Bruder said, "'I kept back nothing that was helpful, but proclaimed it to you, and taught you publicly and from house to house.' Yes, Paul said that to the Ephesian Elders. We follow his example. I was in another town when Fern died, knocking on doors and talking to anyone who would listen."

"And where was that town?" Jenn said.

Bruder's face twitched.

"I won't tell you," he said.

For the first time, Riley noticed a hint of surprise on Jenn's face.

"Why not?" she asked.

"We conduct our lay ministries in secret, so that—"

Jenn interrupted sharply.

"So that 'your Father, who sees what is done in secret, will reward you.' Yeah, I get it, Mr. Bruder. And I respect that. But we're dealing with the murder of your daughter. I don't understand why accounting for your whereabouts at the time of her death should be a problem."

Bruder's face was reddening.

"It *is* a problem," he said. "And I have no intention of telling you any such thing. And I don't believe you can compel me."

Bill said, "I'm pretty sure we can. And I don't think you'd want to face an obstruction of justice charge. But what about the time of the other woman's death—mid-morning yesterday? Where were you then?"

"I was traveling and preaching," Bruder said. "I'll say no more than that."

Riley only half-listened as Bill and Jenn engaged in an increasingly heated exchange with Weston Bruder. She was watching young Bobby Bruder, who had been silent so far. He'd kept his head down and seemed much sadder than the rest of his family.

Now she noticed that he'd taken something out of his pocket and was fingering it gently. She couldn't see what it was, but it was red and shiny.

She said, "Bobby, it looks like you've got something pretty there. May I have a look at it?"

The ongoing argument suddenly stopped, and everybody looked at Riley and the boy.

"Yes, ma'am," the boy said.

He got up from his chair and handed the object to Riley.

It was a keychain with a charm shaped like a heart. The heart was made out of transparent red-dyed plastic and it had bits of glitter in it.

A sparkly red plastic heart seemed quite out of place in this household.

"Where did you get this?" Riley asked the boy.

"Fern gave it to me," he said. "Just last week. A man gave it to her on the train."

Riley's head buzzed. Everyone else in the room remained quiet.

She said, "Did she say who gave it to her?"

The boy nodded.

"Red gave it to her," he said.

The father gasped aloud.

"Red! Red Messer!" he said.

Riley asked Weston Bruder, "Do you know him?"

"Of course I know him. He used to be in our congregation. He's a wicked man. And he—"

He took hold of his son's shoulders and shook him.

"Why didn't you show this to me?" he said. "Why didn't you tell me?"

"I was afraid you'd be mad at me," the boy said.

Weston Bruder stood with his mouth hanging open. He looked like he was about to faint.

"Oh, dear God, he killed our daughter!"

He sat slowly down and said to Riley and her colleagues, "I'll tell you where I was—both yesterday and when Fern was killed. I'll give you names of the people I spoke to, and you can check them out. Whatever you need to eliminate me as a suspect. But you *must* arrest this man. I know that he killed her."

For the first time since she'd been here, Riley was impressed by the man's urgent sincerity.

"Why are you so sure?" she asked him.

"It must be him! He's a sinful, godless man. He hates me, he hates all of us, and he hates our church. He left our congregation years ago. But he still lives right here in Allardt. I can tell you where he lives."

Bill and Jenn went right to work taking information from Weston Bruder—where he'd been at the times of the murders and Red Messer's address.

Holding the keychain, Riley spoke softly to the boy.

"I'm glad you showed this to me," she said. "I think it might be a great help. May I take it for a little while?"

The boy nodded. Then he whispered, "Just keep it, please. Don't ever bring it back here."

Of course, Riley realized, the red plastic heart would never be allowed in this house again. The poor boy was feeling guilty for having brought it here.

"Thank you, Bobby," Riley said. "This could be the most helpful clue we've found so far."

At that, he managed a weak smile. Riley smiled back and put the trinket in her purse.

She and her colleagues left the house and got back into their car. With Bill again behind the wheel, Jenn sitting beside him, and Riley in back, they followed GPS directions to the address they'd been given.

As they drove, Riley was bursting with curiosity about how Jenn had dealt with Weston Bruder just now.

She tapped Jenn on the shoulder and said, "How did you—?"

"Know all those Bible quotes?" Jenn replied. "Well, it's not that I'm especially religious. It's just that ..."

She glanced toward Bill warily, then back at Riley.

Riley immediately got the message—that this had something to do with things in Jenn's background that she couldn't talk openly about right now.

She said, "I was encouraged to read a lot when I was a kid. I found out that knowledge of the Bible could be ... useful."

Riley felt a little queasy. She knew that Jenn had been tutored in the ways of criminality—and of course, a con artist could easily make use of the Bible to manipulate certain kinds of unwitting victims.

Jenn obviously had a vast range of knowledge, far more than Riley had realized. Could she successfully channel that knowledge into enforcing the law rather than breaking it?

Riley could only hope so.

At that moment Riley's cell phone buzzed. She was dismayed to see that it was a text from Bull Cullen.

I'm in Chicago. You need to be in on a meeting about this case. At the RP office in Union Station. Take the next train you can get.

Riley suppressed a sigh.

Chicago seemed like an unnecessary detour, and Bull Cullen was the last person she wanted to talk to right now.

She pulled up the train schedule on her cell phone and saw that the next train for Chicago left Allardt in about an hour.

I guess we can make it, she thought.

But what she really hoped was that she and her team would be making an arrest between now and then. Then that Chicago meeting might be completely unnecessary.

As they pulled up in front of a rather plain but decent-looking

81

brick apartment building, she texted back.

OK. What abt our car?

The reply came through quickly.

I'll have it picked up at Allardt train station.

She texted another "OK," then put her phone away.

Bill said, "Apartment A. Probably right on the first floor."

Jenn asked, "Do you think this is it? Do you think this is our guy?"

"I don't know," Riley said. "But check your weapon. You might be needing it."

She took out her own Glock and clicked the cartridge out and back in again, assuring herself that it was in good working order.

CHAPTER SIXTEEN

Riley and her colleagues moved quietly into the apartment building. Fortunately, none of the residents were out and about, so they didn't have to worry about clearing away unwary civilians. They stopped just outside the door to Apartment A and exchanged uneasy glances.

Like Riley, Bill and Jenn had their hands near their weapons.

Riley knocked sharply on the door. They waited a few moments, but there was no reply.

She hesitated. Of course it was possible that Red Messer wasn't home.

If he didn't answer the door, maybe they should check in with Chief Dolby to try to find out more about him—including where he might be at the moment.

Riley didn't much like that idea. If Messer really was their killer, she wanted to arrest him here and now, before he got wind that they were after him.

Before he could possibly get away.

She knocked again. After another moment of silence, she heard footsteps inside the apartment, coming toward the door.

Then she heard a grumbling voice. "Who is it? What do you want?"

There was a peephole in the door. Riley held up her badge and introduced herself and her colleagues.

"Are you Red Messer?" she said through the door.

"That's what they call me," came the reply.

"We'd like to speak with you about Fern Bruder's murder five days ago. And a similar murder that happened in Illinois yesterday."

A brief silence followed. Riley's hand edged closer to her weapon.

Then she heard the sound of the door chain rattling and the dead bolt turning.

The door swung open to reveal a husky man wearing a bathrobe, pajamas, and bedroom slippers. He had long gray hair and a beard. Judging from his face, Riley guessed that the gray was premature, and that he was actually in his thirties.

She also noticed that he had a distinct odor.

He works in a kitchen, she realized.

There was no sign that he might be armed, and she could see her colleagues relax a little. Riley tried to do the same.

The man squinted as if half asleep.

"I guess you folks want to come in," he said in tired voice, stepping aside so that the agents could all enter. "Make yourselves comfortable."

Riley saw that Bill was watching the man closely as he followed them inside. But Bill made no comment and they all sat down. It was a modest apartment with sturdy furniture that Riley suspected had either come with the apartment or been bought used.

Red Messer looked around groggily.

"Maybe you'd like some coffee," he said.

"I'm fine," Riley said, and her colleagues agreed.

"Well, *I* sure need some," Messer said. "Excuse me just a moment."

As Messer headed for the kitchen, Riley noticed that he walked with a slight limp. He rattled around for a few moments, then made his way back with a mug of steaming coffee and sat down.

He took a sip and shook his head wearily.

"Horrible thing, what happened to poor Fern. If I can help you with it somehow, I'd love to. But I can't imagine how I can help. I sure don't know anything about it."

Riley was startled at his opening up this line of conversation.

She asked, "So you knew the victim?"

"A little. I wish I'd known her better. She was a nice lady."

Riley took the heart-shaped trinket out of her pocket and showed it to him.

"I believe you gave this to her," she said.

The man stared at the trinket for a moment.

"Good Lord," he said in a hushed voice.

Then he looked around at the agents and stammered, "Where did you …? How did you …? I mean, how did you know that I …?"

Riley said, "She gave it to her little brother, Bobby. She told him she'd gotten it from you."

"Yeah, she sure did," Red Messer said. "I told her it was a little piece of heart-shaped love, flaming red like I used to be."

He fingered his hair.

"All this used to be bright red, like a ripe old strawberry. I guess you'd never know it now, but that's why they started calling

84

me Red when I was a kid. My real name's Jesse."

He held out his hand for the trinket, and Riley reached over and passed it to him.

He turned it over with his fingers.

"I told her not to keep it too long," he said. "I told her to pass it along soon to someone else who she thought might need it. Pay it forward, if you know what I mean. I guess that's why it wound up with little Bobby."

He sat staring at the trinket in his hand.

Riley studied his face. Was he a killer? He certainly didn't show any sign of a murderous nature. But Riley knew from hard experience not to judge from appearances or even from first impressions. And she reminded herself of what Weston Bruder had said about him …

"He's a wicked man."

Bruder certainly seemed to believe that Red Messer was his daughter's killer.

Riley needed to find out the truth fast.

"How well did you know Fern's family?" Riley asked.

"Well, in a little town like this, everybody knows the Bruders. But old Weston Bruder and I were never friends. Far from it."

Riley sensed that Jenn was eager to ask the next question. She gave her a nod to go ahead.

"Mr. Messer, can you tell us where you were at the time of Fern's death?"

"Yeah, but if you're looking for an alibi, it won't be much help for mine. You said somebody else was killed yesterday?"

Jenn nodded and said, "A woman named Reese Fisher. She died on the tracks near Barnwell, Illinois. It happened in the morning, about the same time of day as the murder near here."

Messer shrugged and said, "I was here alone asleep both times. I don't suppose that's what you want to hear, but it's the truth. I keep strange hours, because I'm the night shift cook at a local all-night diner. Midnight to eight. I sleep during the day, and I was asleep when you folks knocked on the door. However …"

He pulled up the right leg of his pajamas. Riley was startled to see a prosthetic leg, which had been covered by the pajamas and his bedroom slipper. That obviously explained the limp.

He said, "Maybe this will do for an alibi."

Bill asked, "Iraq?"

Red Messer answered, "That's right."

Riley realized that Bill had picked up on the handicap right away. But she thought that the man had seemed quite mobile despite his prosthesis. Then she remembered the footprints she'd seen at the murder scene back near Barnwell. They'd looked perfectly even. She doubted that they could have been left by a man with a prosthetic leg.

Messer explained, "I lost my leg back in oh-four, during the Second Battle of Fallujah. I was an Army sergeant at the time."

He smiled a bitter, ironic smile.

"I can't tell you how eager I was to go and serve my country. I was afraid the Army wouldn't take me. I had reason to worry. Those were the days of 'Don't Ask, Don't Tell.'"

"You're gay?" Jenn asked.

Messer nodded.

"I wasn't very open about it here in Allardt. Some folks knew and were all right with it, and others weren't so all right with it. As far as the Army goes—well, they didn't ask, and I didn't tell, so I guess you could say I got lucky."

Tapping his artificial leg, he added, "Or not. Depends on how you look at it. But I was glad to do my duty. I'd like to think it was all worth it somehow."

Messer was quiet for a moment.

Then he said, "I was a real mess when I came back home. Mad at the Army, mad at myself, mad at the world. I needed something to make me feel whole again. I decided to check out the Ephesian Elders church, see if maybe some religion could help me."

Messer let out a scoffing sound.

"I didn't know what I was in for. The Sunday I went, Pastor Brayman happened to deliver a hellfire sermon about all the people the church was against—Jews, Catholics, Muslims, and of course homosexuals. No question about it—that wasn't the church for me. I quietly got up from my pew and tried to leave without making too much fuss about it."

He squinted as he remembered.

"But before I could get out, Weston Bruder stood up and pointed at me and told the whole congregation I was one of *them*. Before I knew it, a crowd of folks was blocking my way, and Pastor Brayman was calling on me to repent my ways. I'd already been judged, he said, which was why I'd lost my leg, but it wasn't too late to save my soul. I had a hell of a time getting away from there without banging up any of the congregation. And ever since then,

I've never had much good to say about Weston Bruder, nor he about me."

He paused for a moment.

"Don't get me wrong, I'm still a religious man. I found another church that really helped me through my rough times. But I sure never went back to the Ephesian Elders."

Riley thought hard and fast, trying to assess what she was hearing.

She asked, "How did you wind up giving the keychain to Fern?"

He smiled a little at the memory.

"I was on a train a couple of weeks ago, coming home from a trip to Chicago, when she happened to be in the same car with me. She came right over to me, said how sorry she'd always felt about what had happened to me, and how she had quit going to that church right then. She'd never go back, she said, no matter what her father said."

His eyes moistened.

"Imagine that!" he said, his voice choking a little. "She defied her whole family, her father especially. And all on account of what had happened to me. Right at that moment she seemed like the nicest human being in the world. I didn't have anything on me to give her except this cheap little thing, but I figured it was better than nothing."

He hung his head and added sadly, "And now she's dead. I just don't know what to make of it. What kind of a world is this, anyway?"

Riley remembered something Weston Bruder had said about his daughter.

"She'd been straying away from us lately."

Riley felt a pang of pity at the terrible irony. Fern Bruder had good reason to want to get away from Allardt and make a life for herself in Chicago. But she had lost her life during her efforts to do that.

She also remembered the sadness in little Bobby's face. As young as he was, he wanted to get away too. Fern seemed to have given him the keychain as a gesture of hope. But who did he have to turn to now that his big sister was gone?

She knew that Red Messer had every reason to wonder …

"What kind of a world is this, anyway?"

It was a question that haunted Riley every day.

Red Messer held out the trinket toward Riley.

"I guess you'll want this back," he said.

Riley thought quickly. Was it of any use as evidence?

No, she was sure that it wasn't—as sure as she was that Red Messer wasn't the killer.

"Keep it," she said.

Messer smiled and tucked the keychain into his bathrobe pocket.

Before anybody could say anything else, Riley's cell phone buzzed. She saw that the call was from Sam Flores, the head technician back at Quantico.

"I've got to take this," she said, getting up from her chair.

Then she said something that she hadn't expected to say when she'd arrived here.

"We're all very sorry for your loss, Mr. Messer."

Riley went out into the hall, leaving Jenn and Bill to wrap things up with Red Messer.

When she got Sam Flores on the line, she asked, "What have you got, Flores?"

The technician sounded excited.

"I think maybe I've found a person of interest."

Riley almost gasped with excitement.

"You mean a suspect?"

"No, but maybe the next best thing."

Sam paused and added, "I may have found the killer's next victim."

CHAPTER SEVENTEEN

Riley gripped the phone tightly, excited by what Flores had just said.

"The next victim?" she asked. "What do you mean?"

"My team and I have been monitoring the Internet, looking for any activity that might have to do with the case. There's a lot of buzz online about the murders right now. Of course, we've run across the usual crackpots with crazy theories, including a couple of guys claiming to be the killer. Don't worry, we checked them out, they're just asshole trolls. But ..."

Flores fell silent for a moment.

"There's a woman on Facebook named Joanna Rohm. She's been posting that she's scared she'll be the next victim. She could be just another crackpot, but ..."

Flores paused again.

"I don't know, Agent Paige. I've just got a feeling about what I see here on her page. Maybe the threat is imaginary, but the fear seems genuine."

Riley knew from experience that Flores's instincts were very good.

"Where does she live?" she asked.

"In Chicago. I've already run down her address and phone."

Riley gasped a little. Maybe this wasn't going to be a wasted trip after all. She decided to check Joanna Rohm's Facebook page herself as soon as she got a chance.

"Send that information to me, Flores," she said. "But what about the two victims' cell phones? Have you found anything helpful?"

"Not a thing," Sam said. "Fern Bruder just communicated with friends and family, nobody suspicious."

"What about Reese Fisher?" she asked Flores. "Her husband thought she had a lover in Chicago."

"I know," Flores said. "But if she did we see no sign of that on her cell phone. She didn't use hers much at all for calling or texting. I guess she used it mostly to connect to the Internet and use GPS and such."

Riley thanked Flores and ended the call just as Jenn and Bill came out of the apartment.

"Come on," she said to her colleagues. "We've got a train to catch."

*

A short time later, Riley and her colleagues were in a coach class car on an hour-long train trip to Chicago. Riley told them about the call from Flores, and they all huddled together as Riley opened her laptop and went online.

Riley logged into Facebook, then searched for the name Joanna Rohm. She found her page immediately.

Her horizontal cover photo was a view of Chicago's skyline as seen from Lake Michigan. Her profile image was actually an old photograph of a familiar male face, with a quote superimposed over it:

"A dreamer is one who can only find his way by moonlight, and his punishment is that he sees the dawn before the rest of the world."

Riley didn't recognize the quote, and couldn't quite place the face in the picture.

She asked, "Does anybody know who that is?"

Jenn was the first to speak up. "That's Oscar Wilde," she said. "The quote is from *The Critic as Artist*."

Riley glanced at her younger colleague. She remembered what Jenn had said a little while ago …

"I was encouraged to read a lot when I was a kid."

Riley was impressed. Whatever criminal skills Jenn had learned from Aunt Cora, she had obviously gotten a good education along the way.

Riley wasn't especially surprised that the photo wasn't of Joanna Rohm herself. Riley had several friends who posted sayings or images for their profile pictures instead of photos of themselves.

Bill pointed to the first post on the page. It simply read …

I'm scared for my life.

Bill said, "I guess that's what Flores was talking about."

Riley glanced down the comments thread.
A friend asked …

Why?

An exchange continued between Joanna Rohm and her friends.

Have you heard about the railroad killings in Indiana and Illinois?

Yes.

I think I'm the next intended victim.

Why do you think that?

Riley could see from the thread that Joanna wouldn't say exactly why she was afraid. And when her friends suggested that she notify the police, she said she didn't want to, and that she had her own reasons. The thread petered out due to Rohm's reluctance to share any meaningful information. At least, she hadn't shared anything more in a public thread.

Bill said to Riley, "Check her personal information."

Riley clicked the "About" tag. It showed almost no useful information at all, only a few innocuous "Likes"—music, books, and movies. She didn't even say where she lived, although Riley had already found out from Flores that she lived in Chicago. Rohm only had twenty-six friends.

"Just some crackpot?" Bill asked.

"Flores doesn't seem to think so," Riley said. "At least, it got his attention enough to pass it on to me."

"What do you think?" Jenn asked Riley.

Riley thought for a moment. She was somehow fascinated by what she saw here—or rather what she didn't see. With so few online contacts, Rohm seemed to be borderline reclusive, but she was alarmed enough to make a public statement about it.

Riley said, "Let's see if we can get her to talk to us."

She brought up the message bar and typed a message to Joanna Rohm.

I'm FBI Special Agent Riley Paige. I'm here with my

colleagues, Agents Jeffreys and Roston. We're investigating the railroad murders. We want to know why you're afraid you'll be the next victim.

Riley had no idea how long they would have to wait for a reply. But in a matter of seconds, her message was marked "seen."

Then came a reply ...

How do I know you're who you say you are?

Jenn said, "Sounds a little paranoid."

"Maybe," Riley said. "But as they say, even paranoids have enemies."

She typed again.

Check my own Facebook page.

She knew what Joanna Rohm would find there. Although Riley spent little time on Facebook, her information was very specific about her work and career, and her cover photo showed the FBI's seal and motto. The woman would have to be remarkably mistrustful not to believe her.

After a few moments, Joanna Rohm replied ...

I see it.

Riley typed ...

Do you think you're in danger right now?

Rohm quickly replied ...

No. I think I'm in a safe situation at the moment.

Riley typed ...

We need to talk.

As Riley waited for a reply, Jenn said, "Flores gave you her address. Maybe you could suggest that we meet her there."

"No," Riley said. "It might spook her to know that we've

tracked down that information. Let's just be patient for a few seconds."

Finally the woman typed …

Meet me at the restaurant at the Stott Hotel at 4:30.

Before Riley could type a reply, she saw that Joanna Rohm had suddenly gone offline.

Bill said, "Stott Hotel—yeah, I was there once. It's not far from Union Station."

Riley glanced at the time. Hopefully the meeting Cullen had set up would be over in time for them to meet with Joanna Rohm by 4:30.

Bill added, "It's a swanky place with a really high-class restaurant. This woman could just be some kind of rich eccentric who wants attention."

"Maybe," Riley said.

But she had a gut feeling that the truth was somewhat different.

She also felt sure that Flores was right. Joanna Rohm was genuinely scared.

The question was—of what?

CHAPTER EIGHTEEN

As the train came to a stop at the platform in Chicago's Union Station, Riley heard Jenn let out a growl of disgust.

Riley looked outside and spotted the cause of Jenn's dismay.

Bull Cullen was standing on the platform, waiting for their arrival.

Riley said to Jenn, "Surely you're not surprised to see him. We *are* here for a meeting with him, after all."

Jenn said, "Yeah, but I guess I hoped he wasn't going to meet us right off the train. What a drag."

Riley resisted the urge to say again …

"You're going to have to work with him."

But of course, Jenn knew that already.

Or at least she'd better, Riley thought.

Riley, Bill, and Jenn stepped off the train, and Cullen strode across the platform to meet them. Riley didn't fail to notice how Cullen not-so-subtly leered at Jenn as he approached. Jenn avoided making eye contact with him.

Riley suppressed a sigh.

These two really don't mix, she thought.

She sensed that they weren't going to get through this case without some kind of an altercation between Jenn and Cullen. She could only hope that whatever happened wouldn't be too disruptive of the work that lay ahead.

Cullen grinned at them in his usual cocky manner.

"I've got good news, and some not-so-good news," he said.

"OK," Jenn said in a tight voice. "Give us the not-so-good news first."

"Well, it's not really news, I suppose. We haven't found the killer. But the good news is he's through killing. He's not going to murder anybody else."

Riley exchanged surprised glances with Bill and Jenn.

"How do you know?" she asked.

"You'll find out," Cullen said. "Come on, the meeting is already underway."

Riley and her colleagues followed Cullen through the

concourse into the station's cavernous Great Hall, then up a wide flight of stairs with brass railings. After going up another flight of stairs, they arrived at the offices of the railroad police, where they went into a large conference room.

Riley was startled by how crowded the room was. As soon as she and her colleagues got seated, Cullen took his place at the end of the table and made some general introductions. A number of railroad police investigators from both passenger and freight units were there. She recognized a few of the faces from the Barnwell crime scene. She also recognized some agents from the Chicago FBI field office, including Special Agent in Charge Proctor Dillard, with whom she and Bill had worked in the past.

Riley was anxious to get right down to business.

She asked Cullen, "How do you know the killer isn't going to strike again?"

Cullen grinned and clicked a remote that brought up an image on a large screen. It was a photograph of a vehicle that had been burned to smoking cinders in the middle of a field.

He said, "My guys got wind of a report about this SUV—a Nissan off-road vehicle. Somebody deliberately torched it in a field about twenty-five miles outside of Barnwell. It didn't have a license plate, and it was too thoroughly incinerated to get DNA samples or any other useful information. But …"

He clicked the remote again and brought up two more pictures. One showed the tire tracks Riley had already seen alongside the railroad tracks near Barnwell. The other showed a similar set of tracks, obviously from the crime scene near Allardt.

Cullen said, "The FBI guys compared the tire tracks left at the two crime scenes, and they both were made by the same vehicle. The tracks are consistent with the type of vehicle that got torched."

Riley just looked at Cullen. She didn't quite understand what he was getting at.

Cullen shrugged and added, "What are the chances that the burned vehicle wasn't the one used by the murderer at both crime scenes?"

"Slim to nonexistent," Riley said.

Cullen nodded and smiled.

"Which means that our killer deliberately destroyed his vehicle to get rid of the evidence. And that surely means that he got skittish and doesn't plan to commit any more murders. We still don't know who he is, but all we've got to do is track him down. And we're not up against the clock. Nobody's life is in danger."

Riley glanced across the table and made eye contact with Chief Dillard. He shook his head at her, obviously as bemused by what Cullen was saying as Riley herself felt.

A bit cautiously, Riley began, "I hate to say this, but …"

"But what?" Cullen asked.

Before Riley could continue, Jenn spoke up sharply.

"You're jumping to conclusions. The only thing the burned vehicle tells us is that the killer is smart. He knows that the SUV was going to be easy to track down, and he didn't dare keep it, much less use it a third time. He probably has a new vehicle by now."

Cullen looked baffled.

Before Jenn could really lay into him, Riley silenced her with a stern look.

She changed the subject by asking Chief Dillard, "Has somebody followed up on the alibi that Weston Bruder gave us for the time of his daughter's murder?"

Dillard replied, "We checked out each of the people he said he'd spoken to. We didn't tell them where Bruder had claimed to be, but their responses all backed up his story."

"Has anyone talked to Reese Fisher's mother?" Riley asked.

Dillard nodded. "I sent a couple of my people to Tandy Place, the assisted care facility where she's living. The poor woman is deeply demented and can't fully grasp what happened to her daughter. She certainly couldn't give us any useful information."

Riley nodded and looked at her list of loose ends. There was just one more topic that she'd left a question mark beside.

"I take it the footprints at the two crime scenes also match," Riley said.

"They do. They were definitely left by the same man," Dillard said.

And that man didn't have a limp, she remembered. It wasn't Red Messer. She hadn't thought it could be, but she was glad to have him cleared.

"I'm glad we've cleared up those little details," Riley said. "So now it seems most likely that we are dealing with a serial killer, not a one-off followed by a copycat. That's important information. We weren't sure of it till now."

Bill added, "You brought us from Quantico to give you a profile. And it seems unlikely that we're dealing with the type of killer who's going to stop after two murders. The pressure is still on us. We *can't* let another victim die."

"Are you sure that he'll—" Cullen began.

"You'd better count on it," Jenn said.

Cullen's mouth dropped open and his face reddened.

This isn't helpful, Riley thought.

After all, Cullen was in charge of the railroad police here in Chicago, and Riley and her colleagues had just made him look foolish on his own turf—not only in front of his own agents and detectives, but the Chicago FBI people as well. Tweaking a male ego like Cullen's served no useful purpose in a situation as dire as this.

Besides, Riley knew that Cullen's assumption that the killings were over and done with wasn't stupid—not coming from a law enforcement officer used to dealing with collisions, suicides, and even the occasional murder or terrorist threat. He simply had no knowledge of psychopaths.

Riley said, "Look, I can think of one scenario under which the killer might actually be finished killing. It's not likely, but it's possible. Deputy Chief Cullen, I asked you to have your agents keep track of Chase Fisher, the second victim's husband. How is that going so far?"

Cullen seemed to be regaining his poise.

"My people have been tracking his every movement," he said. "He's not doing anything suspicious."

Riley was anything but surprised.

"Well, keep watching him. There's still a chance—a really dim one, I think—that he killed Reese Fisher because of her infidelity. If so, he could have set up the earlier killing as a ruse, to make us think we were dealing with a serial killer. If that's the case, he might not bother to kill again. As I said, it's not a likely scenario, and we'd better not count on it, but we can't ignore it."

Bill said, "The victims' lives don't seem to have been related in any way, except that they both sometimes rode a commuter train in and out of Chicago. We have to proceed with the most likely assumption. That it's a serial with a more generalized personal motive."

Riley paused for a moment.

Then she said, "Can you bring up pictures of the two victims? When they were alive, I mean?"

Cullen clicked his remote, and ID photos of Fern Bruder and

Reese Fisher appeared side by side on the screen.

Pointing, Riley said, "The women were ten years apart in age—Fern was twenty-five and Reese was thirty-five. One was married, one was single. Still, we can see a certain physical resemblance between them. Both had brown, curly hair, slender faces, aquiline noses. Those similarities might just be coincidental and tell us nothing about the killer's tastes and preferences. But they also might be meaningful. For example, women with those features might remind the killer of someone in his past."

Special Agent in Charge Dillard spoke up.

"Agent Paige, you say that Chase Fisher is a long shot as a suspect. Why is that?"

Riley thought for a moment.

"As Agent Jeffreys just said, it's likely that there's a more generalized motive behind these murders. In serial cases we often encounter killers driven by their own demons, their own compulsions. This man might not want to kill, but can't stop himself, despite intense feelings of guilt. His motives are probably murky, even to himself. But the railroad is part of his obsession somehow. He's triggered by something in his past, and it has something to do with trains."

Riley drummed her eraser on the table. She wasn't very satisfied with what she'd just said. It wasn't much of a profile, and it wasn't much to go on. But in her gut, she was wary of the usual textbook assumptions she might otherwise make. The killer clearly had psychiatric problems, but she somehow suspected that he'd never actually been institutionalized. And since neither victim had been sexually assaulted, the killer didn't seem to be sexually motivated.

Riley's eye was drawn to a tall, gray-haired man who seemed to be lost in thought, jotting down notes on a notepad. He didn't quite seem to belong to any group here—neither the railroad police nor the Chicago FBI.

Cullen apparently noticed who had attracted her attention. He looked along the table at the older man, then grinned and said, "Any ideas you'd like to share with us, Grandpa?"

The man cringed a little, and so did Riley. She could tell by Cullen's patronizing tone that "Grandpa" was a less-than-respectful nickname.

The man looked up from his notepad.

"Just playing around with a little theory," he said.

"Yeah? And what's that?"

The man shook his head.

"I'm not ready to say. I need more data."

Riley's interest was piqued. She wished she could get a look at whatever was written on that notepad.

Cullen chuckled and said, "Well, good luck with that, Grandpa. Let us know when you've cracked the case."

The man looked hurt now—understandably so, Riley thought. Without another word, he got up from his chair, opened the door, and stepped out of the room. He closed the door quietly behind him.

When he was gone, Riley asked Cullen, "Who was that man?"

Cullen laughed.

"His name is Mason Eggers—just a retired old fart who can't accept the fact that he's retired. He was a railroad cop for years, not a bad one in his day. He doesn't seem to know what to do with himself anymore, and he keeps coming around whenever there's a new case. He's always got ideas and theories, and sometimes they're not bad, as long as they don't have to do with anything more serious than vandalism or theft. The poor guy was past his prime years ago, but I let him hang around."

Riley felt a tingle that told her …

Cullen underestimates that guy.

She had an impulse to dash out of the room and catch up with Mason Eggers, but thought better of it.

The discussion at the table shifted to other details. Because both victims had taken trains out of Union Station, the Chicago team had checked and found that no railroad personnel had been at work on both trains.

They'd also pored over platform surveillance tapes, both in Chicago and at their destinations. So far they'd spotted both victims boarding or leaving their trains, but nobody suspicious following them. They couldn't identify any passengers in common for both trains.

Of course, they couldn't discount the possibility that the killer had a good knowledge of the surveillance system and had deliberately escaped detection. And unfortunately, the trains in question didn't have security cameras inside the passenger cars. Such cameras were planned for commuter trains in the future, but hadn't yet been installed.

After some discussion, Cullen made general assignments all around, and the meeting came to a close.

As Riley and her colleagues got up from the table, Bill glanced at his watch.

He said, "If we catch a cab right away, we should be able to make it."

Cullen overheard Bill and said, "Where are the three of you off to?"

Jenn and Bill didn't say anything. Riley didn't want to tell Cullen they were on their way to meet with a woman who thought she might be the killer's next victim. Cullen would surely want to come along, and he and Jenn would wind up at odds again. As far as Riley was concerned, the interview was likely to be sensitive enough as it was without having to deal with all that.

She said to Cullen, "We'll let you know if it amounts to anything."

Riley and her colleagues brushed past him and headed down the stairs. They stored their go-bags in a locker and hurried out of the building.

Within a few moments, they'd caught a cab and were on their way to the Stott Hotel. During the short drive, Riley remembered what Mason Eggers had said about his theory.

"I need more data."

Riley knew just how he felt, and it scared her.

What if "more data" arrived in the form of another murder?

CHAPTER NINETEEN

As their cab approached the Stott Hotel, a line kept running through Riley's mind …

I'm scared for my life.

It was from the Facebook post that Joanna Rohm had shared with her friends. And if Rohm had good reason for her fears, maybe Riley and her team would get their first real break in this case. Maybe they'd be able to stop this ghastly killer before he could strike again.

The cab pulled up in front of the Stott Hotel, and Riley and her colleagues got out. Riley was impressed as she stood on the sidewalk and looked up at the glittering steel and glass building overlooking the river.

"Swanky," Bill had called it.

He wasn't kidding, Riley thought.

She wondered—what did that say about the person they were about to meet?

They took the elevator up to the restaurant, which occupied most of the top floor of the building.

A stylish hostess greeted them as soon as they arrived. Riley said, "We're here to meet Joanna Rohm. Is she here?"

The hostess nodded.

"You'll find her in the lounge," she said, indicating the way.

The three agents passed through the clearly very expensive restaurant. Due to the late afternoon hour, only a few customers were there. When they went into the plush lounge, Riley was surprised to see no customers at all.

Where is she? Riley wondered.

Riley and her colleagues walked over to the bar, where a tall female bartender with blonde hair was cleaning some glasses. She wore a clean white shirt and a necktie.

"Excuse me," Riley said, "but we're looking for Joanna Rohm."

"That would be me," said the bartender.

Riley managed to hide her surprise as she and her colleagues produced their badges and introduced themselves. They sat down on the comfortable, leather-upholstered bar stools.

Riley said, "Now I think I understand why you told us to meet you at four-thirty."

"Yeah, business grinds to a halt right about now," Joanna said. "We can talk privately."

Joanna fell quiet and glanced around nervously.

Then she said, "I'm glad you're here. Like I said, I'm scared."

Riley said, "You said you were afraid you might be the railroad killer's next victim. Why do you think that?"

"I knew Reese Fisher."

Joanna gave Riley a significant look, holding Riley's gaze. Riley squinted, trying to understand what the woman was trying to communicate.

It soon began to dawn on her.

She remembered what Chase Fisher had said when they'd talked to him.

"Reese was having an affair."

Of course! Riley thought.

She said, "You were having an affair with Reese."

Joanna nodded again.

Bill asked, "But why does that make you think you might be the next victim?"

Joanna hesitated, then said, "The last time Reese was here— just before that terrible thing happened to her—she told me she thought her husband knew about us. He was being quiet about it, she said. She was afraid he was planning something, but she didn't know what."

Joanna gulped fearfully.

"Well, she found out what he was planning, didn't she? And now ... I'm scared half to death. Why wouldn't he come after me next? Doesn't it only make sense?"

Riley struggled with her thoughts, wondering what she should say—or not say.

Chase Fisher had told them he didn't know the identity of his wife's lover, and Riley had felt inclined to believe him. Should she say so to Joanna right now, to help put her at ease?

It didn't seem at all appropriate.

But what *was* appropriate under these strange circumstances?

Riley thought for a moment, then said, "Ms. Rohm, I take it

you're aware that there was an earlier murder carried out in the same manner. We now know for certain that the two murders were committed by the same person. This leads us to doubt very strongly that Chase Fisher killed Reese. It's hard to believe that he committed the first murder solely as some kind of preparation for the next one."

Joanna's expression changed. She seemed to be trying to let herself be reassured.

She said, "'Hard to believe,' you said. But not impossible, right?"

Riley hesitated. No, of course it wasn't impossible, but …

"It seems very unlikely," she said.

There was a dramatic change in Joanna's expression. The tension of fear began to give way to an equally terrible emotion.

She said, "I hate being scared. It gets in the way of—"

She choked down a sob.

"Your grief," Jenn said sympathetically.

Joanna nodded and wiped away a tear. Riley understood perfectly. The last thing the woman wanted right now was to be cowering for her life when she really needed to be mourning for someone she loved.

Riley wanted to say …

"Go right ahead and cry."

… but of course, there would be time for that later, probably in another setting.

Joanna cleared her throat and said, "Reese and I met several months ago at an assisted living facility. Her mother lives there, and so does my dad. It's been so terrible to see my dad slipping away from me. He doesn't remember me or my name most of the time anymore. Reese had been going through the same thing with her mother. We just got to talking about it. I'd been feeling so alone about it until I met her."

A tear trickled down her cheek, and she didn't bother to wipe it away.

"Unless you knew her … oh, you have no idea how kind and caring and open she was. She was so outgoing and so full of empathy. She made friends simply everywhere. I fell in love with her right away. You see, I'm a writer—fiction and poetry, mostly. I'm afraid I'm not very successful at it—not yet, anyway. Which is why I work here."

She smiled slightly.

"Yeah, I know the cliché—'Don't quit your day job.' I know better than to do that. But Joanna read my work and said it really touched her. She understood every single word I wrote and just loved it. She was the only person in the world who ever made me believe I could do it—be a writer, I mean. And now …"

An expression of fear started creep over her face again. But Riley sensed that it was a different fear from fear for her life.

It was fear of being alone.

"I don't know how I'll go on without her," Joanna said.

Riley wished she could remember the Oscar Wilde quote Joanna had put on her Facebook page …

Something to do with dreamers.

Joanna was a dreamer, all right. And in Reese Fisher, she had found and lost the only person in her world who had understood her dreams.

Riley fell silent as Bill and Jenn continued to ask Joanna some routine questions. She was quietly amazed by the irony of it all. She remembered the sadness in Chase Fisher's voice when he'd talked about Reese's lover—how he'd hoped that she'd found some rich and cultured man …

"Somebody who could take her to art galleries, plays, symphonies, the opera."

The truth was quite different. Reese's lover was a struggling woman writer, not some wealthy man. Even so, part of Chase Fisher's hope for his wife had proven true. She had found somebody who …

"… could really help fill what was missing from her life."

What would he think if he knew? Riley wondered.

She quickly pushed the question from her mind. It was none of her business, after all.

When Bill and Jenn wrapped up their questions, Joanna asked, "So you really think I'm safe?"

Riley and her colleagues exchanged glances. She sensed that Bill and Jenn felt the same way she did about the question.

What does "safe" even mean?

Of course, an FBI agent's job was to ensure the safety of people like Joanna.

But who could say what might happen to this woman when she left work tonight, or at any other moment in her life?

No, Riley didn't think she was in any danger from the railroad killer. But she couldn't know that for absolute certain.

Besides, the world was full of countless other dangers.

For a moment, Riley flashed back to last night's dream—of trying to save countless bound women from the inexorable, crushing force of an approaching locomotive.

Her whole life's work was like that.

Neither she nor Bill nor Jenn were in any position to make promises.

Instead, she handed Joanna her card.

She said, "Please contact me if you feel like you're in any danger."

Riley and her colleagues left the restaurant and got on the elevator. On their way down, she asked, "So what do we do now?"

Bill looked at his watch and said, "It's getting late, and there's not much else we can do today. Let's stop by the station and pick up our go-bags and get settled into a hotel of our own. Then we can talk about what to do tomorrow."

Riley and Jenn agreed.

As they left the elevator and headed out of the building, Riley found herself thinking about what Red Messer had told her about Fern Bruder.

"She seemed like the nicest human being in the world."

From what Joanna Rohm had said, the same words could be used to describe Reese Fisher. Although Riley was still having trouble profiling the killer, she was starting to get a vivid profile of his victims. And she knew that somewhere, a generous, kind, and vivacious woman had no idea what kind of danger she might be in.

That unstoppable locomotive in her dream was hurtling mercilessly toward her.

And Riley had no way to warn her.

CHAPTER TWENTY

The man waited a little while after the train left the station. Then he got up from his seat and walked from one passenger car to another until he got to the café car. Sure enough, there she was, sitting alone at a table, her eyes focused on her smartphone.

She hadn't noticed him, and he decided not to catch her attention—not just yet.

Instead he stood at the end of the car and looked at her.

Her name was Sally Diehl, and she looked markedly like the other two women—the same slender face, curly brown hair, slight build. It was that resemblance, of course, that had drawn him to her. Her unwariness, too, was somehow seductive. She didn't yet know that these traits and characteristics marked her for death.

He shuddered at the thought.

He felt a strong urge to turn around and make his way back through the cars to his seat.

I won't do it, he tried to tell himself. *Not this time.*

But some palpable force, much stronger than his own will, physically restrained him.

And the audible voice that had been saying *"soon"* since yesterday was whispering …

"It's time."

That palpable force gave him a push, and he stumbled into the café car and into Sally's field of vision.

She looked up with a pretty smile.

"Well—imagine meeting you here!" she said.

She laughed, and he did too. It was a joke, of course. They'd seen each other three times before in this very café car. As far as she knew, it was only a coincidence that they happened to be on the same train from time to time.

He walked over to her table.

"I see you haven't ordered anything yet," he said.

"Hadn't gotten around to it."

"I'll go get us something," he said.

Her eyes twinkled.

"That would be nice, Nash," she said. "I guess you already

106

know what I want."

He walked over to the counter and ordered two sandwiches and a couple of cappuccinos. As he stood there waiting, he wondered why he'd told all three women that his name was Nash. What did it matter, really?

But of course, it did matter.

If any of the women were to escape from his grim intentions, he certainly wouldn't want them to know his real name.

When the sandwiches and cappuccinos were ready, he carried them back to the table and sat down.

"Were you visiting your brother again?" he asked.

Her expression saddened and she nodded. He knew she made these trips between Caruthers and Chicago to visit her younger brother, who was being cared for in a drug treatment center.

"How's he doing?" he asked.

Sally shook her head tiredly.

"Angry this time," she said. "Trevor wants out of there, says he's fine, that thirty days is enough time, and he's ready to get on with his life. I just know that's not true. He's not ready. We've been through this before. He needs the full sixty days. If he gets out now, he'll be using again in a couple of weeks."

She looked into the man's eyes.

"The truth is—well, this is something I don't suppose I'd tell just anyone."

The man was touched that she trusted him.

The other two women had trusted him too, and had felt safe confiding in him. And he'd felt good about that, being able to offer them a sympathetic ear. Poor Fern had been so anxious to tell him about that terrible father of hers, and Reese had longed to talk to someone about the woman she loved in Chicago—someone who would simply listen and not judge her at all.

"I won't tell another soul," he said.

Which of course was true.

Sally let out a little gasp of emotion.

"I'm angry too," she said. "Angry for having to tell him things he doesn't want to hear, because he doesn't have the sense to make these decisions for myself. Angry that he resents it and—and hates me for it. Sometimes, anyway. On days like today."

"Why shouldn't you be angry?" the man asked.

Sally looked a little surprised at the question.

"Because he's ill, of course," she said. "He can't help it. It's a

107

disease. And I also feel …"

Her voice faded.

"What?" the man asked.

"Guilty somehow. Guilty that I didn't wind up the same way. 'There but the grace of God,' as they say. Guilty for being … all right, I guess."

He was rather glad that she was clutching her cappuccino with both hands. Otherwise, he'd be tempted to offer her his own hand for comfort. That would be too much. It would create a bond between them that would hurt him terribly when it finally had to be broken in such a cruel and violent way.

"Survival guilt," the man said. "It's only natural. And as for the anger—well, you've been saddled with all this responsibility. No one else in your family is willing to lift a finger to help him. The whole thing has fallen on you. You're a victim of your own compassion."

She smiled and rolled her eyes a little.

"Oh, I don't know about that," she said.

"Take it from me," he said. "I don't know anyone else who is so warm and caring and generous."

He meant it sincerely—although it wasn't quite the whole truth. He'd known two other women with very similar qualities.

But they were both dead now.

Sally sighed deeply.

She said, "I really appreciate having you to talk to about all this. But … it just doesn't seem fair. It's such a one-way street. You're always hearing about my problems, and you never tell me any of yours."

The man laughed a little.

"Maybe it's because I don't have any problems," he said.

Sally shook her head.

"No, that's not true. I can feel it. You're carrying some kind of awful burden, all the time. You're just … so sad underneath. You keep too much to yourself. And I wish I could help."

She winced at her own words.

"Oh, I'm so sorry," she said. "When will I learn to mind my own business? That was *so* out of line!"

"No, it wasn't," the man said.

After all, she was absolutely right. He was eaten away inside by guilt and obsessions and impulses far beyond his own control. And he wished he could talk to somebody about it—somebody just like her.

He said, "Maybe someday I'll tell you."

He regretted the words the second they were out. It was a lie, of course. He shouldn't have said it. It was wrong.

It was time to change the subject.

"Tell me what else is going on in your life," he said.

She started into some familiar topics—her work as a third-grade teacher in Caruthers, Illinois, and how hard it was to be a divorced woman in a small Midwestern town.

Meanwhile, the voice in his head was whispering to him, reminding him of his plans.

She had no idea that he, too, was going to get off the train in Caruthers. She thought he always stayed on the train to Wendover, where he'd told her he lived.

The truth was, he'd secretly followed her off the train the other times they'd met, skillfully avoiding the station's surveillance cameras, learning her every movement by heart.

He knew what to do, and he knew exactly how to do it.

The voice was saying again and again …

"It's time. It's time. It's time."

He wished the voice would be quiet.

He only wanted to drink in this woman's words.

After today, he'd never be able to do that again.

CHAPTER TWENTY ONE

As Riley and Jenn flagged down a cab in the busy traffic in front of the hotel, Bill looked up at the late afternoon sky that was framed by Chicago's towering structures. He couldn't help feeling that it ought to be dark out by now. It had already been a long day—two long days, actually—and he and his colleagues had nothing to show for all their hard work.

And he was tired—more tired than he ought to be.

Why? he wondered.

The case was wearing him down, of course. But he knew that something else was bothering him. He couldn't put his finger on it exactly.

A cab pulled up and they all climbed into it. The cab driver drove them back to Union Station, the solid-looking building squatting among taller ones. The driver waited while they retrieved the go-bags they'd left in the station lockers.

"Where to now?" the driver asked when they got back into the car.

Bill automatically repeated the name of a modestly priced nearby hotel where he and Riley had stayed during previous cases in the Windy City. He was glad that Bull Cullen hadn't bothered to book a crummy room for them again. This time they could get three simple but comfortable rooms on the FBI's dime.

After they checked into the hotel and dropped off their go-bags in their rooms, they regrouped in Jenn's room to discuss the situation. As they sat down together, Bill felt another wave of tiredness. He realized that he was also hungry.

"Let's order food," he said. "We haven't had anything to eat today since snacks on the train."

"Good idea," Jenn said. "My brain seriously needs recharging."

He called room service and ordered hamburgers and soft drinks. As they waited for their food to arrive, Riley phoned Proctor Dillard, the FBI field office chief they'd met with earlier, to check for updates.

Bill could tell from her expression that Dillard had nothing new.

Riley confirmed that lack of progress when she ended the call. "His people still haven't found any relationship between the two victims, and no indication that anyone had anything personal against them."

Bill shook his head with discouragement. He was all too familiar with the stagnation that could set in during an investigation. Most cases had periods of tediously picking through theories, discarding some and following up others until something pointed them in the right direction. Or until Riley's sixth sense picked up on something that was invisible to everybody else. So far, she hadn't mentioned anything at all about this case kicking in her unusual powers of perception.

He said, "We'd better check in with Coroner Hammond back in Barnwell to find out the results of Reese Fisher's autopsy."

Jenn made that call. When it was over, her expression was as lackluster as Riley's had been. She said, "Nothing new or surprising. Death was instantaneous, of course. Like Fern Bruder before her, she had flunitrazepam in her bloodstream. There were also telltale bruises around her neck."

Jenn growled slightly and added, "So I guess Cullen was right about how the killer choked both victims before injecting them with a date rape drug. I know it's petty of me, but I hate it when the son of a bitch is right."

Their burgers and soft drinks arrived, and the three of them sat down to eat. They also did their best to brainstorm theories and ideas.

They certainly had plenty of questions.

Jenn asked, "Do we think the victims knew the killer at all?"

Bill couldn't think of any reason they could answer that one way or the other. But a glance at Riley told him that she felt differently.

Riley said, "Both victims were charming and outgoing. I know, that might just be a coincidence, like their physical resemblance. But I've got a hunch otherwise. I think the killer engaged their trust. I doubt that either of them had long-term relationships with him. But he wasn't a total stranger. I think they struck up at least one conversation with him."

"Of course, that would make it easier for him to gain control of each prospective victim," Bill agreed.

"On the train, do you think?" Jenn asked.

"Possibly," Riley said. "Or possibly not. Perhaps they met him in Chicago, and he learned everything he needed to know about them there and traveled on his own to Allardt and Barnwell to kill them. Or I guess they might have met him in their home towns …"

Bill shook his head.

"That sounds like a bit of a stretch. I find it hard to believe that he hops from town to town looking for women who happen to commute to and from Chicago."

Jenn agreed. "If he started from their home towns, he'd have to have some more personal reason to look up these particular women."

Riley added, "And either way we're still stuck with the question of *why* these two."

The conversation continued without settling anything. As they all talked, Bill felt his exhaustion taking over, and he had trouble focusing on what was being said. It began to occur to him what at least part of the problem was.

Chemistry.

He knew that he wasn't working well with Riley and Jenn as a unit, at least not yet. He missed the old days when he and Riley were one-on-one partners and had an uncanny ability to connect with each other, sometimes communicating their ideas without even speaking at all. They'd constantly boosted each other's energy. Working with Riley had never drained him or made him feel tired.

In fact, they'd always been best friends, able to confide in each other completely and with absolute trust. But they hadn't even had a private moment to talk since they'd started to work on this case.

Bill bitterly missed that. He wished he could talk to Riley about his own life—his sadness and loss now that his ex-wife, Maggie, had remarried and moved to Saint Louis, taking their two boys away from him. He was losing touch with the boys, and it pained him terribly. And although his PTSD reactions to the debacle in California had subsided over the past six months, he sometimes felt that he still wasn't back to full capacity.

In the old days, he could have turned to Riley for sympathy, understanding, and even wise advice.

Now he felt left out.

Riley and Jenn seemed to understand each other better than he understood either of them.

Bill felt embarrassed to be thinking such thoughts. Was he actually jealous of the rapport that seemed to be growing between the two women?

Was he letting himself feel like the proverbial "third wheel"?

Their conversation shifted to trying to profile the killer himself. They kept coming back to the same old ideas—that the killer was fascinated by trains, that the women reminded him of someone in his past, and that he was acting out of some sort of guilty compulsion. Most of all, he seemed to resist any textbook profiles they might otherwise come up with about him.

As they talked, Bill realized little by little …

It isn't just me.

Riley looked tired, and so did Jenn.

He realized that they both also looked worried.

About what? Bill wondered.

Bill had been plenty concerned about Riley lately. He knew that she'd been taking on huge obligations at home—too much, he thought, for an active FBI agent who was a single parent. The last he'd heard she was in the process of adopting Jilly, and she also had that boy named Liam living with her.

Unless all that's changed, he thought.

The truth was, he didn't know a thing about what was going on with Riley's life, including whether she was still dating that guy named Blaine, who seemed like a decent man. He wondered if he should just come out and ask. But he didn't feel comfortable with that idea, not with all three of them in the room.

And there it was—his concern about that third person. Jenn was still an enigma to him. He couldn't complain about her behavior toward him. In fact, Jenn had covered for Riley on a recent case when he'd had a suicidal spell and Riley has slipped away to help him out.

Bill had returned the favor when Jenn herself had briefly gone AWOL last month.

But he still didn't even know why that had happened. It was obvious that Jenn harbored some sort of dark secret. Apparently Riley knew what it was, but she wasn't willing to confide in Bill about it.

Bill seriously didn't like being left out of the loop.

If something was lurking in Jenn's background that might disrupt everything at any moment, he felt as though he ought to know all about it. In their line of work, information blackouts could be dangerous, even a matter of life or death.

Eventually Riley said, "It's getting late, and we're just spinning our wheels here. I'm heading back to my room. We all really ought to turn in and get some rest so we can be fresh for tomorrow."

Jenn nodded, and Bill agreed gratefully. But as he and Riley got up to leave, he heard Riley's phone buzz.

He paused on his way to the door, waiting to see if the call had anything to do with the case.

When Riley answered the phone, her eyes widened with shock.

She turned pale as she walked back to the bed and sat down.

Bill felt a chill of apprehension.

What's happened? he wondered.

CHAPTER TWENTY TWO

Sitting on the hotel room bed, Riley turned to face away from her colleagues. She was trying to process what April just said.

Jilly's birthday party had been tonight—and Riley had forgotten all about it!

On the phone, April's voice was still explaining, "We all understood that you were on a case and you couldn't be here. But we've been waiting for you to call. When you didn't, I figured you must be in the middle of something serious—a gunfight or something life and death like that, and I hated to bother you. But Jilly's not taking it well."

A painful silence ensued.

In a slow, quiet voice, April said, "Oh, Mom. Please don't tell me you forgot!"

Riley wanted so much to lie, to say something like …

"Yes, I'm sorry, but we had an urgent development and I couldn't tear myself away. But I've been thinking about Jilly the whole time."

But the words wouldn't come, and Riley knew that it was just as well. April knew her mother too well. She'd never believe a lame excuse like that.

Besides, it would be a lie, and Riley couldn't lie to April.

"Can I talk to her?" Riley asked.

The very idea terrified Riley. What was she going to say?

"I'll go see," April said.

Riley could hear April's footsteps as she walked up the stairs carrying the phone. She heard April knock on Jilly's bedroom door.

April called out, "Jilly, I've got Mom on the phone."

Riley could hear Jilly's muffled reply through the door.

"Did she call?"

Riley gulped. She didn't want April to lie. But she dreaded the idea of Jilly hearing the truth.

"I called her," April said to Jilly.

Riley could hear the sound of a sob through the door.

"Leave me alone," Jilly said.

Then came the sound of April's footsteps heading back

downstairs.

"I'm sorry, Mom," April said as she walked. "She's really upset."

Riley sighed miserably.

"*I'm* the one who's sorry," she said. "How could I have let this happen?"

"Face it, Mom. You've done it before."

Riley had to think for a moment about what April meant.

Then she remembered—last August she'd forgotten April's birthday as well.

April had been angry and hurt then, but she didn't sound angry now. She sounded remarkably calm and mature.

Besides, Riley thought, *she's getting used to my screw-ups.*

Riley said, "Please talk to her, April. Maybe she'll listen to you. Just tell her—well, tell her that this isn't about her. It's about me. Tell her about last August. Maybe you can make her understand …"

Her voice trailed off.

Understand what? she wondered. *That she's getting adopted by a terrible parent?*

"I'll do my best, Mom," April said.

Riley didn't know what else to say. She wondered, of course, how the party had gone, what kind of delicious food Gabriela prepared, what kind of gifts Gabriela and April had gotten for Jilly.

But what did any of that matter now?

Everything had been spoiled, and it was Riley's own fault.

April asked, "Are you coming home soon?"

Riley swallowed hard. She wished she could be at home right this very second, trying to make things right.

"I don't know, April," she said. "The case isn't off to a very good start."

"OK, Mom. I understand."

"Tell Jilly I love her," Riley said. "And I love you too."

"I love you, Mom," April said.

The call ended, and Riley's body fell limp with despair. Her brain frantically tried to crank out excuses for herself. She was terrible with dates, she told herself. She was too oriented toward the overall picture to remember calendar details. In fact, she never even remembered her own birthday. It always took April or Gabriela to remind her.

But there was no point in trying to rationalize.

She'd made a terrible mistake, pure and simple.

She heard Bill's voice from behind her, "What happened?"

Riley turned around and saw that Bill and Jenn had been standing near the door during the entire phone call. They'd surely wondered, at least for the first few moments, whether the call had something to do with the case.

"I forgot Jilly's birthday," Riley said. "The family was having a party tonight. Jilly's just devastated."

"You were on a case," Jenn said. "You couldn't be there."

Riley knew that Jenn couldn't understand how serious this was. She didn't have children of her own—and maybe she never even planned to. And Jilly was, with reason, even more fragile than most teenagers.

But Bill reacted differently. He sat down on the bed and patted Riley's hand.

"I know how you feel," he said. "I've screwed up with my boys plenty of times."

Riley shook her head.

"Not like this, I'll bet. I did the same thing to April last August. But this is a whole lot worse. This is the first birthday Jilly has spent with her new family. And now it's ruined—all because of me."

A silence fell in the hotel room.

"I wish I could be there right now," Riley said.

"You should be," Bill said. "In fact, you should go there right now."

Riley looked her partner in the eyes.

"What do you mean?" she asked. "I'm on a case. I can't go anywhere."

Now Jenn spoke up.

"The FBI plane is still at the airport right here in Chicago. We can take you there, and you can fly right back home."

Riley was startled.

She said, "I can't very well say I've got to fly back home because I missed my daughter's birthday."

Jenn smiled a little.

"We'll think of something to say," she said.

Riley stammered, "But—but—"

Bill patted her hand again.

"Jenn's right," he said. "You and Jenn covered for me when I was dysfunctional. And you and I covered for her when she was

117

absent. I guess it's your turn again. Jenn and I can handle things here for a while. And we'll both cover for you. Let's go right now."

Riley felt flooded by a strange mix of guilt and gratitude.

She got up from the bed and said, "I'll go back to my room and get my go-bag."

At that moment, her phone buzzed again. Riley saw that the call was from Bull Cullen.

When she answered it, Cullen said ...

"We've got another body."

CHAPTER TWENTY THREE

Riley felt her stomach sink at what Cullen had just said. She gripped the phone tightly as she began to pace the room. She put the call on speakerphone so her colleagues could hear.

"Where did it happen this time?" she asked Bull Cullen.

"Just outside of Caruthers, a little town in the western part of the state."

Riley glanced at her colleagues and sensed that they were thinking what she was thinking.

The killer is moving westward.

He had started in Indiana, then these two were widely separated in Illinois.

She asked, "A town on a line out of Chicago?"

"Yes, another heavily used commuter line," Cullen said, "Her name was Sally Diehl, and she was killed just like the others, bound by duct tape to railroad tracks a short distance from town, killed by an oncoming freight train."

"So the MO was exactly the same?" Riley asked.

"Yeah, but with one important difference. Her own car was found parked next to the road that runs along the railroad. Either she drove herself there or the killer drove her in her own car."

Riley thought it more likely that the latter was the case. Her brain clicked away, already trying to put together a possible scenario for what had happened.

She asked, "Who's on the scene right now?"

"The local cops headed there as soon as they heard the news from the train crew. I've talked to the police chief, Tanya Buchanan. She thinks the killer may still be in the area, so she's working fast. She says she's already got roadblocks set up. He shouldn't be able to get away this time."

Cullen chuckled and added, "Tanya sounds like one smart cookie."

Jenn let out an audible groan, and Riley shared her disgust.

Tanya?

One smart cookie?

Riley was sure that Cullen wouldn't call a male police chief by his first name like that, let alone describe him as a "smart cookie."

Cullen continued, "I've ordered some of my people to get to Caruthers, and Special Agent in Charge Dillard has sent some of the Chicago FBI people. They're all on their way right now, driving. But we can get there faster. The town's got an airport, big enough for your jet. I need you to make a call and make sure it's ready to fly. I'll pick the three of you up and we'll fly there."

"How soon will you be here?" Riley asked.

Cullen chuckled again.

"Sooner than you probably expect," he said, ending the call.

Hardly a second later there was a knock at the door.

Jenn rolled her eyes and said, "Oh, God—somebody else please answer that."

Riley went to the door and opened it.

Sure enough, Bull Cullen was standing outside, still holding his cell phone in his hand. He was grinning—although his face sobered instantly when he saw that Riley was the one to greet him.

Riley understood the situation right away. As soon as Cullen had found out about the murder, he'd raced right to the hotel and found out Jenn's room number at the front desk. He'd made the call while walking to her room.

Doubtless Cullen had hoped to catch Jenn by surprise alone— yet another immature male stunt of his. Riley was sure it was fortunate that he'd found all three of the FBI agents already gathered there instead.

Jenn looked furious, of course.

Riley said to Cullen, "Agent Jeffreys and I just have to pick up our go-bags."

Jenn had her bag already in hand and actually led the way out the door, with Cullen tagging along behind her.

As she hurried to her room, Riley pulled out her cell phone and contacted the pilot, telling him to have the plane ready for them.

*

A short time later, Riley, her two colleagues, and Bull Cullen were aboard the FBI plane flying to Caruthers. Jenn had managed to claim a seat next to Riley so she wouldn't have to sit by Cullen.

Cullen had settled in next to Bill in a seat facing the two women. He wasn't bothering to hide his ogling of Jenn.

The whole thing exasperated Riley. The last thing they needed was a juvenile-minded guy on this job. She hoped Jenn could keep her own irritation under control, at least until they finished this case.

The flight was mercifully short. The plane barely reached cruising altitude before it started its descent into the Caruthers airport. When they landed, they were greeted on the tarmac by a pair of local police officers who drove them away, sirens blaring and lights flashing.

As they neared the crime scene, Riley could see that the local police had done a good job of closing off the area. Reporters had already gathered, but they weren't able to get past the roadblocks. Even so, Riley wondered—had the barriers been put up fast enough to stop the killer from getting away?

Maybe, she thought. But she suspected that he was too sharp to hang around. He had probably left as soon as he tied the woman down.

Local cops waved the police vehicle through the barriers, where it pulled up behind a small hatchback that had been parked on the shoulder of the road—the victim's vehicle, Riley realized. It was a dark, overcast night and she could see lights darting about nearby. They looked like oversized fireflies.

Flashlights, Riley realized.

Some of the local cops had already gathered there, but flashlights were the only illumination available. Riley took her own flashlight out of her go-bag, and saw that Jenn and Bill had theirs too.

When they walked over to the crime scene area, the moving lights revealed a handful of investigators surveying the area. The spectacle of the beheaded body under the glancing, dancing beams of light looked truly surreal.

A huskily built uniformed woman strode toward them.

She said, "I'm Tanya Buchanan, the chief of police here in Caruthers. I take it you folks just flew in from Chicago."

Riley and the others all introduced themselves. Chief Buchanan shined her flashlight down at the body and shook her head.

"I sure as hell never thought I'd see something like this," she said. "I'd heard about the other murders, of course, but even so I never imagined …"

The woman's voice trailed off and she shuffled her feet anxiously.

Then she pointed along the railroad tracks.

"The train stopped down there about a mile away. The

conductor called us as soon as he and the engineer could get stopped. Those poor guys, they're really a mess. We've already put them in their own motel rooms. A railroad shrink is supposed to get here before too long to help them deal with it."

Riley hoped Chief Buchanan was right. While it was true that Jenn had dealt with the engineer at the Barnwell crime scene delicately and sensitively, Riley and her colleagues weren't here to offer therapy. They were here to solve a crime. And the time between these grisly deaths seemed to be getting shorter.

There had been four days between the first killing and the second one. But this time the monster had only waited a day to carry out another murder. Whatever was driving him must be growing stronger.

That meant they had no time for distractions of any kind.

The first thing Riley noticed was a curve in the train tracks, the same as the Barnwell crime scene. The killer had chosen this spot carefully, knowing that the engineer wouldn't see the woman until it was much too late to stop.

Riley crouched beside the body and studied it with her flashlight. The headless corpse was twisted in a writhing position, similar to Reese Fisher's body. Like Reese, this woman had been all too conscious during the last moments of her life, and she had desperately tried to thrash her way loose.

Riley turned her flashlight toward the head that had rolled down the embankment. Riley felt a chill as the woman's dead, terrified eyes seemed to stare directly into her own.

She quickly noted the resemblance to the other two women— the same thin face, longish nose, and curly brown hair.

The killer is fixated on a physical type, all right, she thought.

She heard Jenn ask her, "What do you think about the car?"

Riley shined her light over at the parked hatchback.

A scenario had been forming in her mind ever since Bull Cullen had mentioned that the woman's own car was found at the scene.

Riley walked over to the car, followed by Bill, Jenn, Cullen, and Chief Buchanan. Riley saw that the passenger door and driver door were both still open.

She felt a welcome shift in her mental focus as she began to get a faint sense of the killer's thoughts and actions.

She walked slowly around the car, telling the others what she was thinking …

"Her car was parked somewhere else a while ago—a place where she often parked The killer knew exactly where to find it, and when to expect her to come back to it. He knew there weren't likely to be a lot of people around. He lay in wait for her out of sight near the car."

She stood beside the driver door and said …

"She took out her keys and opened the driver door. At that moment, everything was right for the killer. No one was watching. He made his move. He subdued her with a blood choke, then injected her with flunitrazepam. As she lost consciousness, he had no trouble pushing her into the car and over into the passenger's seat."

Riley leaned into the driver's seat. She reached out and touched the wheel lightly. "Then he drove directly here. He got out, walked around to the passenger side, pulled the woman out, and carried her over to the tracks. He bound her to the tracks, just as he had the others. Then he …"

Riley paused.

Then he what? she wondered.

He hadn't used the woman's car as a getaway vehicle. Did that mean he'd had his own car parked and waiting nearby? Or did he slip away on foot?

Riley's connection with the killer suddenly vanished.

She stifled a sigh. The feeling had been much too fleeting.

Were her instincts never going to kick in reliably on this case?

She said to the others, "A forensics team will need to scour the car for DNA."

Not that it will probably do any good, she thought.

She had no idea how many people might have ridden in Sally Diehl's car. And she felt sure that the killer wasn't an idiot—he would have worn gloves, so there wouldn't be any of his DNA on the wheel.

She turned away from the car and asked Chief Buchanan, "What can you tell me about Sally Diehl?"

The uniformed woman scratched her head.

"Well, Sally had lived here in Caruthers for two or three years. She taught third grade in our public school. She was single—divorced, I think. Yeah, I believe she told me that she got divorced before she moved here. I don't know where her ex-husband might live. She doesn't have any family here in town."

"What about friends?" Riley asked.

Buchanan smiled sadly.

"Oh, she had friends, all right. Me included. She was sweet and charming. Everybody liked her. Which is why it's so hard to imagine …"

The police chief's voice faded away again.

Riley asked, "Do you have any idea where she was or what she might have been doing today before this happened?"

Buchanan thought for a moment.

"Well, it's Sunday, so she wasn't teaching school. I wouldn't know where she was. But somebody else might. I'll ask my team to talk to people around town who knew her, ask if anybody knows."

Riley's head began to fill up with unanswered questions. She knew which one she wanted to ask first.

"Did she sometimes travel to Chicago?"

Chief Buchanan tilted her head.

"As a matter of fact, she did. I think she had a brother there, and she visited him from time to time. I have the impression that he was in and out of trouble a lot."

"Did a passenger train come into Caruthers from Chicago today?" Riley asked.

"Why, yes," Chief Buchanan said. "About an hour or so before this happened."

Riley looked knowingly at Bill and Jenn.

Jenn nodded and said what Riley was thinking. "The other two victims were on trains from Chicago shortly before they were killed."

Bill said, "Maybe Sally Diehl was on that passenger train."

"We need to find out," Riley said. "If she was, somebody needs to try to find people who were on the train who might have seen her or talked to her. We still don't know whether the killer might have been on the train as well, but we can't overlook the possibility."

Just then Riley heard wailing sirens and saw the flashing lights of several approaching official vehicles. She remembered Bull Cullen saying that he'd ordered his own railroad cops and FBI agents from the Chicago field office to come straight here.

They made it here in a hurry, Riley thought.

In a matter of seconds, a swarm of law enforcement personnel poured out of the vehicles. Led by the Chicago field office chief Proctor Dillard, the FBI people hauled an electrical generator and floodlight stands out of a truck and set them up around the body.

When the lights snapped on, the already surreal crime scene

suddenly became a whole lot weirder. The glare of the floodlights was as intense as sunlight, making the whole place seem like some sort of movie set.

But this scene was all too real.

Riley, Jenn, and Bill helped Chief Dillard organize the newly arrived personnel, assigning them different tasks.

Soon Riley noticed a tall, older man in plainclothes mingling among the others. He was looking around the crime scene with a mixture of horror and intense interest, writing down notes in a notepad.

Where have I seen that man before? she wondered.

Then she remembered.

It was Mason Eggers, the retired railroad cop who had caught Riley's interest at the meeting in Chicago. She remembered being intrigued by his keen concentration at the meeting in Chicago earlier that day.

She also remembered what he'd said shortly before his abrupt departure.

"Just playing around with a little theory."

Riley headed toward him.

It was time to find out what had been on his mind.

CHAPTER TWENTY FOUR

As Riley walked toward Mason Eggers with mounting curiosity, she remembered something that Cullen had said about Eggers at the meeting …

"He keeps coming around whenever there's a new case."

She guessed that Eggers had either driven here as soon as he'd heard about the new murder, or he'd hitched a ride with the railroad police.

Cullen had also said …

"He's always got ideas and theories."

That's what really intrigued Riley about him, and she wanted to hear what was on his mind. Mason Eggers seemed to be lost in thought as Riley walked up to him.

"Hello, Mr. Eggers," she said.

He looked up from his notes, startled.

"Agent Paige," he said.

He looked toward the body and shuddered.

"It's so horrible," he said. "I'd seen pictures of the other two victims. But being right here, seeing all this …"

His voice faded off for a moment.

Then he added, "Back in my day, railroad cops didn't have to deal with this kind of *intentional* thing. What kind of a world are we living in?"

He shrugged and said, "But you're with the FBI. I guess you're probably used to this sort of thing."

You never get used to it, Riley almost said.

Instead she remarked, "Back in Chicago, you said you were working on a theory."

Looking down at his notebook, he said, "It's not much. Nothing I'm sure you haven't thought of already. And it might not mean anything. But now that there have been three victims, you've probably noticed a pattern or two."

Riley nodded and said, "For one thing, the killings are moving westward. That might or might not be an actual trend."

Eggers said, "Yeah, and I'm sure you've noticed something about the town names."

Riley realized that she hadn't had time yet to think about it. She ran the names in her head …

Allardt … Barnwell … Caruthers …

Of course! she thought.

Surely she and her colleagues would have noticed the same thing before too long. But this retired railroad cop had beaten them to it.

She said, "They begin with the first three letters of the alphabet."

"That's right," Eggers said. "The idea started to hit me when I heard the first two names. I'm not sure why it did, just two names wasn't much to go on. It's just that … well, did you ever get one of those really strong hunches?"

Riley almost smiled.

Unexplained hunches were practically her specialty at the BAU.

Eggers said, "What do you think are the chances the town name will begin with a D the next time?"

"The next time," Riley thought with a chill.

There'd better not be a next time.

Even so, she hastily thought it over.

She said, "We still can't be sure that the alphabetical pattern isn't just a coincidence. Even if we were sure, how could we narrow down which 'D' town to look for?"

"I know what you mean," Eggers said. "We're talking about towns to the west of here. Even narrowed down to those with train lines coming through from Chicago—towns that begin with the letter 'D.' I know the railroads through this region like the back of my hand. I can think of a bunch of towns like that right off the top of my head. And if it's just a coincidence, it would be a waste of time to try to check out all of them."

He looked at his note pad for a moment.

He chuckled bitterly and added, "You may have heard that I'm just some annoying old coot whose better days are long behind him. Well, you've heard right. And even in my better days, I never dealt with anything like this. Forget I mentioned it, OK? It's just a harebrained idea."

Riley felt a tingle of interest as he started to walk away.

"Wait a minute," Riley called out to him.

He stopped and turned back toward her.

She said, "You've got another idea, don't you? Aside from the alphabetical pattern, I mean."

He shook his head.

"I haven't really worked it out yet," he said. "I'd just be wasting your time."

"Try me," Riley said.

Eggers looked reluctant, but walked toward Riley again, pointing to his notepad.

Just as he opened his mouth to speak, a sharp yell rang out.

"Hey! You crazy bitch! What's the matter with you?"

She recognized the voice immediately.

It was Bull Cullen.

Riley turned around and looked. The floodlights displayed a truly bizarre scene.

Right near the body, Jenn and Bull Cullen were locked in each other's arms, wrestling viciously while others stood around them gaping with surprise. Cullen was taller and heavier than Jenn, but she was obviously holding her own.

Bill stood nearby, watching but looking undecided about whether to interfere.

"Hey!" Riley yelled, striding toward the grappling pair.

Cullen managed to disentangle himself and threw Jenn down onto the tracks. But she was on her feet in an instant, backing away from him and holding out her hands to warn him off.

"Don't even think about it, creep!" she snarled.

But Cullen ignored her warning. He raised his fist and lunged toward her. Jenn easily dodged his blow and slammed her own fist into his face. Cullen staggered away in pain.

"Ow! You broke my nose, you crazy bitch!"

Riley dashed between Jenn and Cullen.

She yelled, "All right, break it up, you two!"

Cullen was fingering his bleeding nose. He didn't look at all eager to resume fighting. Calling out to the witnesses, he said, "Everyone saw that, right? She attacked me! For no reason at all!"

Riley grabbed Jenn by the shoulders.

She asked, "What the hell is this all about?"

Jenn pointed at Cullen furiously.

"He touched me! The bastard touched me!"

Riley said, "What do you mean, he touched you?"

The young African-American agent was shaking all over, apparently too angry to speak.

Meanwhile, Chief Tanya Buchanan seemed almost to be

128

enjoying the situation. She walked over to Bull Cullen and took his face in her large, strong hands.

"Let me look at that," she said.

"She broke my nose!" Cullen said.

"Naw, it's not broken," the chief said, examining his bleeding nose and speaking as if to a child. "It must hurt though, you poor little thing. We need to get some ice on it. Come on, let's go to my van. I've got a first aid kit, I'll fix you up as good as new. And I can get someone to drive into town and get you some ice."

Thoroughly humiliated, Cullen yanked himself away from Chief Buchanan and stalked off on his own.

Chief Buchanan said to Riley, "I saw the whole thing. Your agent was crouched over the body looking at it real closely when that clown leaned down beside her and put his hand on her back."

Bill added, "Not in an innocent way either, I can tell you that for sure."

Riley could tell that Bill was amused at how the confrontation had played out.

Her mind boggled at Cullen's stupidity. What was he thinking, making a pass at an FBI agent when she was examining a corpse?

And hadn't he learned anything at all about Jenn by now?

She saw Cullen pacing a short way off, holding a handkerchief to his wounded nose.

Riley walked over to Jenn, who was standing stiffly with her arms crossed.

Jenn shuffled her feet and said, "I know what you're going to say—we've got to work with him. I'm sorry."

"No, you're not," Riley said.

The truth was, Riley saw no reason why Jenn should be.

"OK, you're right," Jenn said. "I'm not sorry. But it won't happen again."

Riley glanced over at Cullen, who was now sitting on the ground looking thoroughly shamed and cowed.

Managing not to smirk, Riley said to Jenn, "No, I'm sure it won't. He's bothered you for the last time. I think we can all count on that."

Patting Jenn on the shoulder, she added, "Now get your head back in the game."

Jenn nodded.

"I'll do that," she said.

Riley quickly remembered her disrupted conversation with

Mason Eggers. She looked over to where she'd been talking to him earlier, but he wasn't there. She glanced all around and couldn't see him anywhere. He seemed to have slipped away.

Riley sighed, remembering what Eggers had said about himself ...

"... some annoying old coot whose better days are behind him."

He certainly didn't seem to have a lot of self-confidence. And that was small wonder, considering how Cullen had treated him back at the meeting.

Riley cringed as she remembered Cullen saying ...

"Any ideas you'd like to share with us, Grandpa?"

Riley wasn't really surprised that the old guy had gone away.

All the same, she wished he'd hung around. She wasn't sure why she was so curious about his theories. But she didn't have any of her own at this point. And she had a hunch that Eggers had more insights than anyone gave him credit for—including himself.

Just then one of the local cops yelled over to Chief Buchanan from the police barrier on the road.

"Hey, Chief! Come on over here! We might have a lead!"

CHAPTER TWENTY FIVE

Riley turned quickly at the sound of the voice.

A break in the case? she wondered.

The cop who had yelled out was standing just beyond the barrier among the reporters. Next to him stood a middle-aged woman who was wringing her hands anxiously.

Chief Buchanan said to Riley, "That's Ila Lawrence. Her son Axel is one of my cops. She's a little bit annoying, but she wouldn't come around here if she didn't think she really knew something. Come on, let's check it out."

As Riley trotted alongside Chief Buchanan toward the barrier, the cop escorted Ila Lawrence inside the blocked-off area.

"Is it true?" the woman asked when they got near her.

"Is what true?" Chief Buchanan said.

"That Sally Diehl got killed here? That's what Axel said on the phone. That's why I came over here."

Chief Buchanan gave Riley an awkward glance. Riley understood. The chief was embarrassed that one of her own cops was blabbing crime scene information to his mother.

Chief Buchanan said, "Ila, I'd rather not get into that right now."

Ila's eyes widened.

"It *was* Sally! I'm sure it was! I warned her to stay away from those people!"

Riley's attention sharpened.

She asked, "What people are you talking about?"

"Bums. Hobos. They hang around the train station from time to time, panhandling. They get chased off, but they show up again. They're not really pushy and most folks know well enough to stay clear of them. But Sally kept giving them money—and worse, she kept *talking* to them."

Ila shook her head.

She said, "That woman was just too friendly for her own good. But I kept wondering—what did she talk to them about? I mean, what did she have in common with them? She taught third grade, for goodness' sake! I worried that maybe she was into something dangerous—drugs or something worse. Well, I must have been right. Whatever it was got her killed. I *knew* those bums were dangerous!"

Chief Buchanan shuffled her feet irritably.

"Ila, thanks for stopping by," she said, obviously trying to sound polite. "We'll keep what you said in mind. We've got to get back to work. Meanwhile, I'd really rather you not talk to anybody else about any of this."

Chief Buchanan turned away, and the woman looked startled at getting brushed off so abruptly. As Riley and the chief walked back toward the crime scene, the chief called out to one of her cops.

"Lawrence! Get your ass over here!"

The young cop came toward them, looking apprehensive.

Chief Buchanan said to him in a testy tone, "Did you call your mother and tell her what was going on here?"

The cop stammered, "W-well, no, actually she called me, just to talk, like she usually does around this time of night. When I told her where I was and what I was doing, I guess I—"

"Oh, I know what you did," Chief Buchanan interrupted. "You just hauled off and told her the name of the murder victim. What's the matter with you, Lawrence? You know better than that."

The young cop hung his head.

"I'm sorry, ma'am. It was just that, you know, nothing like this ever happens around here, and I didn't stop to think about what I was saying and …"

He paused and added, "It won't happen again, ma'am."

"Damn straight, it won't happen again," the chief growled. "And when the hell are you going to stop calling me 'ma'am'?"

"Sorry—Chief," the cop said.

As he started walking away, the chief snapped at him again.

"Stay here a minute. Maybe we can find a way to make you useful as well as ornamental."

The young cop fell quiet and stood there.

Riley asked the chief, "What hobos was Ila talking about?"

"Oh, just some transient freight-hoppers, hobos who ride in boxcars. They've moved into the area lately, seem to think of Caruthers some kind of hobo train station. They're a real nuisance. Harder to get rid of than a swarm of flies on a cow's carcass. Like Ila said, they do some panhandling around the station whenever they can get by with it. I'd seen Sally talking to them too, and giving them money. I told her to stop, but she didn't listen. Sally was like that—always interested in other people, it didn't much matter who. She wasn't what you'd call discriminating in her choices of acquaintances."

"Where are they right now?" Riley asked.

Chief Buchanan looked at Riley with a curious expression.

She said, "Surely you don't think those bums had anything to do with Sally's death."

Riley thought for a moment. It didn't seem at all likely that hobos were going around killing women throughout the region.

But even so …

"Sally did *talk* to them," she said. "Right now, I'm interested in anyone she may have talked to. Maybe they know something we need to know. I'd like to check them out."

Chief Buchanan scratched her chin.

"Well, they keep moving around, finding different places to stay nights. My boys shoo them away, but they always find someplace else."

Chief Buchanan pointed along the tracks.

"The last I heard, they were camping up that way, under a place where the tracks pass over a ravine. I'd been planning to send some of my boys to clear them out until … well, until this other thing happened."

Riley decided that she definitely wanted to talk to the hobos. She looked around for Bill and Jenn and spotted them talking with the coroner who had arrived on the scene. They were intent on helping him examine the body. Riley was glad to see the two of them seemed to be working well together.

No need to bother them about this, she thought.

She turned to Officer Lawrence and said, "Do you know this place your chief is talking about?"

Lawrence nodded, looking more than a little disgusted.

Riley said to Chief Buchanan, "I'd like to borrow this man for a little while."

"Be my guest," the chief said.

Riley and the cop made their way along the tracks, shining their flashlights ahead of them.

"Hobos," the cop said, spitting with annoyance as they walked along. "I hate hobos. And freight-hoppers are the worst. The filthy bastards. It had better be worth it—going anywhere near them, I mean. I'll want to take a long shower later on."

Riley fought down a sigh of impatience.

133

The guy definitely wasn't much of a cop—first blabbing to his mother about the murder, and now getting all squeamish about a bunch of homeless transients.

I'd better not count on him for much, she thought.

They'd walked a short distance when Riley noticed a weird glow up ahead. It seemed to be coming up from beneath the railroad ties. They came to a place where the tracks were raised on trestles over a ravine.

Lawrence said, "That's the place right there."

Riley stepped off the tracks and looked down the hillside. She could see a small campfire burning. About eight grubby men with makeshift bedrolls were huddled around the fire talking in quiet voices. Riley guessed that the fire wasn't for warmth, not on a summer night like this. It had to be for cooking and for light.

Riley knew that if she and the cop made their presence known too quickly, the hobos were liable to scatter.

She whispered to the cop, "Let's turn off our flashlights. Keep quiet."

Signaling for the young cop to follow her, she began to make her way down the steep slope into the ravine. They had almost gotten to the bottom without attracting the hobos' attention when the cop tripped and stumbled.

"Son of a bitch!" he yelled.

One of the hobos called out, "Who's there?"

"Just relax," Riley replied. "We're not here to make trouble."

She turned her flashlight back on and shined it on her badge.

"I'm Special Agent Riley Paige, FBI. I just want to talk a little, that's all."

Several of the hobos laughed coarsely.

"The FBI!" one said.

"Holy shit!" said another. "What the hell do you want with a bunch of bums like us?"

Another said, "Does this have something to do with whatever's going on down yonder? We've been hearing sirens for a good while now."

The young cop said, "A woman was killed. Murdered. Run over by a train."

Riley darted a disapproving glance at Officer Lawrence. She wanted to do the talking here. With his lack of basic cop skills, he was sure to make a mess of things.

She said, "The victim's name was Sally Diehl. Is that name

familiar to any of you?"

An uneasy murmur passed among the men.

One said, "Not the *nice* Sally, I hope. Not the Sally we see around the train station from time to time."

"I believe that was her," Riley said.

Several of the men moaned sadly.

"That stinks," said one. "Who'd want to kill a nice girl like that?"

Lawrence said, "That's what we're here to find out."

Riley nudged him with her elbow, hoping he'd get the message to shut up.

She was starting to really wish she'd brought Jenn or Bill with her after all.

Meanwhile, she noticed that one of the men was sitting a short distance off from the others, facing away from everybody.

Why? she wondered.

His effort to go unnoticed was only making him more conspicuous.

She said to the men, "I understand that Sally would sometimes stop and talk with you guys."

There was a low murmur of agreement.

Riley said, "Did she ever tell you about someone she'd met who worried her? On a train, maybe, or anywhere else? Someone who might have frightened her?"

"Not Sally," one of the men said. "She wasn't the type to talk about her own problems."

"That's right," another said. "She was actually interested in us, hearing our stories, offering to help with a little money now and then."

Lawrence stepped forward and said, "You guys had better not hold out on us. Start talking, right now. I've got half a mind to haul all of you into the station."

Riley grabbed him by the shoulder.

"Lawrence, knock it off," she said.

But the damage was done. She could feel a wave of anxiety pass among the men. Gone was any level of trust she'd hoped to establish with them.

"We're not here to make trouble," she'd said.

"I just want to talk," she'd said.

They didn't believe that anymore. She'd never get any meaningful information out of them now.

135

Even as she tried to think how to get the hobos more comfortable with them again, she saw a movement at the far side of the group.

The man who'd been off by himself was on his feet.

He was running away!

"Stop right there!" Lawrence yelled at the man.

The man was scrambling up the slope, on his way out of the ravine.

With another bellow, Officer Lawrence took off after him.

Riley stifled a groan and started after Lawrence. But she suddenly fell to the ground and her flashlight flew from her hand.

She realized that someone had tripped her.

As she tried to get to her feet, a heavy boot pushed her down. She rolled over and looked up.

Riley saw that the group of men had formed a threatening circle around her.

CHAPTER TWENTY SIX

Riley moved slowly to get back on her feet, watching for any attack from the men who had surrounded her. She more than half expected to get kicked back to the ground before she could stand up.

Instead, the circle of men withdrew a couple of steps.

Their retreat wasn't out of fear—she felt none of that in the air.

They just want to give me a fighting chance, she realized.

It wasn't really an encouraging thought. In the dim firelight, these guys looked a lot bigger now than they had when they'd been sitting huddled around their little fire. She remembered that a large percentage of today's hobos were ex-convicts. They would be strong, and they'd learned to be violent in the nation's prisons.

She quickly assessed whether to draw her weapon.

No, she thought.

That wouldn't be a good idea—not in a circle of potential assailants. One might grab her from behind, causing her to lose control of her weapon. She could easily wind up dead.

She fleetingly worried about Officer Lawrence. The aggressive young cop had disappeared out of the ravine in pursuit of the escaping hobo.

Had Lawrence drawn his gun? Did he have the sense not to fire on the fleeing man?

But she didn't have time to worry about that now.

"I don't want any trouble," Riley said.

"Neither do we," the largest of the hobos said. "That's why we want to know—why are you guys after our pal Spider?"

"We didn't come here after anybody," Riley said.

"You got an arrest warrant?" another hobo asked.

"No. We just want to talk, that's all."

The largest guy broke into a sinister grin.

"Talk!" he said with a rough laugh. "We might just get around to that," he said. "Or we might not. Or maybe you and me need to communicate first."

Riley heard a murmur from the others in the circle, but couldn't tell whether it was in support or protest of the big man's attitude.

Then he barked out orders. "Tater, put out the fire. Weasel, grab her flashlight."

"Right away, Dutch," said one of the men.

The two hobos he'd addressed quickly followed their orders. One dumped a cup of water on the campfire. As the fire hissed and smoked, he threw a heavy cover over it.

The other hobo snatched up Riley's flashlight and turned it off.

Suddenly, the darkness was total, and the sound was only that of shuffling feet. No ambient light penetrated into the deep ravine.

Riley knew Dutch was still there, somewhere in front of her. The rest of the men seemed to have stepped back.

Giving us space, she realized.

Riley deliberately slowed her breathing and considered her tactics. Although the hobo called Dutch was a lot bigger and stronger than she was, he was overconfident. His mistake was being determined to fight with her one-on-one. She knew that the darkness didn't give him any particular advantage. She'd fought in total darkness before. She knew what to do.

Riley began to move about randomly—stepping lightly forward, backward, to the sides, ducking and dodging even though no blows were coming just yet.

She couldn't see where her opponent was, but he couldn't see her either. He would hear her moving about, but if she kept moving, he couldn't predict where she'd be next. And he was likely to make more noise than she did.

Soon she heard a heavy step and felt a rush of air as his arm sliced by, then a grunt of discouragement that the blow didn't connect. Another quick swing also missed her widely, and she heard him stumble past her.

Riley knew that she was depending on luck as well as stealth, and that luck wasn't likely to hold out for long. But maybe it wouldn't have to. The guy's very size meant that he was already using more effort and energy than she was, just by flailing about. If she could just evade his blows long enough to tire him, he'd become markedly less dangerous.

She kept her feet moving until a backward step brought her into contact with a body. She'd almost forgotten—the circle of men was still tight around her. Whoever she'd bumped into gave her a sharp push back toward Dutch, who was still swinging at her.

Another blow came, and this time she felt his knuckles graze her cheek.

She heard curses as the big man blundered past her and into his companions. Then for a long moment, she couldn't tell exactly where he was.

Riley began to worry …

Is he tiring fast enough?

She stood still, and she heard a welcome sound.

Dutch was breathing heavily now.

Those sounds were all she needed to locate the position of his head. She drew back her right arm and let fly with her fist.

She felt a sharp pain in her knuckles that shot all the way into her wrist as her fist connected with the man's skull.

Dutch let out an outcry of pain. But Riley could tell by his voice that he was still on his feet.

She fought down a surge of discouragement.

There was a disadvantage to fighting blind that she hadn't reckoned on.

If she'd been able to see, she'd have been able to aim her punch somewhere softer and yet more vulnerable, like her assailant's throat.

Now it was going to take more than one strike to bring him down.

Dutch was groaning and gasping audibly now. She listened carefully, then launched another punch—this time with her left arm.

This hit didn't hurt her hand nearly as much as the last one, and she could both hear and feel something cracking against her knuckles.

Teeth, she realized.

She must have smashed him on the side of his mouth. He was cursing and howling with pain.

The fight was over.

Now Riley drew her weapon. Her hand was hurting, and she hoped she wouldn't have to fire it. She doubted that she would, but she knew that she could fire with her left hand if she absolutely had to.

Dutch yelled, "Light, damn it! I need some light."

The hobo named Weasel snapped Riley's flashlight back on. Another hobo yanked the cover off the campfire and squirted kerosene onto the coals.

Flames leaped up again.

The light revealed Riley standing there, pointing her gun at Dutch. Blood was pouring from the big man's mouth.

"Nobody move," she said sharply. "Dutch, put your hands up on your head."

Dutch looked cowed.

"OK, OK," he said, obeying her order. As he raised his hands, he leaned forward to spit out a couple of broken teeth.

Despite the pain in her right hand and wrist, Riley managed to smile.

She said, "All right, let's pick up where we left off. Like I said, I just want to ask you guys a few questions. Just sit down and make yourselves comfortable. Let's get to know each other."

As the group of men backed off and began to seat themselves again, Riley heard Officer Lawrence's voice. He was talking on his cell phone and making his way back down the slope into the ravine.

"OK," Lawrence was saying. "Just don't let him get away."

He ended the call, and Riley asked, "What about the guy who ran?"

"I couldn't catch up with him," Lawrence said.

Riley saw that his weapon was still holstered.

Well, at least he didn't shoot him, she thought.

Lawrence continued, "But he went running straight down the road beside the tracks. He was actually headed back toward the train station, so I called one of our guys and told him to have a team pick him up. He shouldn't get very far."

Lawrence looked puzzled as he gazed around at the scene. Riley was standing there with her weapon still drawn, and the largest hobo was groaning and fingering the side of his bleeding mouth.

Lawrence said, "Huh—what's been going on here?"

Riley let out a small chuckle.

"Oh, nothing much," she said. "We were just settling down for a nice little chat."

At that moment, Lawrence's phone buzzed. His eyes widened with surprise as he took the call.

"What? Are you kidding?"

He listened for a moment, then added, "OK, we'll be right there."

Lawrence put the phone in his pocket and stared at Riley.

"They caught up with him, all right," he said. "And get this— he was trying to get away in a goddamn Mercedes!"

CHAPTER TWENTY SEVEN

Riley stared back at Lawrence as she holstered her weapon and snatched her flashlight from the hobo who had picked it up.

"A Mercedes?" she asked. "What are you talking about?"

"Some of our guys picked him up in the train station parking lot. It's real close to here, and he must have run straight there when I started after him. He was trying to drive off in the Mercedes when they nabbed him."

Riley shook her hand to try to make the stinging pain from the punch to Dutch's face go away. She knew she should get some ice on it, but none was readily available, and everything else seemed more important anyhow.

The hobos who had been so threatening just a moment before seemed docile now. Dutch, the one who had attacked her, was sitting on the ground moaning softly. One of his buddies handed him a rag that looked reasonably clean to mop up the blood on his face.

Riley quickly decided it wasn't worth trying to arrest any of them—not even Dutch.

"Do you guys have a first aid kit?" she asked.

"Yeah," Weasel said. "We can take care of him."

"Come on," she said to Officer Lawrence. "Let's go see what's going on."

Riley and Lawrence left the hobos behind and scrambled up the embankment. When they emerged from the ravine, a vehicle was already approaching. When it stopped alongside side of them, Riley saw that Bill and Jenn were inside. So was Bull Cullen, who had seated himself safely away from Jenn. His nose was swollen and red but no longer bleeding.

Riley and Lawrence got into the car. There was a rather strained silence in the group, but it took only a few moments to drive the rest of the way to the train station. That explained how the hobo had managed to get there so quickly.

The driver took them to a long-term parking lot near the station, where a couple of local cops were doing their best to keep reporters away from a big Mercedes. Riley and the others got out of the car and had to push their way past a cluster of questioning reporters to reach the vehicle.

A patrol car had pulled up in front of the Mercedes, blocking it from the exit. Beside the car, a couple of local cops were holding a man in handcuffs. Riley recognized him as the hobo who had fled—the one the others had called "Spider."

As they walked toward him, Jenn said, "Do you think maybe that's our killer?"

Riley thought quickly, then said, "I guess it's possible. He's a transient hobo, a freight-hopper. Maybe he gets from one murder location to the next on freight cars, then spots his victims and abducts them. Maybe he steals vehicles to help transport the victims."

She remembered that the killer had used the same SUV for the first two victims, then had abandoned it in a field and burned it. It seemed likely that he'd stolen it to begin with. After all, he'd definitely stolen Sally Diehl's hatchback.

And now, here was a hobo trying to drive away in a Mercedes.

Another stolen vehicle, she thought. At least this time he hadn't gotten away with the car. But did this mean he'd already abducted his next victim?

Might a woman be bound to railroad tracks at very moment, helpless before the next train that came along?

No, it didn't quite all fit together—not if the whole point of stealing the vehicles had been to carry the victims to the murder scenes. And since this car had been left in the long-term parking section of the station lot, it had probably been here for quite some time—days or even weeks.

A couple of local cops were rummaging through the car, so Riley walked over to them and asked, "Have you found out who owns the car?"

One of the cops handed a registration card to Riley.

He said, "It belongs to someone named Timothy Pollitt. He lives in Chicago."

Riley breathed a little easier.

Not a woman, she thought.

The other cop held up a time-stamped ticket. "This was inside too. Mr. Pollitt left his car here two weeks ago." He also produced a printed receipt. "Looks like he paid for a month in advance. I guess he must be off on a long trip."

"And the keys were right under the seat," the first cop said.

"All somebody had to do was jimmy the door. If this perp was able to drive the car right out of here, the owner might not have even known it was missing."

"Dumb luck," the second cop commented.

Riley realized that whoever and wherever Timothy Pollitt was, he was almost certainly not the next intended victim.

But what was this hobo doing, trying to get away in someone's expensive car? Wouldn't it have been smarter to grab something less conspicuous? Or did he have some way of knowing that the keys were inside?

She asked the cop, "Have you searched the hobo for any ID?"

"Yeah, and he doesn't have anything on him—not even a wallet. Just a few loose bills and some change."

Another vehicle was approaching from the direction of the crime scene. When it stopped, Chief Buchanan got out. So did the Chicago FBI field office chief Proctor Dillard, who came toward Riley and the others.

"I just heard the news," he said. "Have we got our guy?"

"We don't know yet," Riley said, handing the car registration to Dillard. "But we need to contact the owner of this car. It's likely that he parked it here himself, but we need to find out if he reported it stolen."

"We'll get right on it," Dillard said.

Meanwhile, Riley noticed that the local police were pushing the hobo into a cop car.

"Come on," she said to her colleagues. "Let's follow them to the police station."

*

A short while later, Riley, Bill, Jenn, and Cullen were facing the seated, handcuffed hobo in the station's interrogation room. At Riley's request, a local cop had given her a small bag full of ice for her hand. She noticed that Cullen didn't ask for one for his nose.

Too proud, she guessed. *Or too embarrassed.*

Riley studied the hobo more closely, now that she could see him better in this light than she'd been able to down in the ravine.

He was predictably filthy, wearing cheap ragged clothes and broken-down shoes. He smelled bad, and he was bearded and his hair was long.

But he struck Riley as somehow different from the other hobos down in that ravine. He was tall, but not as hard and muscular as the others. And something about his manner seemed different. Riley couldn't yet put her finger on how or why.

The man had already asked for a lawyer. According to Chief Buchanan, one was on his way.

"What's your name?" Cullen asked.

"They call me Spider," the man said.

"I mean your real name," Cullen said.

"They call me Spider," the man repeated.

He looked around at Riley and her colleagues.

"So what's this all about?" he said. "Who called in some sort of team?"

"That's what we were hoping you could tell us," Riley said. "For one thing, where did you get that nice car?"

The man smiled. Although his teeth were hardly clean, Riley could see that they were straight and healthy.

"I bought it," he said.

Bull Cullen let out a sarcastic chuckle.

"Yeah, right," he said.

Riley darted Cullen a disapproving look. She really wanted him to keep his mouth shut. She was anxious to hear whatever the man had to say for himself—no matter whether he was lying or telling the truth.

In fact, she figured it might be worth encouraging him in a lie.

"Where did you buy the Mercedes?" she asked.

"In Chicago," Spider said.

"So you didn't steal it?" Riley asked.

"Why would you think I did?"

Riley said, "Well, you hardly strike me as the Mercedes type."

"I might surprise you."

Riley asked him, "Why did you run away from us?"

"I had things to do, places to go."

He chuckled a little and added, "I'm a busy man."

His smiled faded, and a look of anxiety crossed his face.

"You still haven't told me what this is about. I've got no idea. You said a while ago that a woman was killed on the tracks. I don't know anything about that. Whenever it was, I'm sure I've got an alibi. I passed the day panhandling around the station. Then I went down to join up with the vagabonds under the bridge. Those gentlemen can account for my whereabouts."

His wording caught Riley's attention …

"... passed the day ... vagabonds ... account for my whereabouts ... gentlemen."

He sounded like a well-educated man.

She wondered—should she be surprised? Wasn't it possible that a hobo had once seen better days?

Anyway, she wasn't interested in checking this man's alibi with the rest of them. They'd seemed to consider him one of their own, and they'd surely say just about anything to protect him.

Spider continued, "Nobody has said I'm under arrest for anything. Unless you're going to charge me with something, like maybe stealing my own car, I want out of here. I know my rights. And I'm still waiting for that lawyer."

The man was fidgeting a little, and Riley sensed that he was genuinely eager to be released.

Was it because he was guilty of murder? She was having trouble reading him.

Bill asked, "Did you know the victim—Sally Diehl?"

"We were acquainted. All the guys knew her from around the train station."

"Tell us what you knew about her," Bill said.

"She was friendly," Spider began. "She liked to talk to us ..."

As Bill kept the man talking, Riley observed him carefully. His hands were dirty, but his fingernails were neatly trimmed. Although his hair was long and unkempt, it wasn't scraggly or uneven.

She kept wondering ...

What's off about this guy?

Then she remembered what he'd said about the Mercedes.

"I bought it."

In a flash, Riley realized who this man must actually be.

CHAPTER TWENTY EIGHT

Before Riley could tell anyone what she'd just realized, the door flew open, and in came Chief Buchanan and the FBI field chief, Proctor Dillard.

Dillard said to Riley and the others, "You're not going to believe this."

Riley thought …

Yeah, I'm pretty sure I will believe it.

Dillard continued, "We tried to contact the registered owner of the car, Timothy Pollitt. We found out that he's an English professor at Fargate College in Chicago. And here's his picture on the college website."

Dillard held up his cell phone so Riley could see the picture.

The man in the picture was smiling, clean, and respectable-looking.

But even so, the resemblance was unmistakable, just as she'd expected.

Riley looked at the hobo and said …

"You *are* Timothy Pollitt."

The man stared back at her and said nothing.

"There's more," Dillard said. "He's been married and divorced twice, and both of his ex-wives filed domestic violence complaints against him. They both said he made them fear for their lives."

The door opened again, and another man hurried into the room and slammed his briefcase on the table.

He said, "I'm Doug Lehman, and I've been assigned to serve as this man's attorney. I don't know what's been going on in this room, but my client is not going to say another word until we've conferred privately."

Pollitt opened his mouth to speak, and Lehman waved his finger at him.

"Not one word, I said! I want everybody else out of here, right now."

Riley and the others reluctantly filed out of the interrogation room and into the hall.

Bill and Jenn looked thoroughly surprised.

"What the hell?" Jenn said. "I mean, this guy isn't a real hobo?"

"Yeah, I know," Bill said. "This changes everything."

But Riley wondered …

Does it?

Just then she noticed a man sitting on a bench in the hall.

It was Mason Eggers, studying a clipboard with a map draped across it.

She remembered what he'd said about his theory …

"I haven't really worked it out yet."

Riley wondered if maybe he'd worked it out by now. She was beginning to feel sure that they were going to need a new theory.

Riley said to Bill and Jenn, "You guys talk to Dillard. Find out whatever else he knows about Timothy Pollitt. Then get online and see what else you can find. I'll join up with you shortly."

As Jenn and Bill headed away to talk to Dillard, Riley walked over to the bench and sat down beside older man, who looked up from his notes at her.

"Is the hobo a suspect?" he asked.

"Maybe," Riley said. "I know this is going to sound crazy …"

The man let out a short laugh.

"Don't tell me. He's got another life—aside from being a hobo, I mean."

Riley stared at Eggers.

"He's a college professor in Chicago," she said. "He wasn't trying to steal the Mercedes, it's really his. How did you know?"

Eggers said, "Oh, I picked up on that the minute I laid eyes on him. I was a railroad cop for a lot of years, remember. I know the type. 'Scenery bums,' they're called—or 'oogles,' in hobo parlance. They're often successful people with good careers who go freight-hopping as a kind of a hobby—a pretty dangerous hobby, I might add. I hear there are more and more of them these days."

Eggers thought for a moment, then said, "A college professor, you said?"

"At Fargate College in Chicago," Riley said.

"Well, he probably has the summer off. My guess is that he does this every summer. People close to him might know about it. Or maybe not. He might keep it a secret, even from his friends and family."

Riley said, "He didn't have a shred of identification on him."

Eggers tilted his head with interest.

"That's pretty extreme. He must really like to stay off the grid. Scenery bums usually carry plenty of ID, and also credit cards, just in case they get in a jam. This guy must be a serious thrill seeker who likes to live dangerously. I wouldn't be surprised if nobody else knows about this other life of his."

Eggers squinted thoughtfully, then added, "I don't think he's your killer, though. Scenery bums aren't typically violent—unlike your hardcore hobos, who've often done a good bit of prison time."

Riley said, "He's got a history of domestic violence."

Eggers shrugged and said, "Well, maybe I'm wrong. That wouldn't be a first."

He sounded to Riley as though he doubted his own words.

For some reason, Riley doubted it as well.

Eggers pointed to Riley's hand. She was still holding ice on it.

"Speaking of violence, it looks like you mixed it up with somebody."

Riley lifted the ice and saw that the swelling was going down. It still hurt a lot, though.

Riley said, "Yeah, I had a little disagreement with one of his hobo pals."

"I hope the other guy got the worst of it."

Riley remembered the sound and sensation of Dutch's teeth breaking.

"I'd like to think so," she said with a half-smile.

Then she pointed at Eggers's map and clipboard and said, "Show me what you've been working on."

He pointed to locations that he'd marked with his pencil.

"Back at the crime scene, we talked about the alphabetical order of the towns—Allardt, Barnwell, Caruthers. The trouble was, we didn't know if that meant anything. And if it did, how could we figure out what letter D town the killer might choose next? How could we narrow it down? All we knew was that he seemed to be moving westward. But look here …"

He took a drawing compass out of his pocket. Riley was struck by how low-tech he seemed to be—with a folding paper map, pencil and paper, and now an old-fashioned instrument for drawing circles. So far she hadn't seen him use any kind of electronic device.

Definitely old-school, Riley thought.

It hardly seemed surprising that he seemed so out of place among the younger railroad cops. He was like a relic from another time.

He planted the sharp steel point of the compass squarely in the center of Chicago. He opened the instrument so that the pencil reached the town of Allardt. Then he swung the compass westward, drawing an arc as he went.

The arc neatly intersected with both of the other towns—Barnwell and Caruthers.

Riley almost gasped aloud.

"A semicircle," she said.

"That's right. The distances between the towns aren't the same, and they don't seem to have anything in common except that trains from Chicago run through them. But all three are almost exactly the same distance from Chicago."

Riley's pulse started to quicken. This certainly seemed like more than coincidence.

"Show me where the arc goes from there," she said.

Eggers kept tracing—and sure enough, the pencil came to a town with a D at the beginning of its name.

Eggers pointed at the spot and said, "This is Dermott, Wisconsin. I know the place from my days on the job. Like the other towns, it's got a railroad running through it—with trains from Chicago."

Riley's interest was mounting by the second.

It was definitely an interesting theory—or at least the beginning of one.

Eggers shrugged sadly.

"Maybe this is nothing," he said. "This old brain of mine isn't what it used to be. It's terrible how the body slows down—but it's worse that I just can't think things through as fast as I used to. And now …"

His voice faded off, but Riley knew what he was leaving unsaid.

Another woman has been killed.

Eggers said, "Maybe everyone's right about me. Maybe I should take up fishing or something."

Don't even think about it, Riley wanted to say.

Instead she said, "Come on, let's share this theory with the team."

Just as Riley and Eggers got up from the bench, the FBI field chief Proctor Dillard came walking down the hall, accompanied by Jenn and Bill and a couple of Dillard's agents.

149

"Where are all of you headed off to?" Riley asked.

"Home," Dillard said. "Or at least to a motel. Cullen says we've cracked the case and we've got our guy, and he's got no need of FBI help now. So we're through here—all of us. You too, I guess."

Riley started to protest, but then fell silent. The local FBI was clearly in no mood to consider other possibilities, and she didn't feel that she had enough information to block their exit.

She just watched as Dillard and his agents strode past her and headed out of the building.

Riley turned and hurried over to Jenn and Bill.

"We're not through yet," she announced.

They both regarded her with surprise.

"This man has a theory," she told them, indicating Eggers. "And I think it's a good one."

Jenn and Bill looked amazed.

Jenn said, "What are you talking about? Pollitt seems as suspicious as hell to me."

Riley didn't reply. She silently herded her colleagues and Eggers over to the interrogation room. Cullen was standing outside and looking into the room through a one-way mirror. The lawyer was still sitting in there talking to Pollitt.

Riley said sharply to Cullen, "I want a word with you."

Cullen looked at her with surprise.

Riley said, "Mr. Eggers here has got a theory."

Cullen smirked and looked at Eggers.

"Have you now, Grandpa? Well, congratulations. But you're a little late. We've got our guy."

Cullen looked at Riley again and said, "I was talking with your guys and Dillard just now, and from what they told me, this is an open-and-shut case. Not only does Timothy Pollitt have a record for wife beating, he complete disappears every summer. No one has any idea where he goes. The lawyer hasn't let us talk to him yet, but he will soon, and you can be sure that this creep hasn't got any credible alibis for any of the murders."

He chuckled a little and said, "Add to that the fact that he ran away from Agent Paige here and refused to identify himself—well, could he possibly act more guilty? That's because he *is* guilty. It's just a matter of tying up loose ends."

He looked through the window again.

"I've given the bastard enough time with the lawyer. I'm going in there right now and tell him he's under arrest. And I expect the three of you to head back to Quantico ASAP. I wish I could say it's been a pleasure, but the truth is ..."

He darted a nasty look at Jenn.

"All three of you have been a pain in the ass."

Without another word, Cullen opened the door and walked into the interrogation room.

Riley stood staring into the room as Cullen confronted Pollitt and the lawyer.

She was shocked at how brazenly Cullen was displaying his resentment over the bloody nose he'd gotten from Jenn. But what could Riley do about that now?

Orders are orders, she told herself.

After all, she and her colleagues came from Quantico at Cullen's request. And the head railway cop was no longer the least bit pleased with Riley or her team. Of course, she wasn't pleased with him either. And this was now an official FBI case too.

But Riley's brain was crowded with thoughts and ideas. For the first time since she'd started working on this case, she was getting a really powerful gut feeling.

We can't quit now, she thought. *This monster is still out there and he isn't finished yet.*

Her hand wasn't throbbing as badly now—and anyway, she didn't give a damn about the pain anymore. She tossed the bag of ice into a nearby trash bin.

Then she said to Bill, Jenn, and Eggers, "Come on. Let's go find a place where we can sit down and talk."

CHAPTER TWENTY NINE

In a car borrowed from the local cops, Riley drove Bill, Jenn, and Mason Eggers from the Caruthers police station to a well-lighted little restaurant. She was eager to have Eggers show his theory to her two most trusted colleagues.

She knew it was going to be tough to sell, because she wasn't completely convinced about it herself. After all, they had good reason to suspect that Timothy Pollitt was the killer.

Besides, Riley was sure that Jenn felt especially eager to go home and forget she'd ever met Bull Cullen. For that matter, Riley felt the same way, especially about the railroad cop.

But her instincts kept telling her …

We're not through here yet.

While they waited for their sandwiches, Eggers spread his paper map out on the table. Then he again went through his quaintly retro demonstration with a compass. Just as he had for Riley, he showed how the three alphabetically ordered towns all fell on a precise semicircle with its center in Chicago.

He also showed them that a fourth town beginning with the letter D lay in the same path—Dermott, Wisconsin.

Riley could see that Jenn and Bill were impressed by Eggers's calculations.

She also sensed that they were far from sold on the importance of his ideas.

Their meals arrived, and Eggers folded up his map. He tucked the map and compass back into his briefcase, but he didn't give up on his theory even as they ate.

He said, "I know the railroads through this region like the back of my hand. I can remember a precise spot outside of Dermott where I think he'd strike next. I wish I could show it to you …"

Riley couldn't tell whether or not Jenn was actually getting interested, but the younger agent finally got out her laptop computer and started to run a search. In a few moments, she'd brought up a satellite image of the town of Dermott, with a clear photographic view of the railroad tracks running through it.

She showed it to Eggers, and he gaped in astonishment.

I guess he didn't know you could do this with computers, Riley thought.

The old guy really was a relic of bygone days.

He pointed to a spot on the image that was just outside of town.

"Right there," he said. "Can you make that bigger?"

Jenn zoomed in on the area.

"There it is!" Eggers said, sounding excited. "See, right there! A curve—just like the curves where the other victims were killed. The killer chooses curves so the engineer can't see the victims in time to stop. That's the spot he would choose. I'm just sure of it."

Regardless of how Bill and Jenn might be feeling, Riley found herself more intrigued. Maybe picking Eggers's brain could actually point them in the right direction..

She asked, "How do you think he carries out these murders—in terms of time, I mean?"

Eggers paused and wrinkled his brow in thought.

He said, "Correct me if I'm wrong—but weren't all three victims on passenger trains shortly before they were abducted and killed?"

"That's right," Bill said. "Trains from Chicago, as a matter of fact. We think he drugged and abducted them soon after they got off the trains. Then he transported them to the murder sites and bound them to the tracks, where they were killed by freight trains."

"That's interesting," Eggers said. "If he had a particular victim in mind and knew she was on a passenger train, and he knew where she was going to get off …"

Riley put in, "Then he'd know where the intended victim was going to be at a certain time."

Eggers nodded enthusiastically. "And it also means," he said, "that our perp must have known when the next freight train was coming through. But the thing is, freight trains aren't like passenger trains. They don't follow any strict schedule. He must have had a really good knowledge of the general freight train traffic through those areas. Still, his timing had to be awfully precise …"

Eggers drummed his fingers on the table for a moment.

Then he said, "My guess is he's got a scanner—a radio that monitors railroad frequencies. He listens in on conversations between dispatchers and train crews. By listening during the course of a day, he would be able know when to expect an oncoming freight train in a particular spot. He'd be able to determine the time just about exactly."

Riley was fascinated. And despite their doubts, she sensed that the theory was beginning to fascinate Bill and Jenn as well.

"We should tell Cullen about this," Bill said. "He can use this kind of information to investigate Timothy Pollitt."

Riley's patience was starting to wane.

"*If* Pollitt is the killer, Bill," she said. "And that's not an 'if' I'm comfortable with, are you?"

Jenn said, "Pollitt sure seems guilty to me." She hesitated, then added, "Guilty of something, at least."

"Right," Riley said. "He may be guilty of a lot of things. But we're still not *sure* that he's the killer we've been looking for. And if he's not, we're wasting valuable time. If our serial is still out there, he seems to be speeding up his game. We could lose another life while we're all waiting to make sure it's Pollitt."

A silence fell over the table.

Bill finally said, "What do you want us to do, Riley? We're officially off the case. And Cullen's in no mood at all to put us back on it. The whole thing is out of our hands."

"We've got to do something," Riley muttered bitterly.

Bill shook his head and said, "Well, it's late, and there's not a damn thing we can do about it right now. Let's all get a good night's sleep and talk about all this in the morning."

Riley hated to admit it, but Bill was making good sense. It had been a hell of a long and frantic day, interrupted by a lot of travel. First there had been a two-hour morning drive to Allardt. followed by interviews with Fern Bruder's family and a war veteran, and then Cullen had summoned them to a meeting in Chicago, where they met with Reese Fisher's lover before checking into a Chicago hotel where …

Riley winced with guilt as she remembered April's words to her over the phone.

"Oh, Mom. Please don't tell me you forgot!"

Jilly, Riley thought. *I forgot her birthday.*

Jilly had every reason to be angry, and Riley still hadn't made peace with her.

And at the moment, she had no idea when or how she might be able to do that. It was too late to make a phone call to see if Jilly would talk to her now. Tomorrow was a school day and the girls should be in bed.

She felt a wave of exhaustion and despair.

She realized that she was in no frame of mind to think

rationally about the case—or about anything else, for that matter.

"OK," she said to Bill and Jenn. "Let's go find a place to stay the night."

Riley paid the bill for their meals, and Bill asked the server for directions to the nearest motel. When they arrived there, Riley saw familiar official vehicles parked outside some of the rooms. It looked like Cullen and his team had checked into this same motel, and so had Dillard and his Chicago FBI agents.

Probably all asleep by now, Riley thought.

No doubt about it—she needed a good night's sleep herself.

*

Riley was grappling with the minute hand of a gigantic clock.

She felt it pushing against her, inching around the dial as the massive machinery cranked away in deep-voiced clicks.

I've got to stop it, she thought.

She pushed against the enormous minute hand with all her weight and strength, her shoulder hard against it. But the hand was much heavier than she was, and the machinery was vastly more powerful. To make matters worse, the effort was causing her hand to hurt again.

She heard a familiar voice from somewhere nearby.

"What do you think you're doing, girl?"

It was her father's voice.

"Are you trying to stop time dead in its tracks?" he asked with a grim laugh.

Yes, that's exactly what I'm trying to do, Riley thought.

But she didn't say so aloud.

She couldn't spare the energy—not with such a huge task at hand.

Now she heard another sound. It was the roar of an approaching locomotive. She knew that somewhere nearby a woman was tied to train tracks, and the train was coming nearer by the second.

She knew that she couldn't stop a locomotive.

And that was why she had to stop time.

But click by click by click, the minute hand kept pushing its way along.

Worse, she could hear the machinery speeding up.

The hand was moving faster.

155

But how was that even possible?
She finally let out a wail of despair.
"It's cheating! Time is cheating!"
She heard her father chuckle again.
"Is that any surprise, girl? Time cheats and lies and swindles constantly, and it always screws you in the end. There's only one thing in the world that's bigger and stronger and more damned crooked and mendacious than time. I think you know what it is."

Evil, *Riley thought.*
That's what the locomotive really was.
Pure, unstoppable evil.
"What can I do?" Riley called out to her father.
He repeated words that she'd heard him say before.
"Your job. Do your goddamn job. Just don't get any ideas that you'll do any good."

Riley's eyes snapped open.

Everything was quiet. It took her a moment to realize that no locomotive was bearing down on a helpless victim.

At least not here and now. She was in her dark motel room.

There was a clock, however.

She turned to look at the lighted digital clock on the bed stand. It was 2:13 in the morning.

She lay there thinking.

Time is cheating! No way to stop it.

She remembered what Bill had said earlier in the restaurant.

"Let's all get a good night's sleep …"

But Bill had been wrong. Now was no time to sleep.

Like the clock hand in her dream, the killer was moving faster and faster.

What would stop him from killing again tomorrow?

Nothing, Riley realized. *Nothing except us.*

She felt sure that the time to act was now.

Right now!

We've got a job to do.

CHAPTER THIRTY

Riley switched on a light and sat up in bed. She was wide awake now.

She could hear no sounds of activity in the motel. Could she be the only one not sleeping? The urgency of the nightmare was still with her, and she knew she would probably have to wake up the other members of her team.

First, she needed to check out certain information.

She picked up her cell phone, went online, and searched for the coming day's passenger train schedules between Chicago and Dermott, Wisconsin. She found only one inbound train from Chicago. It was scheduled to arrive in Dermott at 12:30 in the afternoon. It was scheduled to depart again at 1 o'clock.

Less than ten hours from now, Riley realized. That train would arrive in a different town in a different state. Was the next victim going to be on it?

She heard an echo from the dream in her mind. *"It's cheating! Time is cheating!"*

She couldn't stop time. She needed to get ahead of it.

Riley knew that she needed more details. She needed help.

She called the motel desk and asked to be connected to Mason Eggers's room. A moment later, Eggers answered the phone.

"I'm sorry about the hour," Riley said.

"Don't worry," Eggers said, not sounding the least bit groggy. "I wasn't able to sleep myself. I've been worrying about when the killer might strike in Dermott."

"Me too," Riley said.

She told him what she'd just found out about the passenger train.

"That's right," he said. "That's the one that's worrying me."

She asked, "Do you think somebody on that train will be in danger?"

"That depends on when the next freight train will pass through there. Like I said earlier, freight trains don't follow a strict schedule, but ..."

Riley waited for him to finish his thought.

"I've got a dispatcher friend, Hank Deever, who's on night duty right now. He's got a lot of information at his fingertips. He might be able to give me some idea. I'll give him a call."

"Please do that," Riley said. "What's your room number? I'm coming right over."

"Fifteen," Eggers said.

"Just a few doors down," Riley replied as she hung up.

She hastily put on her clothes without bothering to straighten her hair. Then she hurried outside and down the sidewalk to Eggers's room and knocked on the door.

Still in his pajamas and a rather old-fashioned robe, Eggers was holding his out-of-date folding cell phone when he answered the door.

"I just talked to Hank," Eggers told her. "He says a freight train runs through Dermott most days at around two o'clock—about an hour after the passenger train from Chicago departs again."

Riley felt a chill of apprehension.

Those two trains followed the same pattern as passenger and freight trains had for the other three murders.

Eggers shook his head and added, "Look, I know I'm just a an over-the-hill railroad cop, and maybe I'd do the world more good if I just gave up this kind of work and took up fishing. But I've got a really bad feeling about this."

Riley was struck by the expression on Eggers's face.

She had a strong gut feeling …

This guy knows exactly what he's talking about.

She simply had to trust his instincts.

"Get dressed—fast," Riley said. "Then come to my room—it's number seven."

She already knew that Bill and Jenn were in rooms on either side of hers. She hammered on each of their doors, demanding that they get up and get dressed and come to her room. A few minutes later, Bill, Jenn, and Eggers were all in Riley's room.

Eggers was the only one aside from Riley herself who seemed especially awake. He took a look at the others, then went about setting up the coffeepot that was in the room. In a few moments, the smell of fresh coffee filled the air.

Riley paced the floor, hoping she could persuade her colleagues to agree with her. As she told them about the passenger train and the freight train that would follow soon after it, Eggers passed around cups of coffee.

Then Riley said, "The killer is working faster. And he's going to kill again tomorrow, in Dermott. We've got to do something to stop him."

Jenn said, "Not if we've caught him already. Not if he's Timothy Pollitt."

Riley flashed back to the interrogation room.

She remembered what Pollitt had said when Bill asked him about Sally Diehl.

"She was friendly. She liked to talk to us."

Riley realized something.

Those were the only words that Pollitt had said that sounded truly sincere.

Riley realized that some parts of the puzzle were falling into place in her mind.

She blurted, "Timothy Pollitt didn't kill Sally Diehl. He didn't kill anybody. Don't ask me how I know that, I just do. I'm absolutely sure of it."

A silence fell in the room.

Am I going to have to beg? Riley wondered.

Jenn looked confused and indecisive.

But Riley noticed a welcome and familiar change in Bill's expression. After working together for so many years, they'd learned to give each other the benefit of the doubt. And Riley could see that Bill was ready to do that.

He finally said, "OK, what do we do next?"

Riley thought for a moment.

Then, without another word to the others, she picked up the motel phone, called the front desk, and asked to be connected with Bull Cullen's room. Seconds later, she heard the groggy sound of Cullen's voice.

"Agent Paige? What the hell do you want?"

Riley said, "Cullen, you can't take the FBI off the case."

"Do you have any idea what time it is?"

Riley ignored the question.

"My colleagues and I think there's an excellent chance that the killer will strike tomorrow just outside of Dermott, Wisconsin, sometime around two o'clock."

Riley heard a groan of annoyance.

"You really don't know when to quit, do you, Agent Paige?"

Cullen hung up the phone.

Riley immediately called the front desk again and asked for

Cullen's room number.

Then she put the phone down and headed for the door.

"Come on," she said to the others.

"Where are we going?" Jenn asked.

"To wake Cullen up."

Followed by Bill, Jenn, and Eggers, Riley strode down the sidewalk toward Cullen's room.

She pounded on his door.

A voice inside called out, "Who is it?"

"You know who it is," Riley yelled.

"Go away," Cullen replied.

Riley pounded on the door again. This time a handful of tired-looking people poked their heads out of other motel room doors, grumbling about calling the police.

Riley ignored them but she saw Bill flash his FBI badge. The complainers disappeared back into their rooms.

"Damn it, Cullen," she yelled. "This is your wakeup call. We've all got work to do. And we've got to start right now. Get up and open the door."

A moment later, a bleary-eyed, pajama-clad Cullen opened the door, and Riley and her colleagues filed inside.

"You guys are being ridiculous," he said. "We've got our guy and you know it."

"Has Pollitt confessed yet?" Riley asked.

"No, his lawyer won't let him talk. And why do you think that is? Why do you think he tried to run in the first place?"

Riley could think of too many reasons to mention. The guy had a domestic abuse record, for one thing. And he had a secret life that he'd gone to a lot of trouble to conceal from everybody. The last thing he wanted to do was talk to any cops. And in any case, no lawyer was going to let him do that.

It doesn't mean he's a murderer, she thought.

In fact, she now felt absolutely sure that Pollitt wasn't a murderer. Certainly not the one they were looking for.

Cullen rubbed his eyes.

He said, "I know what I'm doing, believe me. There are lots of people we can interview who knew the victims. Sooner or later, we'll find a connection between Pollitt and all of the victims. We'll find corroborating evidence."

Riley could hardly believe her ears.

What made Cullen so sure that there *was* a connection between

Pollitt and the victims—even if he really was guilty of the murders?

He really doesn't have the first idea of what he's doing, Riley thought.

Cullen was starting to seem more awake now. He was grinning smugly.

"You guys really can't deal with this, can you? That I'm going to wrap up the case, I mean. Without the FBI's help. You're going to get outshone by a railroad cop. I'll get all the glory, and you'll look like idiots. Well, that's just too damned bad. You're off the case. Orders are orders. And *I'm* giving the orders here."

Cullen finally seemed to notice Mason Eggers's presence in the room.

"What's old Grandpa doing here?" he asked.

"He's come up with a theory," Riley said. "And a damned good one."

Cullen's eyes lit up.

"So Grandpa's got a theory! This I've got to hear!"

Mason Eggers's hands and voice shook nervously as he spread his map out on a table and explained everything to Cullen. Cullen didn't stop grinning during Eggers's whole explanation. Riley could tell by Cullen's expression that he thought the theory was complete nonsense.

When Eggers finished, Cullen crossed his arms and shook his head.

"You guys are really grasping at straws, aren't you? Listening to this over-the-hill old coot. You can't even come up with an idea of your own!"

Riley suppressed a moan of discouragement.

What's it going to take to get through to him? she wondered.

She said, "We've got to set up a stakeout in Dermott. And we've got to get to work right now. If you don't want to be involved, my people are going to do it anyway."

Suddenly Cullen's expression changed. He chuckled and said, "OK."

Riley was startled.

OK? she thought.

This had been easier than she'd expected.

Cullen added, "Let's get moving. Let's wake everybody up. Just one thing, though. I want Grandpa to come along."

Now Riley understood.

Cullen expected the stakeout to be a bust, and he wanted to see

161

all of them made fools of—Riley, Bill, and especially Jenn, for having bloodied his nose.

And of course, he wanted to make a fool of Eggers too.

But that didn't matter to Riley.

What mattered was stopping a killer—and saving a life.

CHAPTER THIRTY ONE

As the FBI jet took off from the small Caruthers airport, Riley sat staring out the airplane's window. Dawn was breaking, and she felt uneasy about what this new day was going to bring.

They finally might have a chance to stop this serial killer once and for all.

She hoped they could do that.

If not ...

She didn't want to think about what might happen otherwise.

She closed and opened her right hand a few times. She felt some twinges now, but no pain to speak of. The injury she'd gotten from punching the hobo named Dutch was healing up nicely.

That was a good thing. She might need to function at full physical capacity very soon.

The small plane's cabin was more crowded than usual. Riley had taken a window seat, and Mason Eggers had sat down next to her. Bill and Jenn were both on board, of course, and so was Chicago FBI field chief Proctor Dillard.

Bull Cullen was on the plane as well. He'd managed to seat himself a safe distance away from Jenn. The leering interest he had shown toward her before was completely gone. Now he looked scared that Jenn might punch him in the nose again at any moment.

Riley wondered ...

Is that a good thing or a bad thing?

Well, it was certainly good that Cullen wouldn't be harassing Jenn anymore. And Riley was pretty sure that Jenn had gotten her hostility toward Cullen out of her system. Riley only hoped that Cullen wouldn't get so jittery about Jenn that his mind wouldn't be on the case. Right now, the team needed all the brainpower it could get, even his. She didn't think he could have become this area's Deputy Chief of Railroad Police if he was a total idiot.

But then Riley thought about Carl Walder back in Quantico. Somehow, that bureaucratic flunky had managed to become the Special Agent in Charge. And Walder was a constant drag on Riley's work.

As soon as the plane reached cruising altitude, Riley managed to get Dermott's Chief of Police, Royce Ulrich, on the phone. The poor guy sounded sleepy and confused, but he promised that someone would meet Riley and her team at the airport. And he assured her that she'd have the full support of his department.

Riley was about to tilt her seat back and try to sleep a little when she noticed Eggers's face was pale and he was gripping the armrests of his chair.

She asked him, "Are you scared of flying?"

He nodded and said, "It's bad enough in those big commercial airliners."

Riley smiled sympathetically.

"I guess you've never been in a plane this small before," she said.

"I flew once in a little Piper Cub many years ago. It was a lot smaller, but this is even worse somehow."

Riley said, "Well, this plane is pretty much no frills as far as service is concerned. But I could go get you a drink of water if you think that would help."

She almost added …

And I'm pretty sure we can find a paper bag somewhere.

But she realized that the mere suggestion of vomiting might be enough to induce it.

"I'll be OK," Eggers said.

Riley wondered if maybe she should try to strike up a conversation with him. That might distract him from his apparent fear of flying.

After all, she knew almost nothing about him.

She'd noticed earlier that he was wearing a wedding ring. This had struck her as odd, since he seemed so insistent on following railroad police cases all over the place. At his age, wouldn't he prefer spending more time with his wife and family?

She said, "I see you're married."

As if by reflex, Eggers covered up the ring with his right hand, and a pained expression crossed his face.

Riley immediately understood her mistake.

A widower, she thought. The loss of his wife was surely the last thing in the world he wanted to talk about.

"I'm sorry," she said.

Eggers simply nodded.

Riley quickly tried to think of some way to change the subject.

But then it dawned on her …

He doesn't like to talk about himself.

He was a lonely old man who managed to stave off boredom and grief by staying involved with railroad cases. That was all Riley knew about him, except she was sure that he had a better mind than Cullen and the newer generation of railroad police gave him credit for. She respected his insights and his expertise, and she felt sure that he understood the nature of this case as well as anybody else—perhaps even better.

And the truth was, that probably was all Riley had any reason or right to know about him. He valued his privacy, and she needed to respect that.

She looked out the window and saw a landscape of forested hills dotted with lakes that shimmered in the early morning light.

Tourist country, Riley realized.

It certainly was a beautiful view, and it was unsettling to think about the implacable monster who was probably lurking down there somewhere at this very moment, scheming to corrupt all that beauty.

But Riley told herself ...

We'll be on time.

This time we'll be able to stop it.

She tilted her chair back and closed her eyes, hoping to catch just a little sleep before the plane landed—which was going to be very soon.

*

When Riley and her colleagues got off the plane at the little Dermott airport, a police SUV awaited them on the tarmac. Riley was surprised to see who was standing beside the car. She could tell by his uniform that he was none other than Chief Royce Ulrich himself. He'd come in person instead of sending any of his local cops.

As Ulrich opened the SUV doors and escorted everyone inside, Riley noticed that the man didn't have the face of a law enforcement official. He had a certain slick, plastic look that Riley quickly found a word for:

Commercial.

Ulrich looked like a male fashion model, or a salesman, or a tour guide. And Riley could understand why. In this beautiful part of Wisconsin, law enforcement typically had little to do except cater

165

to tourists' needs and troubles. A police chief here had to be as skilled in PR as in law enforcement—more so, probably.

As the chief drove the short distance into downtown Dermott, he said, "I thought you'd caught that serial killer already—over in Caruthers."

Riley was briefly startled. But she realized she shouldn't be surprised. The news about the arrest of a seeming hobo must be all over the news by now.

What should she say to Ulrich?

Riley glanced uneasily at Bull Cullen, who of course still believed that Timothy Pollitt was the real killer and that coming out here to Dermott was a waste of time and resources.

Cullen smirked at Riley but said nothing.

Riley said to Ulrich, "We've got a new lead. We need to follow up on it."

It wasn't a satisfactory answer and Riley knew it.

Chief Ulrich said, "How many people know about this? That you're trying to catch a murderer here today, I mean?"

Riley thought for a moment and said, "Just the people in this car."

Ulrich nodded and said, "I'd like to keep it down to the smallest number of people possible. I haven't even mentioned it to any of my own cops just yet. Let's keep things on a need-to-know basis. This town is right next to a state forest. Tourism is our whole local economy. If people get scared to come here, this town could be in serious trouble."

Riley understood his concern, but she knew she couldn't promise him anything.

She also wanted to keep the stakeout as secret as possible in order not to tip off their target. But afterward, especially if they caught their killer, they would all be all over the news.

*

In Ulrich's office at the police station, Riley and her colleagues stood looking at a large computer screen, surveying a satellite image of the local train tracks. Eggers pointed to the curve in the railroad track and explained his theory—that the killer would try to stage his next murder there, because the engineer wouldn't see the victim soon enough to stop the locomotive.

When Eggers finished, Riley said, "We need to monitor that

stretch of tracks. But we need to do it without being noticed."

Ulrich seemed thoroughly engaged now.

"I think I know how to do it," he said.

He got up from his chair and pointed to a spot on the screen. It was a square-shaped object in the woods.

Ulrich said, "That's an old wooden tower, built for looking out for forest fires. Its base is at an altitude of two hundred fifty feet, and it's sixty feet tall. You can see twenty-five miles in all directions from it—including that entire length of railroad track."

Riley was pleased.

She said, "We'll post a couple of people up there, and we'll also put several people on the ground, hiding in the woods near the tracks. The tower lookouts can alert the ground people by radio if they see anyone suspicious, and the ground people will move right in and apprehend the perpetrator. He can't possibly get out of a trap like that."

Riley noticed that Bill was squinting at the screen, looking slightly dissatisfied.

He said, "All this assumes that we catch our killer after he's *already* abducted his victim. That's OK as a last resort. But we should do everything we can to keep him from abducting anyone in the first place. We need to take a two-pronged approach."

Riley agreed.

She said to Ulrich, "Have you got good surveillance cameras on the platform where the trains arrive?"

"We sure do," Ulrich said.

"OK, then," Riley said. "We'll have somebody watching the surveillance feed when the twelve thirty train arrives from Chicago. We'll also have three people in plainclothes on the platform itself. Everybody will be linked by phone, and they'll watch all the passengers who get off the train, looking for a woman who resembles the other murder victims. We're pretty sure the killer is obsessed with that particular appearance."

Cullen looked skeptical.

He said, "And what do we do when we see a woman who looks like the others? Use her as bait and see if the killer comes after her?"

Jenn said, "What's the alternative? Yank her aside and tell her a killer might be after her, when we can't even be sure of that yet? She'll be traumatized right there and then, and probably for a long time afterwards, and we're liable to cause a panic among the people around her."

"Jenn's right," Bill said. "We simply won't let her get in any danger. The second a threatening man comes after her, we'll swoop in and catch him. If we can do it deftly and quietly enough, bystanders might not even realize it has happened."

Those words rang in Riley's mind …

Deftly and quietly.

Those qualities were going to be especially necessary right there on the train platform.

She said, "I want Bill and me to be on the platform, coordinating with two plainclothes officers. Jenn, I want you to be nearby watching the surveillance feed, alerting us the second you see anybody. Dillard and Royce, I want the two of you to run things up in the tower, communicating with the men on the ground near the tracks."

Then she noticed Mason Eggers.

Let's not leave him out, she thought. She knew by now that he had a shrewd eye for detail.

She told him, "I want you on the lookout in that tower with Royce and Dillard."

Bull Cullen spoke up in a petulant voice, "What about me?"

Riley glanced at Jenn and Bill. She knew they were all thinking the same thing …"

What about *Cullen?*

None of them trusted him much at this point—and with good reason.

He had a lot invested in the failure of this operation.

She certainly didn't want him with her on the train platform. And she absolutely didn't want him sitting in a booth with Jenn watching the surveillance feed. Nor would it be a good idea to stick him up in that tower with Mason Eggers, given his open contempt for the older man.

If Riley had her way, she'd bench him altogether.

But that really wasn't an option.

She said, "Cullen, I want you with the team on the ground near the tracks."

Then she said to Chief Royce pointedly, "I want four of your best people down there as well."

She noticed that Cullen cringed at her words—and the implication that he wasn't the "best" in her estimation, at least for the job at hand.

Royce brought a select few of his local cops into his office and gave them their assignments. Riley thought they also looked more like movie stars than cops, but they all seemed to understand what the chief was telling them very well.

They'll do fine, she told herself.

Within an hour, everyone was at an appointed post. And just in the nick of time, too. It was almost 12:30 by the time Riley, Bill, and the two plainclothes cops stepped out onto the train station platform to mingle among unsuspecting people.

Riley spoke into her hidden microphone, "Can everybody hear each other?"

Bill and the two cops answered in the affirmative. So did Jenn, who was sitting in a nearby room watching the surveillance feed.

Now we wait, she thought.

The few remaining minutes seemed to take forever. But soon she heard a train whistle and the dull, monotonous roar of the locomotive.

Riley's heart started to pound as the train approached the platform.

CHAPTER THIRTY TWO

Riley's heart pounded harder as the train slowed to a stop. Her breathing quickened.

Why am I so nervous? she asked herself.

After all, this was hardly the first stakeout of her long career.

But then she realized—it was extremely rare to catch a perpetrator in the very act, in the moment before a crime was committed. Opportunities like this didn't arise very often.

We'd better not screw it up, she thought.

She glanced around to make sure that Bill and the two cops were well positioned to see who would come out of the train cars. In a matter of moments, passengers were climbing down the steps from the cars.

After a few minutes, the stream of passengers slowed to a trickle.

Just when she thought almost no one was left on board, Riley's eyes lighted on one woman in particular.

At that moment, she heard Jenn's voice over her earpiece.

"I see someone. She's coming off the fifth car back from the engine."

It was, in fact, exactly the same woman Riley had just spotted.

She looked remarkably like the three victims—thin body, thin face, long nose, curly brown hair.

Riley murmured into her hidden microphone, "Does everybody see her?"

Bill and the other two cops said yes.

"OK," Riley said. "Let's follow her. Stay at a radius of about twenty-five feet. Try not to be conspicuous."

She could see Bill and the other cops start moving into their positions. There were enough people clustered around—mostly passengers and people greeting them—to help camouflage their actions.

Carrying a small suitcase, the woman continued on inside the small brick train station.

Riley said to the others, "We'll go single file through the door, with me in the lead, and Agent Jeffreys right behind me. Keep about ten feet away from each other."

When she led the way into the train station, Riley saw that the woman was continuing on through the building and heading out through the front door. Sure that her companions were behind her, Riley followed the woman out into the parking lot.

An SUV that was moving through the parking lot slowed as it approached the woman. Riley could see that a man was driving it.

Riley's hand neared her weapon.

"I see a man in a vehicle," she said to the others. "Get ready to move."

The SUV came to a stop. The man looked out the window and waved at the woman.

She knows him, Riley thought.

Of course, she'd realized early on that the murdered women might have known their captor.

But then the side doors of the SUV slid open, and two small children bounced out—two little girls yelling, "Mommy, Mommy!"

The woman put down her suitcase and welcomed the children with a hug.

The man looked out the window and said to her, "The girls have missed you."

The woman laughed and said, "I can see that. I've missed you too. All of you."

The woman reached for her suitcase and picked up the smaller girl with her free arm. The other girl scampered alongside the woman, and they all got into the SUV, laughing and chatting together.

The SUV drove away.

Riley's mouth dropped open from shock.

Was it possible? Had they been wrong?

She asked Jenn over the phone, "Did you see any other passengers who resembled the victims?"

"Not even close," Jenn said. "And I got a good look at each and every one of them."

"Are you sure they're all off the train?"

"Yeah. The departing passengers are already starting to board."

Bill and the other two cops joined Riley in the parking lot.

"This isn't over," Bill said to Riley. "Maybe he's made some adjustments to his MO. The killer's next victim might not have been on the train at all. He might be abducting her somewhere else as we speak. Or …"

171

Riley finished his thought.

"*Or* the killer might not be sticking to his usual type, and we may have missed the real victim when she got off the train. Maybe he's already abducted her."

Riley said to the two local cops, "Agent Jeffreys and I need a ride to the lookout tower."

One of the cops dashed away toward a parked vehicle.

Riley spoke again to Jenn through the microphone, "Bill and I are heading on over to the tower. Stay on the surveillance feed, just in case something new comes up."

"Like what?" Jenn asked.

Riley suppressed a discouraged sigh.

"I don't know," Riley said. "Just keep watching."

The cop who had walked away a moment before drove up in his vehicle. Riley told the other local cop to stay at the station and keep in touch with Jenn. She and Bill got into the car, and the driver took them out of Dermott—as fast as he could move without drawing attention to the car. Even without the use of sirens and lights, just minutes later they were entering the lush forests of the neighboring state park.

As the car wended its way into the beautifully forested hills, Riley looked at her watch. It was about time for the passenger train to leave the station again. According to Mason Eggers's dispatcher friend, the freight train would come through in about an hour.

But she also remembered what Eggers said about freight trains …

"They don't follow any strict schedule."

How soon might the freight train follow after the passenger train?

Riley had no idea.

The road that wound up through the hills seemed interminable, even after the huge wooden tower came into view above them. Riley's spirits sank further when she realized that they had to park the car at the base of a cliff about seventy-five feet below the tower itself.

She flung the car door open and raced up flight after flight of wooden stairs up the side of the cliff, with Bill close behind. Then they climbed another several flights of stairs to reach the top of the sixty-foot tower itself.

Riley's chest and legs were hurting by the time she and Bill reached the top. For a few moments, they both stood gasping for breath.

Three men armed with binoculars were already there on the highest platform of the wooden tower—the Dermott police chief, the Chicago FBI chief Proctor Dillard, and Mason Eggers.

All three looked astonished to see Riley and Bill.

"What's going on?" Dillard asked.

Struggling to bring her breathing under control, Riley gasped, "We didn't see the victim get off the train. Either we missed her or …"

She was too out of breath to finish her sentence.

She leaned against the railing for a moment, dizzy and exhausted, her heart pounding fiercely. She couldn't help noticing that the view from the tower was truly astonishing. Lakes were visible in the distance, and so was the town of Dermott. Even without binoculars, Riley could see that the passenger train was no longer at the station platform.

Bill asked the three men, "What have you seen so far from here?"

Mason Eggers said, "The passenger train passed through a little while ago, right on schedule. Now we're waiting …"

Before he could finish, Dillard called out, pointing into the distance.

"Here it comes—the freight train."

Riley borrowed Eggers's binoculars and looked up the tracks.

Sure enough, she could see a locomotive coming toward Dermott, pulling what appeared to be about thirty cars. She gasped and turned the binoculars to the curve in the tracks where they expected the killer to strike.

No one was there—neither a man nor a victim.

She scanned the entire length of the tracks all the way back to Dermott. She saw nothing suspicious at all.

She watched as the freight train passed through the station in Dermott, then continued on into the forest, rounded the curve, and rolled away into the distance.

Nothing had happened.

Nothing at all.

Riley was swept by a flood of confusion.

She couldn't help but feel relieved that the killer didn't seem to have seized another victim.

But what could this mean?

She and Eggers had both been so positive that the killer would strike again right now, in this very place. This would have matched his previous pattern so exactly.

How could they have been so wrong?

Had they somehow given away their presence to the killer?

Then she heard Bill's voice.

"Riley, I think we've got trouble."

Riley looked down to see what Bill was pointing down at.

Several vehicles were pulling in near where the police car was still parked, all the way down the cliff below the tower. As people climbed out of the vehicles, Riley realized with dread …

Reporters!

CHAPTER THIRTY THREE

Bill's heart went out to Riley as he watched her staring down at the crowd of reporters far below. He'd seldom seen such a defeated expression on her face.

He touched her on the shoulder and said, "Come on. We'd better go deal with them."

Riley simply nodded, then started down the stairs. Bill followed her, with Dillard, Ulrich, and Eggers right behind him.

As they made their way down, Bill kept wondering …

What the hell went wrong?

Riley had been so positive that this would be the time and place of the next murder. And her instincts were nearly always right. In fact, she was famous in law enforcement for the reliability of her gut feelings.

Maybe this is my fault, Bill thought.

After all, he had let Riley talk everybody into this stakeout, even though he hadn't fully shared her conviction.

Maybe he should have overruled her.

But then he thought …

Overrule Riley?

He almost smiled at the very idea. He couldn't remember ever being able to talk Riley out of anything, not when she'd really set her mind to it.

When they reached the base of the cliff, the reporters crowded around them, shouting one question on top of another.

"Why did you hold a stakeout here?"

"Did anything come of it?"

"We'd been informed that another suspect was in custody."

"Does the murderer have an accomplice?"

"Is there a copycat killer?"

Bill was surprised with the force in Riley's voice when she shouted them down.

"No questions! *I've* got a question to ask *you*!"

Startled, the reporters fell silent.

Riley said, "Who the hell told you anything was going to happen here? How did you know about the stakeout?"

A murmur passed among the reporters as they protested that they had no intention of revealing their sources.

Just then a voice called out from nearby.

"False alarm, folks. There's nothing more to see."

Bill turned and saw Bull Cullen emerging from a path that led back into the forest.

An angry sneer took form on Riley's face, and Bill knew what she was thinking.

This is all Cullen's doing.

After all, Cullen had been sure all along that Riley's hunch was wrong. Not only had he been looking forward to seeing Riley fail, he'd obviously alerted the media to make her that her failure was as public and humiliating as possible.

He'd told them exactly where and when to show up.

Worse still, Cullen hadn't even been at his post during the stakeout. He'd stayed in the woods close to the tower so he'd be able to greet the reporters when they arrived.

That son of a bitch, Bill thought.

He started toward Cullen, his fist clenched and ready to punch the man out.

Riley reached out and stopped him.

"Don't, Bill," she said. "Things are bad enough as it is."

Meanwhile, Cullen was basking in the situation, holding court among the reporters and offering his own full explanation for what was going on.

"Yes, we *do* have another suspect in custody. A good, solid, suspect. His name is Timothy Pollitt, and we expect to bring charges against him soon. But FBI Special Agent Riley Paige here had her own theory, and we felt compelled to follow up on it. As you can see, it didn't pan out. But we didn't want to leave any loose ends."

He looked at Riley and Bill with a gloating smile and added, "On behalf of the railroad police, I want to thank Agent Paige and her FBI colleagues for their help. Now, of course, the FBI's work on this case is through, and they'll be flying right back to Quantico."

As Cullen continued to talk with the reporters, Riley said to Bill, "We can't quit yet. We just can't."

"There's nothing left for us to do," Bill said.

"Yes there is! I'm sure we aren't wrong. We just made a mistake about the time. We need to find out when the next freight trains will be coming through. We need to keep this stakeout going. Let's go talk to Dillard. Maybe we can convince him—"

Bill interrupted her.

"Riley, listen to me. Even if you're right about the killer's plans, there's no way he'll strike here now—not now that reporters have arrived and our cover is blown. Besides …"

Bill hesitated.

"Besides what?" Riley asked.

Bill sighed and said, "I think we need to face facts. In all likelihood, Timothy Pollitt really is the killer. There really is nothing more for us to do here."

Riley's stricken expression broke his heart.

Before she could say anything, her phone buzzed. Riley looked at it and rolled her eyes in despair.

"Jesus," she said. "It's Carl Walder."

Bill could hardly believe it.

As if things weren't bad enough, he thought.

He remembered all too well the countless conflicts Riley had had with Walder. The incompetent, baby-faced bureaucrat had suspended and even fired Riley on more than one occasion.

This is too much, he thought.

"Let me take that," he said to Riley, taking the phone away from her.

Walder sounded surprised to hear a male voice instead of Riley.

"I'm trying to reach Riley Paige. Who is this?"

"Bill Jeffreys here. Riley isn't available at the moment."

"What do you mean, not available?"

"Just what I said," Bill said.

Bill heard a growl of disapproval.

Then Walder said, "Listen, I got a call from Deputy Chief Cullen of the railroad police a while ago, and he said Paige has gone off her rocker and is determined to pull some kind of cockamamie stakeout even though you've already got the killer in custody and—"

Bill interrupted, "It's over, Chief Walder. The stakeout, I mean. We came up empty."

Walder growled again.

"OK, then. I hear that Agent Roston is also on Paige's team. I want the FBI plane back here in Quantico tonight, with the three of you on it."

"Should we report to you when we get there?" Bill asked.

"No, damn it. I don't even want to talk to any of you—not yet, anyway. I've got to take some kind of disciplinary action against Agent Paige—and from what Cullen told me, against Agent Roston as well. It's sounds like Roston is a serious loose cannon, following right along in Paige's footsteps. I haven't decided what to do yet. Just take a couple of days off, all three of you. That's an order."

Walder abruptly ended the call.

Bill shook his head and thought …

He's mad enough already. Wait till he sees what the media's going to do with this.

He handed the phone back to Riley and said, "It's really over, Riley. Walder's making this personal, and we can't buck his orders. We've got to fly back to Quantico. Right now. Come on, let's get a ride back to Dermott. I'll call the pilot on the way."

Riley nodded silently. As they both walked toward the car they'd arrived in, Bill remembered what he'd said to Riley just a moment ago …

"In all likelihood, Timothy Pollitt really is the killer."

For some reason, he really wished he hadn't said that.

Deep down, his own instincts were starting to nag him, telling him …

This really isn't over.

CHAPTER THIRTY FOUR

As the FBI plane flew back toward Quantico, Jenn wished she could talk to either Riley or Agent Jeffreys. The flight seemed interminable, and the monotonous drone of the engine wasn't helping her spirits. She doubted that it was making her two partners feel any better either.

It made Jenn uncomfortable that Riley was sitting behind her, alone in the back of the plane, obviously brooding over the terrible blunder of the failed stakeout.

Agent Jeffreys was across the aisle from Jenn, staring out the window. He'd had little to say since they'd boarded the plane.

Are they angry with me? Jenn wondered.

She told herself that was a self-centered sort of worry, but she still couldn't help but wonder.

After all, her own clash with Bull Cullen hadn't helped the case go smoothly.

She seriously wished she'd found some more dignified means of dealing with him—something other than punching him in the nose.

Maybe she could have simply brushed him off and filed a complaint at an appropriate time.

Then she thought …

Stop doing this to yourself.

Cullen himself had been the real problem. And she was certain that he'd been a problem long before she met him.

Although Jenn hadn't been an agent for very long, she already knew about some of the pitfalls of being a female agent. One of those was accepting inappropriate responsibility for the actions of others—especially men.

It really was Cullen's fault, she told herself. *It's not mine.*

Surely Jenn wasn't the only woman who had felt his unwelcome hands wandering across her body. She knew perfectly well that it would have gotten worse if she'd just let it go—the same as it had surely gotten worse for other women in the past, and would for more women in the future.

Jenn decided to file a complaint the next chance she got. It was time someone called the man on his behavior.

Not that her decision made her feel any better.

Other worries kept crowding into her mind. She remembered what she'd said to Riley over the phone just before this case had started …

"Maybe I should just turn in my badge."

It had only been two days ago, on Saturday, but it seemed much longer. At the time, Jenn had just gotten a vaguely threatening phone call from Aunt Cora. Jenn had convinced herself she could ignore the lurking figure from her past.

And yet …

It was as though Aunt Cora was still pulling and tugging at her.

Jenn realized that pull was because of this very case, and how unfinished it seemed, and how hard Jenn knew it must be on Riley.

Because the truth was …

Aunt Cora could help.

It was a chilling thought—but true.

The woman's criminal tendrils were everywhere, and she had access to information that even the FBI couldn't dream of.

If there still was a killer out there, Aunt Cora could help find him.

Jenn took her cell phone out of the pocket and stared at it.

She's just a text message away, she thought.

Maybe she could get Aunt Cora's help without either Riley or Agent Jeffreys ever being the wiser.

Maybe there would be no consequences—this time.

But Jenn felt a shudder of realization …

This is exactly what Aunt Cora wants. For me to need her help—and to accept her help.

Once Jenn let that happen, she would again be in debt to Aunt Cora.

Jenn put the phone back in her pocket.

Maybe she could sleep a little during the rest of the flight.

But she doubted it.

*

Riley sat staring out the cabin window thinking about how much she hated certain aspects of flying. The landscape far below always seemed to creep by at a snail's pace, as if the plane were barely going anywhere.

Not that she really looked forward to landing. She didn't feel ready to face whatever she might be returning to.

Not at BAU and not even at home.

She smiled a little at the thought …

By the time I'm ready to face the world, the plane will run out of fuel.

The flight seemed especially torturous today, given what had just happened …

… or rather what *hadn't* happened.

The same question had been rattling through Riley's brain ever since they'd flown out of Dermott.

What went wrong?

Riley had suffered setbacks and even failures before, but in the past she'd at least been able to make sense of them.

This time, she couldn't seem to get a rational grip on things.

Even after the freight train had gone by without incident, she'd kept right on thinking …

I was right.

And she wasn't the only one who was right.

So was Mason Eggers. At the very least, she had the overwhelming feeling that Eggers understood the case.

And she still couldn't help telling herself.

We were right.

We were in the wrong place at the wrong time, but even so …

… we were right.

It was a weird paradox, and she couldn't get her mind around it.

She also kept thinking …

Poor Eggers.

She remembered how broken and defeated he'd looked the last time she'd seen him, when he was getting into Dillard's SUV for the drive back to Chicago.

The man's confidence had been shaky to enough to begin with, and Riley kept thinking about something he'd said.

"Maybe I'd do the world more good if I just gave up this kind of work and took up fishing."

Now he surely felt that he had no other choice.

But was life in retirement, fishing his remaining years away, even possible for a lonely old railroad cop like Mason Eggers?

Riley doubted it.

She felt certain of one thing—the failure of the stakeout was going to be even harder on Eggers than it was on her. She doubted that he'd ever recover from it.

As for herself, she was surely due for a reprimand at the very least. A suspension seemed more likely. She'd already thanked Bill for taking that call from Carl Walder, buffering her against that toady-in-charge's newly kindled rage.

According to Bill, Walder wanted nothing to do with Riley or her team for another couple of days, which at least gave them a temporary reprieve.

The plane lurched a little, and Riley noticed a change in the cabin pressure. The pilot announced their descent toward the Quantico airstrip.

Soon Riley would be home, dealing with a whole different set of problems.

The most daunting would surely be Jilly, who must still be mad at her.

Mad and hurt, Riley thought.

And no doubt about it, Jilly had good reason to feel both mad and hurt.

Riley wondered if maybe, when she drove home from Quantico, she should stop somewhere and buy Jilly a belated birthday present.

But no, whatever gift she might find in such a rush simply wouldn't do. It would seem lame and perfunctory, and it would probably make Jilly only feel worse than she already did.

Riley needed to talk to Jilly face to face, do or say whatever it would take to make amends.

And it wasn't going to be easy.

Through her window Riley could see the buildings of the Quantico facility getting larger by the second.

The case she and her colleagues had left behind seemed a long distance off indeed—far away, but anything but solved.

Deep down in her gut, she felt absolutely sure of one thing:

Timothy Pollitt was not the killer.

Whoever the real killer was, he was surely planning his next murder.

And there wasn't a damn thing Riley could do about it.

CHAPTER THIRTY FIVE

As soon as she got off the plane, Riley sent a text message to April saying she was on her way home from Quantico. So when Riley pulled up to her townhouse, she knew that her arrival wouldn't be unexpected.

The trouble was—what should *she* expect?

Was Jilly still angry with her?

Did Riley have whatever it took to be the good mom and work everything out?

When she walked through the front door, April was right there to meet her.

Riley put down her bag and returned her daughter's big hug.

Then April wasted no time getting to the point.

"Jilly's in the family room. You should go talk to her."

Just as she had been on the phone, April sounded remarkably calm and grown up.

I guess that's what I've got to be too right now, Riley thought, fully aware of the irony of the situation.

As Riley walked through the house, she noticed a delicious smell wafting from the kitchen. Riley was curious about what Gabriela might be making, but now was no time to stop and ask.

Riley felt a swell of sadness as she reached the family room. After all, this was where Liam had slept during his short time as a member of the family. And now he was gone.

Jilly was sitting at a table, quietly working on some pages of algebra problems.

Riley sat down facing her.

"Jilly, we've got to talk. I—"

Jilly interrupted, looking up from her homework, "No, stop, Mom. Just stop. I've got something to say first."

Riley gulped hard. It sounded like this might be even worse than she'd expected.

Jilly looked her directly in the eyes for a moment.

Then she said, "I'm sorry."

Riley felt as though she'd been pushed into a cold shower of sheer confusion.

"What?" she asked.

"I'm sorry," Jilly repeated.

Riley shook her head.

"No, Jilly, no. You've got nothing to be sorry for. It's me. I was wrong. I forgot your birthday. I—"

Jilly interrupted her again.

"Just tell me what you've been doing. Since you've been gone, I mean. All about the case."

Riley sighed and shrugged.

"Oh, that doesn't matter …"

"Just tell me."

Why does she want to know? Riley wondered.

Jilly certainly seemed sincere about it.

So Riley started telling her younger daughter about everything that had happened, starting with the phone call from Meredith on Saturday. When she started describing the first crime scene, Jilly stopped her again.

"Give me all the details. I want to know what that poor woman looked like."

"Oh, Jilly, I don't know."

"Please. I really, really want to know."

Riley paused for a moment. Was this some kind of morbid, adolescent curiosity on Jilly's part? No. Riley could tell by her face and her voice that Jilly really wanted to understand the whole thing—and how Riley herself had felt having to deal with it.

So Riley went ahead and told her all about it, sparing no details—not even from herself.

It was a strange experience, not at all like filling out some formal report—which Riley reminded herself that she still needed to do. This was personal and deep. She was sharing a dark, troubling part of her life that she'd become all too used to keeping private, hidden from everybody except Bill and an occasional therapist. And a curious realization came over her.

I need this.

She'd spent too many years keeping these terrible experiences to herself.

It had been harder on her than she'd realized.

But was this the right thing to do—sharing such horrors with a girl who had just turned fourteen?

But as Jilly kept listening with intense interest, Riley realized something else. Jilly had experienced her own horrors—a childhood so terrible that she'd almost sold her body to escape from it. Jilly was surely better equipped emotionally to deal with the shocking facts of Riley's work than most adults were.

As Riley got to the part about the ill-fated stakeout, she felt her own frustrations rising again over leaving the case unsolved. But strangely, it felt good to give voice to those frustrations—something she hadn't even done with Bill or Jenn.

Riley finished her story, and Jilly sat looking at her for a silent moment.

Then Jilly smiled and said, "Thanks, Mom. That's the best birthday present I could possibly want. And I'm really sorry I made a fuss about things. I shouldn't have given you something so stupid to worry about when you were dealing with something so important. And anyway, I had a really nice party."

Riley was stunned. She simply didn't know what to say.

Jilly tilted her head a little.

She said, "You really don't get it, do you, Mom? I've never in my whole life had anyone to look up to, someone I wanted to grow up to be like. This is a huge change for me. It means more to me than you can imagine."

Riley's throat tightened and her eyes started to fill.

Jilly said, "Don't cry, Mom. Crying's for wusses."

Riley brushed away a tear and laughed a little. It felt good to hear Jilly sound like an ordinary teenager again.

Riley said, "Well, no matter what you say, talking about murder and mayhem is *not* a proper birthday present. I'll make it up to you somehow. We'll do something together soon, just the two of us. I promise."

Jilly looked pleased.

"OK, Mom," she said. And maybe someday I'll have something so important to do in my life that I'll forget *your* birthday."

Riley laughed a little.

"Then I guess we'll be even," she said. "But I hope it will be something pleasant."

"Oh, and another thing," Jilly said. "You're still going to solve that case. I just know it."

Riley felt herself tear up all over again. Jilly seemed so sure about it.

She wished she felt the same way.

At that moment April poked her head into the family room a bit cautiously. She took a look at Riley and Jilly, then said, "Gabriela's got some treats for everybody. Is that OK?"

"Come on in," Riley said.

April came inside, followed by Gabriela, who was carrying a tray full of freshly baked *empanadas de leche*—a custard-filled Guatemalan pastry.

"I heard you were coming home," Gabriela said. "I can heat up dinner leftovers if you're hungry."

"Just these will be wonderful," Riley replied. *"Muchas gracias."*

As everybody settled down to enjoy the delicious empanadas, April said to Riley …

"Blaine called yesterday. I guess he wanted to know how the case was going and when you'd be back."

Riley felt a bit jolted at the sound of Blaine's name. She'd sent him a brief text during the flight out to Illinois, and he'd texted back wishing her luck. The truth was, she hadn't given a thought about him since.

Strange, she thought.

She'd not only forgotten Jilly's birthday—she'd forgotten about her boyfriend.

It was definitely time to settle back down into ordinary life.

*

After the snacks were eaten, Gabriela went down to her apartment and the girls scattered to their own rooms for bed.

Riley was glad to go to her room alone. She was tired from the long awful day, but she did want to touch base with Blaine.

She typed a text in her cell phone …

Hi Blaine—
Solved the case and I'm home.
It'd be nice to see U.
When can we get together?

It was fairly late, so Riley hardly expected a reply until the next morning.

But within seconds the text was marked "read," and Blaine replied …

How about tomorrow?
I'll call you in the morning.

Riley smiled.

Sounds great!

Feeling a bit like a schoolgirl, she put "<3" next to her message—a little heart.

She had hardy set her cell phone down when her house phone rang.

When Riley answered it, she heard a woman's voice.

"Is this Riley Page? Special Agent Riley Paige?"

Although the woman spoke in a kindly tone, Riley didn't reply. She knew better than to identify herself to an unknown caller.

"Well," the woman said cheerfully, "I hope it's OK for me to call you Riley."

"Who is this?" Riley finally asked.

A silence fell. Riley almost hung up the phone.

Then the voice said, "I thought it was time we got acquainted."

Shock ran through Riley's mind as she realized who she was listening to.

"Aunt Cora," she said, almost in a whisper.

The woman chuckled and continued, still sounding perfectly friendly. "After all, we've both been mentors to a brilliant young woman. I must admit, though, to a certain pang of jealousy that she's left my nest, and she's now in your charge. But that's life, isn't it? Things change. And it's healthy that things change. Healthy and natural."

Riley almost asked …
How did you get this number?
But of course, it was a ridiculous question.

From everything Jenn had said about Aunt Cora, that woman would have no trouble at all tracking down a simple home phone number.

Aunt Cora continued, "I've been following that case you've been working on. It must be frustrating—getting stymied like that, knowing that the killer is still out there. How are you holding up?"

Riley started to feel a new worry, but Cora seemed to anticipate it.

"Before you get upset … no, Jenn hasn't been in touch, isn't

187

reporting to me. She's being a perfectly good girl, very discreet, loyal to you and the FBI, keeping me at a safe distance. I'm just nosy, that's all. I like to know what's going on. And ..."

For the first time, Riley heard a slightly sinister sound in the woman's voice.

"... and I have my ways of finding out whatever I want to know."

Riley felt an icy chill.

Was Cora in touch with any of the local cops Riley had dealt with? Or someone with the railroad police? Or the Chicago FBI?

Or all of them?

Riley couldn't imagine the extent of Aunt Cora's criminal web.

Cora continued, sounding as warm as before.

"Such horrible murders, so shocking. Not so shocking to you, I don't suppose. But do you ever get used to it? Do you have any idea what drives someone to do such ghastly things?"

Riley said nothing. She wondered what to do.

Just hang up?

No, something told her that she'd want to hear whatever this woman had to say.

The voice on the phone went on, "You meet some interesting people working on a case, don't you? I hear you've met a nice widower. So sweet, so lonely. Any sparks between you? Any possibility of romance? Well, I suppose he's a bit old for your taste ..."

Riley's stomach felt uneasy at the obvious reference to Mason Eggers.

The woman knew a lot—too much for Riley's comfort.

Cora continued, "I'm sure you hope you've seen the last of that young railroad cop. Such an obnoxious character, isn't he? Can't keep his hands to himself. Doesn't treat women with proper respect. I wonder. A man who harasses female colleagues like that—it makes you wonder, what else might he be capable of?"

She knows about Cullen too, Riley realized.

But she determinedly kept her silence.

Finally, in a sweet, chirping voice, Aunt Cora said, "Well, I'm so glad we had this pleasant little chat. Let's do stay in touch. I always want to know how dear little Jenn is doing. Such a remarkable girl!"

Aunt Cora abruptly ended the call.

Riley sat there with the phone in her hand, feeling completely baffled.

Cora had said …

"Let's do stay in touch."

… but she hadn't told Riley a thing about how to reach her.

Not that Riley wanted to know.

It was surely best for her not to know.

But why had Aunt Cora contacted Riley?

A *"pleasant little chat,"* she had said.

It certainly hadn't been pleasant at all for Riley.

But surely Aunt Cora had called with some purpose in her mind.

Riley began to replay the one-sided conversation over and over in her head.

Little by little, an idea started to take form in her mind. There was something she should look up, something she'd never checked on because it had never seemed even remotely relevant.

Her heart beat faster as she turned on her computer and ran a search.

In a matter of moments, she'd found an old newspaper clipping with a photo.

Riley gasped aloud.

I know who he is.

CHAPTER THIRTY SIX

Juliet Bench had just sat down at a table in the train's lounge car when she saw the man come in from the next car.

There he is again, she thought.

Shortly after she'd boarded the train, the same man had walked past her seat and stopped in the aisle to look at her—just long enough for her to notice—and then he had continued on his way.

And now he stood at the far end of the lounge car, looking at her again.

Do I know him? she wondered. The face didn't seem familiar.

He was gazing downward now, his hands in his pockets.

Acting like he doesn't notice me, Juliet thought.

But he looked up at her again and walked straight toward her table.

Juliet wasn't sure how she felt about that. She didn't travel much, especially by train, and she didn't like to travel. Would talking to a total stranger make things any better? She doubted it.

When the man reached her table, he said, "Excuse me, but … I see that you're sitting alone, and …"

Rather surprisingly, the shyness in his voice put her somewhat at ease.

"Please, have a seat," she said.

The man smiled timidly and sat down.

"Have we met?" Juliet asked.

The man wrinkled his brow curiously.

"I don't think so," he said. "But you *do* look remarkably like someone …"

His voice trailed off.

Then he said, "Do you have any family in Dunmore?"

"No," she said. "I'm from Chicago originally, and my blood relatives are all there. Now I live in Keadle with my husband and two daughters."

The man's eyebrows rose.

"Keadle. Well, I don't know anybody there. I guess it's just a coincidence—the resemblance, I mean. So were you visiting family in Chicago?"

Juliet felt a stab of sadness. For a moment, she couldn't say anything.

"Oh, I'm sorry," the man said. "It's something sad, isn't it? Never mind, forget I asked."

Juliet managed to smile faintly.

"No, it's all right. My dad passed away. I spent some time with him before he died and stayed for his funeral. He'd been ill for a long time—prostate cancer—so it wasn't a shock, but still ..."

She fell quiet.

The man said, "It's always sad to lose someone you love. I know what it's like."

Juliet noticed a melancholy look in his eye.

Yes, he does know what it's like, she thought.

And she had to admit, it was nice to talk to someone who knew and understood.

"His passing was peaceful," Juliet said. "Hospice is such a blessing, and he was able to spend his last days at home, with family all around. My mother was holding his hand during his last moments."

"Did your husband go to Chicago with you?" the man asked.

"No, he wanted to. Kent and my dad were very close. But someone had to stay at home with the children. Jenna is five, and Amy is seven. Jenna especially is having a hard time understanding that her grandfather is gone. I thought about bringing them along to say goodbye and for the funeral but ..."

She paused for a moment, wondering again over something that still worried her.

"Kent and I decided against it. Do you think we were wrong?"

The man shrugged a little.

"I never had children, so I'm afraid I'm not the right person to ask. But ... well, five and seven sound *awfully* young to me. My guess is that you did the right thing."

Juliet felt a smile form on her face. It was really nice to hear someone say that.

She said, "I was just getting ready to order a glass of wine. Would you ...?"

The man smiled.

"I'd love to. Allow me to get it. What will you have?"

"Just an ordinary red wine."

The man got up and walked toward the bar and ordered the wine.

It now seemed to Juliet that this was turning out nicely. A little friendly company was what she really needed after those sad days in Chicago. She reminded herself that she still had to make the drive home from the station, but it was short and very familiar. One glass of wine wouldn't hurt.

The man came back with two glasses of red wine and sat down.

"By the way, I don't believe I know your name."

She lifted her wine glass with a smile.

"Juliet Bench," she said. "What's yours?"

CHAPTER THIRTY SEVEN

Riley sat staring at the picture on her computer screen—a newspaper photograph of a smiling young woman with a slender face, an aquiline nose, and curly brown hair.

She kept reading the name in the caption over and over again …

Arlene Eggers

… the name of Mason Eggers's wife, who had died fifty years ago.

Riley kept murmuring aloud to herself …

"I can't believe it. I can't believe it. I can't believe it."

But that wasn't true.

She *did* believe it. She believed it completely.

She just didn't *want* to believe it.

Aunt Cora had triggered Riley's research effort with her words about Eggers.

"I hear you've met a nice widower."

It had been a hint, of course.

So Riley had checked to see how the retired railroad cop had been widowed. And she had discovered that the victims of the serial killer looked very much like the wife Eggers had lost.

Aunt Cora had also said …

"I've been following that case you've been working on."

Now Riley realized that the mysterious woman had also been doing her own research, coming up with her own theories.

Riley shivered deeply.

All this hinting and teasing.

So much like Shane Hatcher.

In fact, this was too much like Shane Hatcher for comfort. Was another criminal mastermind trying to gain control of an FBI agent? Did Aunt Cora already have her hooks in Jenn? Was she now working on Riley?

There was no time to figure that out now. But she couldn't avoid the main question in her mind.

Why didn't I know all along?

Surely the thought should have occurred to her at the third murder scene, when she'd wondered how the killer had escaped from the scene of Sally Diehl's murder without taking the car he had stolen.

He hadn't escaped at all.

He'd been right there, talking with Riley.

How had her instincts failed her so badly?

Then it dawned on her ...

My instincts didn't fail me.

From the very first time she'd seen Eggers at that meeting in Chicago, he'd stood out to her. Unlike everyone else in the room—especially Cullen—she'd sensed that he had some special insight into the case.

She'd sought him out for that very reason.

She also remembered how he'd reacted when she'd said ...

"I see you're married."

... how he'd covered up his wedding ring with a look of pain.

Right then she'd sensed the depth of the grief of an elderly widower.

She remembered, too, something she had decided about him.

He doesn't like to talk about himself.

She'd been right about all of it.

Mason Eggers was all that he seemed to be—intelligent, kindly, restless, lonely, misunderstood ...

But he was also something else.

He was also a murderer.

Riley just hadn't looked hard or deep enough.

And the reason she hadn't was very simple. She'd actually felt a kinship with him, thought of him as a colleague, and something of an oddball like herself, someone whose best work and ideas often seemed to others like pure craziness—at least until facts bore out those ideas.

She didn't want to see that he harbored his share of demons ...

Just like I do.

... for Riley could remember surrendering to her own internal darkness with acts of brutality against her adversaries. She remembered how she'd killed one especially vicious man who had captured and tormented April—how she'd beaten him savagely to death with a rock, smashing him in the face time and time again.

To this day, she had no regrets about it.

She'd do it again in a heartbeat.

Riley shuddered deeply, then reminded herself …

I'm different.

I'm not like Mason.

I kill monsters.

I don't kill innocent women.

But why did Mason Eggers kill innocent women?

Riley reread the newspaper article, looking for some hint of explanation.

Fifty years ago on this very night, Mason Eggers's wife, Arlene, had committed suicide by lying down on railroad tracks in front of an oncoming freight train just outside the little Michigan town of Dunmore.

She'd just left the home of some friends, who had said she seemed very sad when they'd last seen her. They hadn't known why.

It seemed that everybody in Dunmore liked Arlene Eggers, and she liked everybody in return.

But all of her friends and loved ones used the same word to describe her.

"Sad. So often sad."

She'd been a chronically melancholy person, and no one could understand why—least of all her loving husband, a respected and well-liked local cop named Mason Eggers.

Riley felt a stab of sympathy for the poor woman—and for her husband, too.

She knew that fifty years ago clinical depression was poorly understood, its ravages and terrors underestimated. Today's antidepressant drugs didn't yet exist. People routinely died from depression, often by their own hands, without anyone knowing why.

Mason Eggers had carried this terrible loss with him for years. He'd surely felt guilty for his wife's death. How could he possibly understand why she might kill herself, unless it was somehow his fault?

And now, she could see into the killer's mind for the first time.

She could actually feel his anguish. The sensation was so strong that for a moment she almost believed he was in the room with her. After he'd retired guilt had started pressing in on him again.

And with a deep chill, she realized something else about him.

195

Something was wrong in his mind. Something, whether physical or emotional, had twisted his perceptions. And as that horrible fifty-year anniversary came nearer, his demons had taken over, and he'd begun to kill.

Tonight, Riley realized. *He's going to finish his work tonight.*

He was going to kill one last time—on the same date, in the same place, where his beloved wife had taken her own life.

It was the most powerful gut feeling Riley had gotten on the case so far.

But was it correct?

She couldn't risk being wrong again.

She brought up a map and saw that Dunmore was just a short distance from Detroit. Then she searched for a train schedule and saw that a passenger train had already left from Chicago on a four-hour trip to Detroit.

He's on that train, she realized.

He had to be stopped as soon as he arrived in Detroit—before he had a chance to abduct anybody, much less kill again.

She needed help—but who could help her?

Who would even listen to her theory?

Proctor Dillard, she thought.

She and Bill had worked with the special agent in charge of the Chicago FBI Field Office. If anybody would listen to her, he would. And he could alert agents at the Detroit FBI Field Office to arrest him straight off the train there. Eggers wouldn't even make it all the way to Dunmore.

She found Dillard's emergency phone number.

When she got him on the line, she said, "Agent Dillard, this is Riley Paige. Please listen to me. I know who the killer is. I know where he's going to strike next. He's going to kill tonight. I need for you to—"

Dillard interrupted her.

"Agent Paige, just stop. Whatever it is, I can't help. My hands are tied."

Riley could hardly believe her ears.

Dillard continued, "I got a call from Carl Walder in Quantico today. He was very specific. I'm not to have anything more to do with you, at least pertaining to this case. He really meant it."

Riley suppressed a growl of rage.

That bastard Walder!

She said, "*Listen!* The killer is Mason Eggers!"

A long pause fell.

Then Dillard said, "Agent Paige, you know I've got all the respect in the world for you. But everybody knows you've been off your game on this case. And I've known Eggers too many years to think he could possibly be a murderer."

"But Agent Dillard—"

"And anyway, it's out of my hands. Orders are orders. I don't want to lose my job."

"Please listen—"

"I'm sorry, but I'm hanging up now."

He ended the call.

Riley felt about to hyperventilate from frustration. She struggled to calm herself. There had to be some way to handle this.

Who else could she call?

Could she try contacting Walder himself, try to make him understand her theory?

Impossible, she thought. *He'll never listen.*

And even if she could make him listen, she'd lose precious time in the effort.

But who else was there?

Bull Cullen?

No, the very idea of trying to persuade him was laughable. He wouldn't even take her call, much less seriously listen to her.

Who, then?

Of course! The Detroit police.

They could catch Eggers as soon as the train arrived there.

She quickly found the phone number and punched it into her cell phone.

When a voice answered, she said, "I need to talk to whoever is in charge there right now."

"How can I help you?"

"This is Riley Paige with the FBI. I'm calling to report—"

The voice interrupted, "Wait a minute! Riley Paige? The FBI woman I saw on the news today, the one who screwed up so bad in Wisconsin?"

She heard him call out to someone else nearby, "Hey, guys! I've got that batshit crazy FBI woman on the line!"

Riley felt her face redden with rage and humiliation.

She wondered—how long would it take to undo the damage her reputation had taken during this case?

She ended the call. What else could she do?

She sat down slowly behind her desk, trying to collect her nerves.

It's up to me, she thought. *I've got to stop him myself.*

Nobody else is going to.

She ran a computer search for plane schedules and found what she needed. If she left right now, she could catch a late-night commercial flight from Reagan International Airport. She'd arrive at Detroit's Wayne County Airport about an hour and a half later—before Eggers's train reached that city.

She could stop him right then and there at the Detroit train station.

She wondered …

Should I contact Bill and Jenn?

Of course, she realized. They at least deserved to know what she was trying to do. She typed a text message to both of them that included a link to the article she'd found. She briefly explained her theory and gave them her flight schedule.

She scribbled a note to her sleeping family explaining that she had gone away to work on the case again. She grabbed her gun and car keys, left the note on the living room coffee table, and raced out the front door.

CHAPTER THIRTY EIGHT

When Riley arrived at the flight desk, she was breathless from haste and anxiety, and her head was spinning with dangerous scenarios and possibilities. Her mind boggled at the realization that had sent her here—and with thoughts of what she was going to have to do to stop Mason Eggers from killing again.

She kept telling herself …

I won't know exactly what I have to do until I have to do it.

Just when she finished buying her ticket, she heard a familiar voice behind her.

"Hey, Riley!"

It was Bill's voice.

She turned and gasped aloud as she saw Bill and Jenn hurrying toward her.

"What are you doing here?" she said.

Bill grinned at her as Jenn started to buy her own ticket.

"What do you think we're doing? You didn't think we'd let you go alone, did you?"

"But how did you …?"

Riley was about to ask Bill how he and Jenn had gotten here so quickly. But of course, the answer was obvious. It was a shorter drive for them from Quantico than it was for her from Fredericksburg. As soon as they'd read her message, they'd gotten together and driven straight here.

Riley felt overwhelmed. Their arrival here was much, much more than she had dared to hope for. She couldn't find words to begin to express her gratitude.

She wouldn't have to do this alone after all.

Later, she thought. *After we've caught the killer.*

When all three agents had their tickets, they hurried to the departure gate, where the plane was already boarding. They showed their badges to the flight attendant and told her that they'd need to deplane as soon as possible after landing in Detroit. The attendant quickly found them three seats together near the door. Jenn sat between Bill and Riley.

The three agents were still winded when the plane took off a few minutes later.

"So," Riley said breathlessly, "you believe my theory."

Bill and Jenn looked at each other, as if surprised by the question.

Bill said, "Hey, that article you linked us to was pretty convincing."

Jenn added, "And the victims all resemble his wife so strongly. It's surely no coincidence. And now, this is the anniversary of her suicide."

Riley shook her head and said, "I wish I could get someone else to believe me. And I've still got all kinds of questions of my own …"

When the plane reached cruising altitude, Jenn got on the Internet to do some research.

She said, "I'm finding out more about Mason Eggers. He left Dunmore soon after his wife's death, then moved to Chicago where he became a railroad cop. He never remarried."

Bill asked, "Has he ever had any trouble with the law?"

"Just the opposite," Jenn said. "He had a distinguished career with the railroad police and got several commendations. As far as I can tell, he's never hurt a fly."

New doubts started to creep into Riley's mind.

"I can't make sense of that," she said. But then she remembered the feeling she'd had that something had gone wrong in the man's mind. She added, "He seems to have gone through some kind of serious psychiatric change. Schizophrenia, maybe?"

"Maybe," Bill said. "But as I understand it, schizophrenia typically starts in late adolescence or early adulthood—not in old age."

Jenn's fingers danced on her tablet computer as she brought up more information.

She said, "Schizophrenia is rare at that age, but not unheard of. It's sometimes called very-late-onset schizophrenia when it occurs after the age of sixty. But older people can suffer from delusions, hallucinations, and mental confusion for other reasons. There's a condition called Charles Bonnet Syndrome that involves visual hallucinations. And of course, he might be suffering from some physiological brain disorder—brain cancer, maybe, or early stages of Alzheimer's or even Parkinson's. There really are lots of reasons why his mental health might be failing."

The three agents thought in silence for a few moments.

Finally Bill said, "It's still hard to understand his behavior—as it relates to us, I mean. I know he put us onto that stakeout as a ruse. But some of his suggestions seem to have been genuine, even helpful—like how he listens to scanners to figure out freight train schedules. And the last town, Dermott—it really does begin with a D, following the alphabetical pattern he described."

Again, Riley felt an alarming surge of uncanny empathy with Eggers.

She said, "Part of him wants somebody to stop him, and part of him wants to get away with his murders. Part of him is trying to help us, part of him is trying to trick us. He's at war with himself. As lucid as he seems in person, he's slipping into some kind of dementia, and he doesn't know which he wants more—to go free or to face justice."

Bill scratched his chin and looked at Riley.

"I'm just wondering one thing," he said to her. "What made you look for that news story in the first place? Checking into that kind of ancient history is a pretty big intuitive leap—even for you."

Riley gulped. She couldn't very well tell him about Aunt Cora's phone call.

She stammered, "It—it was just a wild hunch."

Jenn locked eyes with Riley. The younger agent looked worried.

Riley was sure …

Jenn has guessed what happened.

They would need to talk about this sometime—but not now. Riley realized that she wasn't eager to ask all of her many questions about Aunt Cora anytime soon.

Coffee was served, and the three agents continued to quietly brainstorm. Jenn also arranged to rent a car at the airport so they could drive directly to the train station. But as the time for their landing neared, they heard the pilot's voice.

"Folks, I'm sorry to say that our landing is going to be delayed a bit. There's some bad weather down in Detroit, so we'll have to circle for a little while—probably about twenty minutes."

As the pilot went on to assure his passengers about connecting flights, Riley and her colleagues exchanged looks of despair.

"Twenty minutes," Riley said. "We'll be too late to meet the train when it arrives. He'll abduct his victim after all."

Bill said, "Can't we get somebody to pick him up at the platform?"

Riley suppressed a groan as she remembered her desperate phone calls.

"We won't get any help from the Detroit cops, believe me. We don't even have a warrant, and we'd never get one soon enough—even if this were still an open case, which it isn't."

Jenn got busy on her tablet computer again.

"We need to change gears," she said, bringing up a map.

She pointed to the map and explained, "We're coming in west of Detroit, and Dunmore is also to the west of the city. But he'll be arriving on the other side of Detroit. He'll have to drive through the city to get back to Dunmore, but we'll be able to drive straight there. We can get there as soon as he can. With any luck, before he does. "

Riley stared at the map, hoping Jenn was right.

But her worry was still building up.

She knew that, tonight, Eggers was going to transport a victim to the very place where the tragedy of his life had taken place fifty years ago.

We've got to be there too, Riley thought.

We've got to get to the train tracks in time to stop him.

But was that possible?

CHAPTER THIRTY NINE

As soon as the plane taxied to a stop at Detroit's Wayne County Airport, Riley and her colleagues were out of their seats and on their feet. The flight attendant made sure that they were the first passengers off the plane. They ran through the jet bridge and into the terminal, flashing their badges at startled security people as they went.

The terminal wasn't busy at that hour, so they were able to make an unbroken dash to the front of the building. Even so, Riley had the terrible feeling that time was slowing down and they were moving in slow motion.

It seemed impossible that they would get to their destination in time to catch Mason Eggers.

Worse, just as the pilot had warned—it was raining outside where their rental car was waiting for them. That hardly boded well for their efforts to spot and stop a killer.

Riley got behind the wheel of the car, with Jenn next to her and Bill behind them. Hardly a word was said during the short drive to Dunmore, but Riley was well aware that her colleagues must be as anxious and worried as she was.

The rain lessened to a drizzle as Riley drove, but the sky remained ominously dark and overcast, despite the fact that morning was near.

When they reached the outskirts of Dunmore, Riley turned on the vehicle's GPS system to navigate through the quiet streets of the little town. They were soon making their way through the neighborhood where Mason and Arlene Eggers had once lived.

The area struck Riley as appropriately sad, full of rundown little houses that had seen happier and more prosperous days. Lights were coming on in a few of the windows as people were just beginning to stir. No one was out and about yet, which was just as well.

Riley quickly found the road she had already chosen—one that ran parallel to the train tracks. High streetlights shed some light on overgrown empty lots and the occasional shabby buildings that separated the tracks from the road. None of the buildings

203

themselves were well lighted.

Riley pulled the car to a stop at the side of the road, and she and her colleagues stepped outside. The rain had completely stopped now, but the air and the ground were still wet, and the sky was still dark.

The three agents moved quietly and spoke in hushed voices, knowing that the killer might be anywhere. They couldn't let him know that they were here, looking for him.

Riley pointed to the tracks and whispered, "Eggers's wife committed suicide somewhere along this long curve in the tracks. The newspaper didn't say exactly where. And we sure don't have time to go searching through old police records to pin the place down."

They all looked around, hoping to catch some hint of the killer's presence. But Riley knew that it was of no use. He could have parked a car in any secluded place, and he could be anywhere. He might already be dragging a drugged woman onto the tracks.

Jenn whispered, "This is a long section of track and the visibility is really poor. The three of us won't be able to watch the entire curve—not from here. Actually, not from any single point. Maybe we should roust up some local cops and raid the whole area with lights and guns."

Bill shook his head.

"No," he said. "If he sees anyone coming, he's likely to just kill the woman and disappear for good. He knows his way around here. Anyway, we don't have time for that."

They all were silent for a moment, then Jenn said, "I've got an idea, but neither of you is going to like it."

Riley immediately guessed what Jenn was thinking.

She said, "You think we should split up, check out separate sections of tracks."

Jenn nodded and added, "We can text message each other when we see something."

"You're right," Riley said. "I don't like it."

But as she stood there she realized …

What's the alternative?

And they had to get moving.

She said reluctantly, "OK, Jenn. You cover this area. Bill and I will drive on ahead and find our own sections."

Riley and Bill got back into the car as Jenn made her way among the lots and buildings, heading toward the tracks. Riley drove a short distance down the road and dropped off Bill. Then she continued on to find her own spot.

After she parked and made her way between a couple of storage buildings, she saw just how difficult a task they all faced. She had arrived at the tracks, but there was no lighting out here. She could only see a short distance in either direction. She didn't dare turn on her cell phone flashlight for fear of alerting Eggers to her presence.

Now she knew that she and her colleagues had no choice but to stumble along the tracks until ...

Until what?

The sun would come up soon, but the early morning was still and quiet—too still, deathly quiet.

It seemed impossible to imagine that there was anybody but Bill, Jenn, and her for miles around.

Just as Riley was trying to decide which direction to explore, a chilling sound broke the damp, dark silence.

It was the wail of a faraway train whistle.

It has to be now, she realized with a shudder. *He must be somewhere near here.*

Her phone buzzed. She looked at it and saw a single-word message that Jenn had sent to both her and Bill ...

Here!

She's found him! Riley realized.

Riley broke into a run in Jenn's direction.

*

When Bill saw the message, he also took off running. He knew he was closer to Jenn than Riley was.

He still hesitated to turn on his cell phone flashlight, which would announce exactly where he was. At least the sky was clearing up and a faint lightness overhead showed that dawn was on the way.

Taking care not to trip on the railroad ties, he ran along as fast as he could.

Finally he saw something moving on the tracks ahead. In a few more strides he could see two struggling figures.

Jenn and Eggers! Bill realized.

He switched on his light and dashed in their direction. When he reached them, he could see that a woman was already bound to the tracks beside the combatants—completely motionless, still unconscious from the drug.

Jenn seemed to be prevailing over her opponent, but Eggers suddenly escaped her grasp. He started away alongside the tracks, with Jenn close behind him.

Bill looked down at the helpless woman at his feet. The sound of the locomotive was growing louder.

Much too close, he realized.

And the woman was taped to the track just as the others had been.

He yelled at Jenn.

"Leave him! I need help here!"

Jenn whirled around. She hesitated but then dashed back and crouched beside Bill.

"He's getting away," Jenn complained.

"We won't let him get far," Bill said. "Help me with the woman."

Bill and Jenn both kneeled on the train track. They opened their pocketknives and desperately cut into the dense coils of duct tape that held the woman down.

The woman groaned aloud and murmured, "Where am I?"

By the time they got her loose, she was regaining consciousness.

Suddenly she writhed and kicked, and Jenn shouted out …

"Damn it!"

The writhing victim was free now, and she was terrified. Bill briefly struggled with her and finally managed to heave her completely off the tracks. She rolled over, crying, but stayed where she was.

He heard Riley's voice call out …

"Bill! Jenn!"

"We're here!" Bill yelled back.

Now the locomotive's headlight was visible in the distance. The train was rounding the far end of the curve in the tracks.

Riley yelled, "Get off the tracks!"

Bill moved to do that, but Jenn screamed.

She was still lying where they had struggled with the victim, and Bill could see what was wrong.

The heavy sole of her shoe was wedged sideways under the

steel rail.

She couldn't pull herself loose.

"It's no use," Jenn moaned. "Get off."

Bill's mind flashed back to another young agent, Lucy Torres, who had died right before his eyes.

Not again, he thought. *Never again.*

With his pocketknife, he worked to slice the leather shoe, to free Jenn's foot.

Then Riley was beside him, tugging at Jenn's leg.

But the light was blinding now.

Bill glanced up and saw the terrifying shape of the locomotive hurtling toward them.

"Go!" Jenn yelled.

For a long moment, it seemed that they would all die there.

Just then, Bill saw Jenn's whole body lift and turn. The movement twisted the shoe loose from the rail.

Bill looked up and saw Mason Eggers standing over them, lifting Jenn up off the track, turning her whole body so that her foot came free.

Then he tossed Jenn off to the side of the tracks.

Bill and Riley both dove off the tracks into the dirt beside Jenn.

A shattering whistle shook the air.

Then there was the scream of metal on metal as the engineer hit the brakes.

Bill looked back from where he lay and saw Mason Eggers still standing in the middle of the tracks, his arms outstretched, the full glare of the headlight bathing his body in dazzling whiteness.

Looking straight at the engine, Eggers shouted—so loudly that Bill could hear his voice over the roaring engine—

"Arlene!"

Then the locomotive roared past, and Eggers was gone.

CHAPTER FORTY

As she sat and waited on the stage of the school auditorium, Riley felt an odd chill up her back.

Fear, she realized with some surprise.

Not deep fear, and certainly not panic. Even so, it seemed silly to be fearful at all under the circumstances—especially given all that she and her colleagues had survived just a week earlier.

Besides, it wasn't the first time she'd spoken in front of a group of people. She'd taught plenty of classes at the BAU. Still, public speaking in front of an audience of mostly strangers always stirred up a certain degree of anxiety in her.

She reminded herself …

This is good. This is a good thing to be doing.

After all, this was a celebration of something very important to her. Today Jilly was finishing middle school. Although the school held no formal graduation ceremony, the PTA had arranged what they referred to as a little inspirational gathering.

They had asked Riley Paige to be the speaker.

And of course, she felt honored to be asked.

The school principal was at the podium now. His rather cliché congratulatory remarks seemed to be taking forever, and Riley had trouble paying attention to his words.

She couldn't help thinking about Mason Eggers—the terrible crimes he had committed, and the terrible death he died.

There hadn't been much left of his body for the medical examiners to work with. Even so, they'd found a malignant tumor that had started to grow in his brain. Just as Jenn had suggested, this must have caused him to have terrifying hallucinations.

Judging from his medical records, his condition hadn't yet been diagnosed. He might have been aware of encroaching symptoms, like headaches, disturbing physical sensations, and cognitive lapses, without ever realizing what was causing them.

He surely hadn't known why such terrible impulses were taking control of his life—why mysterious and irresistible voices were commanding him to revisit his wife's suicide again and again, brutally sacrificing live victims in her stead.

It must have been horrifying for him, Riley thought.

After all, he wasn't evil. He'd been a good man who had lived a good life. But unbidden evil had invaded his mind, destroying him and ending the lives of four women.

Riley tried to imagine how he must have felt in those last seconds of his life.

Maybe it wasn't so terrible, at least not for him.

She found it easy to imagine that, in the deepening confusion of his mind, the headlight of the locomotive was the tunnel-light of the hereafter. Perhaps he'd known for sure that he was about to be reunited with his beloved Arlene at last.

After all, her name was the last word that escaped his lips before he died.

Or maybe he was thinking …

Who knows? Riley thought.

She tried to put such sad thoughts aside by thinking about something that made her feel much happier—the letter of apology Bull Cullen had been forced by his superiors to write to Jenn about his atrocious behavior.

Whether it would change Cullen's future actions remained to be seen, but Jenn had done exactly the right thing and had gotten good results.

Riley also remembered with pleasure the cowed and demoralized expression on Carl Walder's face when he had managed to stammer out his congratulations to her for solving the case. And now she saw that same expression whenever she encountered him around the BAU these days.

Poor guy, she thought—without meaning it.

Now everybody in the FBI knew about how he had done his level best to thwart Riley just when she was on the very brink of stopping a serial killer.

In fact, news of her success had spread throughout the law enforcement community far and wide. Riley's reputation was restored, as sterling as it had ever been.

But now it was time to put all such thoughts aside—no matter how boring and longwinded the principal was being. After all, some of the people Riley most loved in the world were right here waiting for her to speak.

Jilly was seated in a special section along with the others who would be moving on to high school next year. April was in the general audience, along with Gabriela. So were Bill and Jenn—it

209

had been so sweet of them to come! Jenn was still on crutches from the terrible sprain she'd suffered on the railroad tracks, but she said that she was mending nicely.

Riley was grateful that Blaine was here too. Although he had no child in middle school, he'd said it was important to spend as much time as possible with Riley whenever she was home.

All in all, Riley's world was good right now. The girls had made it through the stress of finals and were looking forward to the summer off. They had heard from Liam that he was happy in his new home.

At long last, the principal was bringing his speech to a close.

He said, "Now I want to introduce one of our own parents. Agent Riley Paige has had a distinguished career in the Federal Bureau of Investigation, receiving too many medals and commendations to name here. Instead, I will let Ms. Paige speak for herself."

As the audience applauded, Riley's fear magically evaporated.

The moment just seemed too right to be afraid of.

She got up from her chair, walked toward the podium, adjusted the microphone, and began.

"Let me talk to you about opportunities, and the wonders that await you in life—more wonders than I can even imagine …"

*

Riley was feeling quite wonderful when Blaine drove them all home after the ceremony. Her speech had gone over well. It was a Friday, and she was looking forward to a few days of vacation with her family and her boyfriend.

Even the sight of an express letter in the mailbox didn't disturb her contentment. She carried it inside with the other mail—most of it advertisements and junk mail.

She put the mail down on the living room coffee table, and Jilly leafed through it.

"This one is from Phoenix," Jilly said.

The word jolted Riley a little.

Phoenix.

That was where Riley had found Jilly. The skinny and unkempt girl had been shut out of her home and was hanging around with hookers at a truck stop. Riley had found her in the cab of a truck, waiting for a trucker to return and pay her for sex.

Fortunately, another girl had tipped Riley to the child's plight. Riley had taken her to a social services facility, but in the longer run it had become obvious that she needed to take care of this girl herself.

And today, she felt blessed and grateful that she had done just that.

But a letter from Phoenix …

… was that good news or bad news?

Riley nervously opened the envelope. She saw that the papers inside were to inform her of a court date in the near future. There was an attached note from Brenda Fitch, the social worker who had put Jilly in Riley's care.

> We've been trying to handle all the paperwork here to finalize your adoption of Jilly Scarlatti. But as you can see, we've run into a snag. Albert Scarlatti, the girl's father, is refusing to give her up. He's not only challenging the adoption, he's even threatening to charge you with kidnapping for taking her away. He says he's charging us as accomplices.
>
> We know that being with you is the best possible solution for Jilly. We've managed to arrange a hearing in front of a decent judge. I know this is short notice, but if we have to change the hearing date I don't know who we'll get. We really need for you and Jilly to appear at this one. In fact, please get here ahead of time so we can go over our case together.

Riley's heart was beating hard and fast.

She found herself thinking about what Jilly had said to her a week ago when Riley had felt so demoralized and defeated.

"You're still going to solve that case. I just know it."

Jilly had been absolutely right.

And those were exactly the words Riley had needed to hear.

Riley felt a knot of emotion in her throat. How things had changed since Jilly had come into her life!

Back then, Jilly had needed Riley.

Now Riley needed Jilly just as much as Jilly needed her.

I can't lose her, Riley thought. *Not ever.*

With a deep sigh, Riley put the note down and looked at Jilly, who was waiting to hear what was in the letter.

"You and I have to go to Phoenix," she said.

ONCE TRAPPED
(A Riley Paige Mystery—Book 13)

"A masterpiece of thriller and mystery! The author did a magnificent job developing characters with a psychological side that is so well described that we feel inside their minds, follow their fears and cheer for their success. The plot is very intelligent and will keep you entertained throughout the book. Full of twists, this book will keep you awake until the turn of the last page."
--Books and Movie Reviews, Roberto Mattos (re Once Gone)

ONCE TRAPPED is book #13 in the bestselling Riley Paige mystery series, which begins with the #1 bestseller ONCE GONE (Book #1)—a free download with over 1,000 five star reviews!

In this dark psychological thriller, a wealthy husband turns up dead, and his abused wife is charged with the crime. She calls Riley for help—and yet it seems clear she is guilty.

But when another wealthy, abusive husband turns up dead, the FBI is called in, and FBI special agent Riley Paige wonders: is this all a coincidence? Or could this be the work of a serial killer?

What ensues is a game of cat and mouse, as Riley Paige realizes she is up against a brilliant and unpredictable killer, one without a clear motive—and one determined to keep on killing until he is caught.

An action-packed thriller with heart-pounding suspense, ONCE TRAPPED is book #13 in a riveting new series—with a beloved new character—that will leave you turning pages late into the night.

Book #14 in the Riley Paige series will be available soon.

Book #2 in THE MAKING OF RILEY PAIGE series will be available soon.

Blake Pierce

Blake Pierce is author of the bestselling RILEY PAGE mystery series, which includes twelve books (and counting). Blake Pierce is also the author of the MACKENZIE WHITE mystery series, comprising eight books (and counting); of the AVERY BLACK mystery series, comprising six books; and of the KERI LOCKE mystery series, comprising four books (and counting).

An avid reader and lifelong fan of the mystery and thriller genres, Blake loves to hear from you, so please feel free to visit www.blakepierceauthor.com to learn more and stay in touch.

BOOKS BY BLAKE PIERCE

THE MAKING OF RILEY PAIGE SERIES
WATCHING (Book #1)

RILEY PAIGE MYSTERY SERIES
ONCE GONE (Book #1)
ONCE TAKEN (Book #2)
ONCE CRAVED (Book #3)
ONCE LURED (Book #4)
ONCE HUNTED (Book #5)
ONCE PINED (Book #6)
ONCE FORSAKEN (Book #7)
ONCE COLD (Book #8)
ONCE STALKED (Book #9)
ONCE LOST (Book #10)
ONCE BURIED (Book #11)
ONCE BOUND (Book #12)
ONCE TRAPPED (Book #13)

MACKENZIE WHITE MYSTERY SERIES
BEFORE HE KILLS (Book #1)
BEFORE HE SEES (Book #2)
BEFORE HE COVETS (Book #3)
BEFORE HE TAKES (Book #4)
BEFORE HE NEEDS (Book #5)
BEFORE HE FEELS (Book #6)
BEFORE HE SINS (Book #7)
BEFORE HE HUNTS (Book #8)
BEFORE HE PREYS (Book #9)

AVERY BLACK MYSTERY SERIES
CAUSE TO KILL (Book #1)
CAUSE TO RUN (Book #2)
CAUSE TO HIDE (Book #3)
CAUSE TO FEAR (Book #4)
CAUSE TO SAVE (Book #5)
CAUSE TO DREAD (Book #6)

KERI LOCKE MYSTERY SERIES

CPSIA information can be obtained
at www.ICGtesting.com
Printed in the USA
LVHW02s2149010818
585625LV00023B/262/P